TOPE OMOTOSHO

Once Upon a First Love

(First Love Series Book 1)

LEVERAGE
PUBLISHING

Editing by Ekklesblue Media +234 809 822 1673

Cover Design by Raymond 'Ray'Em' Emamezi +234 706 064 7493

Author Photograph by Ajibola Animashaun Photography +234 803 844 1396

www.lifegodandlove.com

First edition

*This book was professionally typeset on Reedsy.
Find out more at reedsy.com*

To the Lover of my soul, my First Love,
Thank You for giving me this message to write.

Acknowledgement

To my husband, Dapo, and my son, Mayowa. You guys were pillars while writing this. Thanks Dapo (Sweet Caramel) for all the times you had to hold on to Mayowa while I locked myself in the study to write. The times when you dealt with my mood-swings while writing. The times when you encouraged me to keep going. I love you much! Thank you Mayowa for making me smile when I was down. *kisses*

Mrs Efe Ogunnaiya, you will never understand how much I'm grateful for your input.

My financial partners and helpers too numerous to mention that said yes to God, may you enjoy great intimacy with Him always.

Makes for an interesting and compelling read.
*- **Abimbola Dare (Best Selling Author of the Accidental Wife)***

This book has the transformative power of God to restore children of God who have strayed from their First Love. It is romantic and sweet, but it also deals with real life issues Christians face. I will recommend it to anyone who wants to grow deeper in their relationship with God, and anyone who wants an awesome Christian love story.
P.s - It doesn't end the way you expect!
*- **Ejiro***

Chapter 1

PEJU

Peju Adams rang the doorbell and let out a slow, calming breath. No answer. She raised her hand to the bell again, right when he opened the door.

Her heart leapt at the sight of him. Just like it always did. Smiling, he shifted aside to let her in.

"I didn't think you would show up," he said.

"Neither did I. I guess I couldn't help myself."

He was casually dressed in jeans and a black t-shirt. Black had always been his favourite colour. On his feet was a new pair of Nike sneakers. She took a seat on his leather sofa, restraining herself for the millionth time that week from pulling him close and wrapping her lips around his. She was curious to know if her body would still respond as it did years ago.

"Yeah, I've missed that."

"What?" *Was I thinking out loud?* She quickly turned her gaze to his apartment. The décor screamed *rich bachelor pad*, just like the kind in movies.

"I've missed you checking me out. It feels good to know I still appeal to you." He smiled. "So what would you like to drink? Water, a soft drink, hot chocolate.... me?"

She raised a brow at his cheekiness. "Mr Layeni. Water is fine. Ice-cold please."

He nodded and headed to the fridge to pull out a bottle of water, a premium brand. He handed it to her ever so gently. "You can start talking when you're ready."

"Abdul -" she said wearily.

"When you use that tone, it makes me feel weird."

She ignored him. "What happened back in school needs to stay there. Our love was just *play-play*. Nothing serious."

His expression suddenly grew solemn. "I don't want to believe you mean that. It was never like that for me. Why do you think I sought you out when I arrived?" He inched closer. "I'm back now. Back for you."

She shook her head in disbelief and dropped the bottle beside her on the dark, marble tiles. "Can you hear yourself? Time has passed, Abdul. We can't just pick things up from where we left off. We have both grown. Things have changed, and we don't have the same values."

"What values?"

The words *Christian values* hung loosely on her tongue, but she held back.

Abdul moved even closer, enough to caress her burning cheek. She flinched at his touch, and it wasn't because his hand was cold.

How do you do this to me, Abdul?

"Nothing matters but us. Plus, it's not like we didn't keep in touch, at least for the most part. You're still the same person I left in Nigeria years ago, only older and sexier," he teased. She elbowed him back, gently, "And I'm more in love with you than ever before. We can make this work. No restrictions. No barriers. Give us another chance, Habeebah."

The name sent shivers down her spine. He called her that during their most intimate of moments.

"Abdul. Please. This isn't secondary school. This isn't a movie script or a novel. This is —"

"Love, Peju. This is love."

He cupped her chin, willing her to look at him. She gazed into his eyes and found some of her answers there, but not all. Yes, she loved him. Yes, she would like to be with him forever. What they had was now, and if there was anything she learnt from her late father, it was she had to seize every opportunity when it presented itself. Tomorrow could be too late.

Damning the quiet nudge in her heart not to, she made the move to kiss him and was glad when he responded with as much urgency.

Come out from among them and be ye separate.

The words were whispered against her heart but her desire took over. She didn't stop. Couldn't stop. Even her gospel-themed ringtone couldn't interrupt, no matter how hard it tried. She would call whoever it was later.

Maybe tomorrow.

* * *

FEMI

Earlier that day, in the afternoon...

After sorting out his bill, with a very generous tip, Dr Femi Alakija received the cup offered and smiled back at the waitress.

"Pretty," Osaz, his colleague turned friend, chipped in. His eyes followed her as she left their table.

"Yes, she is."

"Maybe you should ask her out."

Femi's eyebrow rose a notch. "Excuse me?"

"It's only a suggestion, my brother. You never know what can happen."

Not when there is Peju, Femi thought. Memories of last night rushed into his mind. She looked beautiful in her red, flowy dress. He had known, from the day their eyes locked at *His Glory Centre* that she was someone special. The woman he had spent years waiting for. She was warm and kind, and also feisty if the occasion called for it. But beyond that, he knew there was a certain softness he would find if he dug deeper. And he wanted to dig deeper. He was done searching and believed God approved of their relationship. Peju's friend, Eliana, had been kind enough to introduce him to her weeks back. Now, Peju just needed to let him woo her.

"Oluchi sends her love by the way," Osaz interrupted his thoughts.

Femi nodded and took a sip of his steaming, black coffee. "How is she?

And the twins?"

"They are fine, but I swear I'm almost running mad in that house. One child will cry and the other will follow suit. Then I have to run up and down for Madam, and now Mama has joined the picture."

"Do they get along?" Femi asked, referring to Oluchi and her mother-in-law.

"I don't know. *I no fit kee myself on top their mata.* But I think they do." He picked up his phone off the table and glanced at it briefly. "Last night, they were watching Africa Magic and talking about the travails of promiscuous husbands. I just exited before they pounced on me and made me their victim."

Femi coughed out a laugh as he reached out for his glass of water. *I wonder if Peju and Mum would have gotten along?* "When conversations like that start, it's best to not be there."

"Hehe. I can't wait to hear you vent about things in your marriage. Scratch that, I'm done waiting."

Not again.

"You and I both know you aren't getting any younger. You're clocking the big three-seven soon. I already know what I'm going to face planning my kids' future and all the money I will spend. It means I'm probably going to be working till I'm like -"

"70?"

"What? God forbid. Maybe until I'm sixty. But my point is, if I planned, I would have married on time and not dragged my feet up and down."

"With all those girls you were chasing back then?"

Osaz waved his hand in dismissal. "Don't change the subject. Oluchi and I are concerned about you. You keep saying there's a girl you have spotted. That was a year ago and up till now, I haven't laid eyes on her. *Abi na spirit you dey chase?* Make I carry you go my church for deliverance."

"Joker."

"*Na true na.* When are we seeing this mystery woman?"

"Soon and very soon." He wiped his hands with a napkin and immediately stood up. "Lunchtime is over. Let's get back to work."

4

Osaz rose as well. "Work that only you enjoy the fruits of. If there was a Mrs. in the picture, different story."

Femi was done with this conversation but still maintained his calm. "So you expect me to just pick a random woman, marry her and start a family? You of all people should know better."

Osaz sighed.

"Patience. She will come around soon enough."

As his friend drove them back to the hospital, his thoughts shifted back to Peju. *What is she doing right now? Is she thinking about me?* He was supposed to call her but he didn't want to do so when he was tired and worked up. *She deserves my full attention, after all.* He could have called during his break but he didn't want Osaz listening in. He would call later on in the evening.

Chapter 2

PEJU

Her alarm went off. Again.

You've got to be kidding me.

Peju was tempted to hit the snooze button but decided not to. It had been a tough night of constant heat and opera-singing mosquitoes. And right when sleep showed up, the morning came with a rude awakening.

Grudgingly, she pushed herself off the bed and dragged herself to the bathroom. Getting to work late was not an option, even if her boss was her ex. Or lover. She hadn't decided yet.

Saturday night memories with the ex/lover were beautiful. No, they didn't go past kissing, cuddling, spooning. Instead, they talked all night, catching up on each other's lives and the latest movies. Being the perfect gentleman, he dropped her at home early Sunday morning, right in time for church. And their kiss goodbye? It felt unreal. A part of her longed for more as she watched him drive off, her heart firmly in his grasp. He'd had it since she was sixteen. What they had was teen love. Puppy love. But love nonetheless. The highlight - the night she gave herself to him. She had shed a few tears from the pain of having her virginity taken from her, but the pleasure that followed after made up for it. Notably, she was also his first, making the moment even more magical.

With time, they made plans to marry. Little did they know they were basking in a bubble life was set to pop.

CHAPTER 2

Many are the plans in a person's heart, but it is the Lord's purpose that prevails.

Peju shook her head as the scripture came to mind. She recognised that soft prompting anywhere, the same that told her not to kiss him.

Maybe we aren't supposed to be together at all.

She pushed the thought aside and brushed her teeth. *Peju, you're late for work. Think later.*

Twenty minutes later, she was standing in front of her bedroom mirror, admiring her black dress. She took in a deep breath to reassure herself. No, she wasn't longing for Abdul's eyes to sweep her frame when he saw her. No, she didn't want his eyes to light up at the colour. It was a simple dress, and that was that.

As she stepped out of her apartment, en route to the bus stop, her phone rang. Femi. She closed her eyes and gently tapped her forehead. *Crap.* She forgot to call him back on Saturday.

"Hello?"

"Hey, Peju. Good morning. Hope I didn't call at a bad time."

"Hi, Femi. Well, I'm heading out of my house now."

"Oh. I assumed you would be on a bus."

She looked at her watch. *Crap times two.* She should have left the house fifteen minutes ago. "I woke up late. Had a tough night."

"*Pele* dear. Would you like if I called you back?"

"Yeah, sure. You can call back later."

"Time?"

"Fifteen minutes is fine."

"Alright then. Talk to you soon."

He ended the call and she hurried out of the house. It was scarcely dark yet the streets were swarmed with yellow-black tricycles. How she flew to the bus stop, she couldn't tell. And thankfully, the queue hadn't built up much.

Femi called back when she was entering the bus.

"So what happened? Why did you have a rough night?"

She swiped stray hair from her face. "You know Nigeria *nau*. Mosquitoes,

7

heat, generator noise. *All join.*"

He laughed. "You must be really tired. Hope you're seated."

She smiled. "I'm seated."

"Good." He paused a bit before clearing his throat. "I've been meaning to ask. Can I take you out soon for another date? Say Friday?"

Hmm, wahala. "Can I get back to you on that?"

"Sure. Just let me know the time and I'll clear my schedule."

"Okay." She bit her lower lip. "Oh, and Femi?"

"Yes?"

"I'm sorry I didn't call you back. I was preoccupied and later forgot."

"No worries, Peju. Have a great day."

"And you too."

Sigh.

Minutes after the call, she got a text.

Hope you had a restful night. I missed you a lot...Looking forward to when we can spend more days and nights together. See you soon love.

P.S. I dreamt of you in a white dress looking beautiful. Could that be a sign?

Double sigh. She had an important decision to make, her heart racing at the truth behind the thought.

Her close friend Eliana, had recently played the role of matchmaker, hooking her up with a fine gentleman in their church named Femi. Asides from his good looks, he ticked off some boxes in her mind.

Patient. Check.

Mature. Check.

A good listener. Double-check.

The ten-year age gap was a bit of a concern, but not a complete red flag. Admittedly, they had a good time during their date at a fancy restaurant in VI, and he made her laugh. One would think he was still in his early thirties. But was that it? Was that enough for her to have butterflies in her tummy and fall in love?

Peju wasn't sure.

Motion stopped. Piercing insults followed, from the market women surrounding her. They were loud outbursts from the top of tired lungs, in a range of Nigerian dialects. Peju asked the man seated next to her what happened. The bus driver had parked at the side of the road and hurried off to ease himself. The man took her question as a cue to make conversation but she nipped it at the bud by thanking him and facing the window. From the corner of her eye, she spotted a huge rat scamper into a house through the gutter. She didn't want to be rude, but she was in no mood for small talk. She needed to plan her life.

See, if I can't picture myself with a man ten years from now, then there's no point being with him. Can I confidently say I'd be happy with Uncle Femi, sorry Femi, as a husband? Not sure.

Not like I was with Abdul.

She once asked her mother what it felt like to be in love when she was in her second year in university.

"How do you fall in love? How do you know if that person is right for you?"

"You just feel it deep within you that that's the person you want to spend the rest of your life with. Love is unpredictable. It can happen when you least expect it and it is a bondage that can not be easily broken once you entangle yourself in it."

Peju frowned. "So is it wrong to love?"

Her mum shook her head and Peju saw beads of sweat travel from her mother's brow to her chin. She wiped them as she stirred the yam porridge. The smell of it was making Peju want to break her fast. "It's not wrong to love. But it's wrong not to love the right way."

Honk! The bus driver was back and so was her present-day reality. She looked out the window and watched as hawkers got ready for the day. Not far from them was a young boy, barely a teenager, kneeling in front of his goods with lips moving. *Why can't life be so simple?* she wondered. But she knew better. Life itself had taught her better. Her mind drifted eleven years back to when the lessons began.

Peju and her friends were seated at the far end of their large classroom. They had just finished their third term exams and were excited about the holiday and what they had planned to do together. Peju knew she would spend most of her time at her mother's shop; washing plates, cleaning and attending to customers. Most of them were annoying and condescending. She was still thinking of how she would make out time for herself when her friends stopped talking and smiled at each other. Their sudden silence, strange to her.

"Why are you guys smiling?"

"Abdul just walked in," Antonia answered with enthusiasm.

Peju made a face. "And so? Is that why you just stopped talking?"

"Yes! I mean, look at him. He's so fine."

Peju hissed.

"Am I lying? Stop acting like you don't have feelings."

"I have something better than feelings and it's called common sense." She turned around to look at the object of her friends' attention. He was seating on a desk with a leg on a chair and another on the ground. Laughing at something, he turned his gaze to hers and winked. Peju quickly looked away.

"I think he's crushing on you," Titi said.

Why would you think that?"

"Because he's been stealing glances at you since he walked in. I heard he's having a party at his house. One of his friends invited us."

"All these silly rich boys that like to waste their parents' money. You girls have fun. I'm helping my mum at the shop today."

"Ahn-ahn nau." Titi spoiled her face. "Come with us. It'll be fun."

"No, and when were you two going to tell me about the party? It doesn't matter sha. I'm not going. Eat, drink and enjoy yourself but don't go and quarve anybody sha."

Antonia laughed. "I'm surprised you even know the word. You always act like you are better than all of us. What's wrong with having a little fun? We have finished our exams and now we can play. Just come with us jor."

Peju was ready to give a curt reply when Titi said, "Shut up! He's coming here." Antonia and Titi gave a friendly smile, but Peju didn't blink in his direction.

"Hello Antonia and Titi. What's up, Peju?"

Peju waved briefly before flipping through the novel Titi gave her.

"I came over to personally invite you guys to my party this Saturday. It's at 2

pm. Hope to see you there. Especially you Peju."

This time, Peju turned around to look at him. "Why?"

"Because... I would like to see you."

She raised a brow at him. "That's not a good reason."

Peju distanced herself from her thoughts. Quite frankly, time was not on good terms with her. She would have to reminisce much later.

* * *

PEJU

She dashed into the office at 8.30 am, thirty minutes behind schedule. Luckily, Abdul's leather seat was empty. She settled in her corner of his office to do the needful - put on her high stilettos, adjust her dress and put the unruly strands of her weave back in place. It wasn't long before the brown office doors flung open. It was Abdul. Her heart fluttered at the sight of him in his tailored black suit and navy blue tie.

"Good morning Miss Adams," he said loud enough for the employees to hear and closed the door. "Nice dress." He added with a lowered voice. "You look ravishing. How was your night?"

"Fine. I didn't sleep too well but I'm here. Thank God."

With a concerned look, he asked, "Oh no, why didn't you sleep well?"

"Mosquitoes. They kept me up all night."

He was in front of her now, his cologne filling her senses. His gaze pierced her soul. "How did you get to work?"

She shifted her gaze to the door. In her mind, it was far too early to entertain unholy thoughts. "How the average human gets to work – public transport. But enough about me. Let's begin your day, shall we?" She pulled out his schedule and scanned through her notes. It was an arduous job

11

being a personal assistant, let alone, his. At her last job, she had worked as a secretary in a tax office. The pay was less, the job unexciting. But she did her job well. It was a given for her to put her back into whatever she was doing.

"So, you have a meeting with Chief Ojukwu at 10 am. An investor is set to come by thirty minutes later, and you'll need to put a call through to your —"

"I'm getting you a car."

"Uh, no."

She looked up at him and smiled to ease the blow of her rejection. He was still her boss after all. She also knew it was a rare word for him. Not many people had the guts to say it to his face. "I don't really need one right now. But thanks."

He sighed. "Okay. No problem."

Back to Assistant mode. "Then, you have a meeting with some of the directors coming in from the States. That's at 2 pm. Then later in the evening, you should be on a flight to Aberdeen. That's at 10 pm. So your meeting can last only for two hours so you can head straight to the airport. Have you packed your luggage?"

He shook his head as he backed away from her, heading to his office. "Nope. That's your job. And pack yours too."

She blinked, confused at his statement.

"I'm not taking no for an answer this time."

"I don't have a visa."

"Handled." He pulled out a passport from his suit pocket. Hers. He had requested for it a week after she resumed work. For official documentation, he said. Now she knew better.

"We leave at 7." He winked at her, answering a call as he went into his office.

She stood there, boiling. *Peju, what have you gotten yourself into?*

* * *

12

ABDUL

He sat not too far from the entrance so he could keep an eye out for her. He had hoped she would come. He had spoken to one of her friends to make sure of it. But still, all he could do was hope. And now, there she was, at his house.

Abdul couldn't place why he liked her. She wasn't his type looks-wise with her petite, busty frame. Her natural hair, flying all over the place. Perhaps it was her tough exterior that had him hooked. It was different from what he knew. His mother was ever at his father's beck and call and never riled up for an argument. She never had anything of her own except what was given to her.

Right from when he was slightly mature enough to have a girlfriend, he knew he wanted someone different. Someone he could relate with. Someone bold and blunt – not like the few girls he had come across. A woman who could hold her fort without him but then was vulnerable enough to want him.

His mother had always said he was too wise for his age.

"It's good to see you, Peju. I'm happy you came." He walked up to her, hands in his pocket. She stood with friends, but his eyes were locked down on hers.

She said dryly, "Thanks for inviting me. I hope it's worth the trip." She looked anything but happy to be at his party.

"Don't mind her," Antonia nudged Peju's arm. "Thanks for inviting us."

"You're welcome. What would you like to drink? Fanta, Coke, juice, Chapman or water?"

"Chapman works," her friends answered.

"Cool. Peju, please follow me to the kitchen. I can't carry everything by myself."

Scowling, she opened her mouth but a slight push from her friend made her feet shuffle forward.

Alone with her in the kitchen, he jokingly asked, "Is it all guys you hate? Or just me? Keep squeezing your face up and down, or you h —"

She slapped him. Right there and then, she slapped him But he wasn't angry. No, more like amused.

"Don't talk to me like that again." She withdrew her palm. "Is this why you invited me? To run your mouth anyhow?"

I love this girl. "No, but I just wish you smiled more around me." He paused.

"Because I like you."

"You like me? Why?"

"You're independent. Smart. Pretty. I even like your sharp mouth." Then he said the next thing that was on his mind. *"I would love to be your boyfriend if you let me."*

She blinked for a moment then burst out in laughter. "Just like that? I didn't say I like you back."

"You don't have to, Peju. I know you do."

She raised a brow, her lips pouted. All he wanted to do was pull her face to his and taste those lips. But he knew what would follow next and his cheek couldn't take another hit. "You do? How?"

"Two reasons. One, you didn't say you hate me and two, you're still talking to me."

"Mr Layeni?"

Abdul turned around in his swivel chair to face the love of his life.

"How was the meeting with Ojukwu?"

"Not bad. The partners are warming up to me. They've bought the vision of me running this place. A few concerns but nothing we can't handle —"

"I can't go with you to Aberdeen."

He sat up then, resting his back on the chair. In a dismissive tone, he continued, "Just grab a few clothes, or you can do some shopping over there. Anything you like."

She folded her arms against her chest. "It's not about clothes. And stop throwing your money in my face."

Same old Peju. The words were at the tip of his tongue, but he refrained from giving a retort. He concluded she was on her period, and from experience, he knew it would be a terrible mistake.

She sighed. "Abdul, what are we doing?"

"Retracing steps, Habeebah." He rose from his seat and moved to where she stood. "Come with me. Let's figure out what *this* is together." He placed a hand on her arm, loving the feel of her soft skin against his fingers. "Please."

Peju looked into his eyes. Warmth looked back. "I.. I...."

"Good. Then, it's settled. Pack your bags and we will meet up at the airport. I'll have the driver get you."

Abdul pulled her into his arms. Letting her go once was a mistake he would never make again in his life. When he told her about his plans to relocate abroad, the thought of a long-distance relationship scared her, so she asked him to end things. She believed it would only end in heartbreak for both of them. He never accepted it and fought hard to keep in touch for the first two years. Schoolwork and life won, leading to her long-winded email on a breakup. All efforts to reach her after that were futile.

Thankfully, the past was past. He was back. Fate had given them another chance to be together. It was almost magical, the way their paths crossed at their secondary school reunion almost a month ago. He didn't think she would make it. But she did, looking as stunning as ever in a white dress that accentuated her beautiful curves.

They were together again. That was all that mattered.

Meanwhile, back at Peju's desk, her phone vibrated. It was a text message, from Femi.

* * *

OBA

On the other side of town, Oba Afolayan was in a predicament. Ten text messages, and all from a *Nene*.

This girl won't kill me. He placed a call quickly, releasing a familiar sigh.

She answered on the third ring.

"Baby!"

"Hey, babe. Sorry, I just read your messages." *All one million of them.* He listened on. "Sure, I'll come by and pick you up when you're done. Just text me when you're ready. Okay love?"

"Thank you, baby. I didn't want to call earlier on," She sighed, "But I don't know why my car keeps giving me issues."

"Have you called a mechanic?"

15

"Yes, he came by to pick it up. What I wouldn't give for a new car… hmm. Let me get back to work. Kisses, baby. Love you!"

"Love you too." He got her message loud and clear.

"*Love you too*," Timilehin, Oba's cousin, mimicked in a high pitched tone from the stairwell. "When are you asking the big question?"

"Which question?"

"Will you marry me?"

"God forbid. Why would I marry you?"

Timilehin raised his left hand at Oba and splayed his five fingers in front of him. "You're sick."

Oba laughed. "Don't mind me. I don't know *jere*. Still thinking if I should. We've been together for two years now, you know. That's got to count for something"

"True true. Your anniversary was last month or so *abi?*"

"Yup. Treated her to a spa weekend and restaurant in Mauritius."

Timilehin's eyes opened wide. "Sorry, what?"

"She's worth it." What he also said to comfort himself after going broke that week.

About half an hour later, Oba and Timilehin set out to a nice *bukka* joint. The *Amala* and *gbegiri* he was going to order had been on his mind all day, long before Nene's texts. They hopped into Oba's car and talked some more on the way.

"I just want to be extra sure. This marriage is a lifetime thing and I don't want to make any mistake."

"Wise decision." Timilehin smiled, but deep down, he wasn't Nene's biggest fan.

"Yeah. I'll keep you updated *sha*. But enough about me. How far with you? Any babe?"

"Nothing serious yet, but there's this babe I'm *eyeing sha*. She's really pretty."

"Nice. And where does her boyfriend work?"

Timilehin raised his hands in surrender. "What's that supposed to mean?"

"That you always go for girls in relationships. Am I lying?"

"Yes. Yes, you are! The last time was just a coincidence *jor*. I don't know if this current babe is in a relationship but I will find out and prove you wrong."

Oba smirked as they pulled up in front of the joint on the busy Lagos Marina stretch. It was his last day before his trip to Ibadan, where his parents lived, and he planned to make the most of it. Lunch with the Cousin first, and then he would head out to see Nene.

$$* * *$$

OBA

"Oba, thank you so much for coming to pick me," Nene said as she wore her seatbelt. "You're the best." She leaned over and kissed him on the cheek, not caring for the extra stares from the outside. He didn't mind as well. Oba liked PDA, no matter where.

He also like what she had on, particularly the grey skirt that drew up to her slim thighs. All he wanted to do was take it off, her blouse too, and do crazy things to her as she screamed in appreciation.

His mind went into planning mode as he joined the traffic. Reaching his goal was tough considering all the obstacles to face. Traffic to Victoria Island was light but he knew it was going to take another thirty to forty minutes before they got to her house. Also, her parents were home. There was no use. He aborted his mission, his face was sunken.

"How was your day with Timilehin? Were you able to rest?"

He shook his head. "No. We played basketball, went to eat, *gisted*… that's about it."

"Sounds like a typical guy day. And all set for tomorrow?"

"Yeah, babe. Can't wait."

"Great. I wish I could follow you to Ibadan to see your parents."

He knew as well as she that that was a lie. Nene had no problems with his father, but with his mother? That was another situation entirely. The two were like oil and water. Like Tom and Jerry. Like the Nigerian sun and an Eskimo. They just could not get along.

Nene was innocent, as always. It was his mother's fault; the thought of him dating an Igbo girl, a bitter taste in her mouth.

"I also got some things for Mum. I hope she would like them."

Oba spared a smile and fixed his gaze back on the road. "That's nice. Thank you, love." Knowing Mrs Afolayan, she would most likely give them to their house-girl.

"Again I ask, why do you want to marry this girl?"

He raised his brow, wondering if she was the one dating her, or he was. "Mummy, please let's not do this again. I like Nene."

"Because she has big breasts and nyash?"

Oba almost choked on his bowl of garri. He looked at her, but her face was numb like she said nothing out of the ordinary.

"No. I assure you."

She snorted. "Tell that to yourself. You men are like that. Your eyes lead you first before your head." She hissed and walked out of the parlour leaving him confused.

"Oba, did you hear me?"

"Sorry, what did you say?"

"I said you should let me know when you arrive tomorrow."

"Sure."

He couldn't blame her. He was also worried about his mother's next move. For all he knew, she had a Yoruba woman ready for him at home.

Chapter 3

FEMI

Death always carried its tune.

Femi dropped his phone and rubbed his eyes with the back of his hand. He was exhausted from a long day of seeing patients. But he wasn't just physically tired, he was emotionally drained as well. He had lost a long time patient earlier in the morning. A ten-year-old boy with kidney problems. It had been hard watching the parents mourn the loss of their firstborn. Femi had prayed every day for the boy to be healed, or receive a kidney donor.

But there were complications.

God, did it have to be this way? Couldn't something have been done?

Rejoice in the Lord always... I say it again rejoice!

The scripture was soothing to his heart.

Yes, Lord. I praise You for You are the giver of life and nothing happens without You knowing about it. You are the Almighty. He knew James was resting in the bosom of the Lord. Yet, death was always painful. Even his history in the medical field couldn't help him come to terms with its blow.

Could anyone?

To date, his mother's death was the most gripping experience in his life. She lost her cancer battle years ago. He wished she had lived long enough to see his kids. He felt bad and yet, he knew God's timing was best.

Yes, there were times he doubted God cared, or was interested in him. Why was he still single after so long? Why was he all alone? Why didn't he have a family? Despite his moments of uncertainty, God had shown

Femi countless times He was faithful and enough for him. His siblings were married and had children of their own. All except one who had been waiting on God for the past three years. She was on a low and her husband's family was breathing down her neck. Occasionally, she had called to share her burdens with him. She had done tests that showed she was fertile but still, the waiting game continued. All they could do was wait on God.

There was an urgent knock on his door and he looked up as a nurse walked in, file in hand. "Good afternoon Sir. There's a patient here to see you. I know you're off duty now but she says it's a pressing issue."

Femi signalled for her to come closer and collected the file from her. He read through. The patient had an abortion done last week, but there were complications. "Dr Kola's supposed to handle this case. Alright, let her in but please no more patients. I'm heading out after I see her."

"Yes Sir."

A young woman walked in. Dressed in a polished navy blue pantsuit, she appeared to be deeply troubled. "Good evening Sir."

He glanced at his watch. "Good afternoon, Miss Ali."

"Oh, I'm sorry." She glanced at her fine leather-strapped watch as well and turned back to him, apologetic. "Just a lot of things going on. Good afternoon."

He smiled. She also had a distinct accent. Femi guessed she was Fulani. "It's fine. Please, have a seat. What seems to be the problem?"

"Well, I've noticed red spots in my urine which I assume is blood, but I would love to be wrong."

He opened the file and wrote a few things down. "Any burning sensations when you pass urine?"

She nodded. "Yes."

"What else?"

"Sometimes I have pains in my stomach. Serious pains."

Femi nodded. "Can you show me where?"

She placed her hand on her pelvic region and he saw her wince.

"That's fine. It says here you had an abortion last week?"

"Yes." He wasn't sure but he thought he heard her say she didn't have a choice. "I told Doctor Kola and I asked for painkillers to suppress the pain. I didn't think it would be anything serious."

"Okay, were you tested for any sexual infection before or after the abortion? Have you ever had any sexually transmitted disease?"

Her eyes widened. "Sexual infection *ke*? No *o*. I didn't. I haven't had any STDs in my life. I just had the abortion done and that was it. Is there something wrong?"

"I can't say at the moment, but I'll need you to do a few tests to rule out some things. Is that okay by you?"

"Yes Sir."

"Great. Don't get yourself unnecessarily worked up. I'm sure you're already worried."

She nodded. "I just hope there's no problem."

He said softly, "Worry or fear doesn't make the problem go away." He jotted a couple of things in her file. "Just meet the nurses and they will draw up blood. You can come back in three days for the result. I would advise you to abstain from any sexual activity within the next few days until this is sorted out." He handed the file to her while she rose to her feet, adjusting her bag strap on her shoulder. She seemed less flustered than when she arrived at his office minutes ago.

"Thank you very much, Doctor - ?"

"Alakija. Femi Alakija."

She gave an easy laugh, her smile, revealing beauty that caught Femi's attention. "Really? Are you the owner of the hospital?"

Femi nodded. "Guilty as charged."

She nodded, thanked him once more and left. He rose from his seat once she walked out.

Femi stretched. His back ached. His head hurt. He needed a hot meal, a warm bath and a cold bed. He also needed to see Peju. Lately, she seemed preoccupied. She was either busy or avoiding him.

He prayed it was the former. *But what if she doesn't want to see me?* He shook his head. Why would she be avoiding him? He knew she enjoyed herself on their date. He was just worrying over nothing.

***

ELIANA

4th of November, 2015

The village missionary trip was amazing, with lives being won for Christ. I know it's all the Holy Spirit's doing and I'm so grateful He used me.

We visited a village just south of Abeokuta. It was a small village with very few social amenities available. Then, there was the toilet "situation". I wasn't interested in pit-latrines so I had to poo in nylon. I'm bad at throwing things because, on two occasions, it landed on someone's roof instead of the bush! When it started smelling, I didn't know how to act innocent and shocked. Thank God it rained. Showers of blessings, showers of blessings we plead. Mercy drops round us are falling, but for the showers, we plead.

I loved teaching the children about Jesus and teaching them songs. They were a joy to be with. There was this cute baby boy who always wanted me to carry him every time I met with the children. I won't forget his name in a hurry. Light. I pray he bears the true meaning of his name.

I came back home a week ago. Life has been interesting since my return. First, my dad finally agreed to lend me money for a course on interior design. (That was after sounding it in my ears that I wasted his money reading English in school). He doesn't want me sitting at home all day. He's also really worried about my obsession with God and zero love life after my breakup with Kene. Maybe it's because he doesn't want me to be a nun?

"I'm reading from Zechariah 8 verse 2, New Century Version. This is what the Lord All-Powerful says, *"I have a very strong love for Jerusalem. My strong love for her is like a fire burning in me."* In Kings James Version it says, Thus saith the LORD of hosts; *I was jealous for Zion with great jealousy, and I was jealous for her with great fury."*

Stella, Eliana's Bible study leader for that evening, raised her head before continuing, "Our topic tonight is the Jealous Lover, in line with what we have been discussing in our Love series." She clasped her hands. "I love the passage we just read. It stood out to me, after praying for God to lead me on what to share tonight. I was brimming with excitement when different scriptures popped up in my spirit. So let me just go straight to it so we have time to discuss."

"The word *jealous* usually has a negative meaning. It says in Galatians 5 that people harbouring jealousy in their lives can't see the Kingdom of God. So you may think, why is God described with such a negative word? But that's not the case. Jealousy in this text, or in any text where it gives reference to God, simply means zealous. God is zealous over me. God is zealous over you. Do we follow?"

Eliana nodded along with others in the small group. The fatigue from earlier in the day had waned considerably; her body was still recovering from the village life. If it wasn't in such an intense atmosphere, where God's presence felt so tangible, she would have dozed off. She had missed the sessions during her missionary trip and was glad to be back. She had also missed Stella's deep teachings.

"God is guarding us so intensely and closely that He doesn't want anyone to steal our hearts. Especially anyone who's not worth it. Zechariah 8 says God has a strong love for me, Stella. His love for me is like a fire burning in Him." She paused briefly as she spoke in tongues and a few ladies shouted 'Hallelujah'

"Sisters, that's pure love. That's true love. It's not the love this world has to offer. It's not the love my husband gives me, though he's working on becoming more like Christ every day. It's a love that just is. He loves you and me so much that He doesn't want us to be tainted. He loves us intensely and passionately. And you know what? He expects us to love the same way."

On her way home, after the study, Eliana digested the lessons. She wondered how anyone could be like Paul and serve God so wholeheartedly in this day and age. How could a person be so passionately in love with Him? Eliana felt ashamed and guilty somewhat. For a while now, her thoughts were centred on how a man could love and care for her, amongst other things. It wasn't about how *she* would care for God, or how she would care for her future husband.

She was mostly thinking of herself.

Forgive me, Lord, if I have been selfish. I love You, Lord. I adore You. My life is absolutely nothing without You. Two hours later, she was back at home. She took a quick inventory of her day's activities. The highlight - her morning design classes which had been tasking but exhilarating. Eliana loved everything about it, anxiously waiting to put her skills to work. She closed her eyes, but in her heart and mind, it was full of thanks to God. He was just too good to her.

* * *

OBA

"Baby, what's up?" Nene asked, placing her head on his bare chest. Strands from her Peruvian weave lightly tickled him. He rubbed her back in circular motions, loving the feel of her skin against his fingers.

"Nothing. Just thinking *jare.*" He couldn't tell her what was on his mind for fear of hurting her or driving a bigger wedge between her and his mother.

"What's the time?"

He grabbed his phone from his bed stand. "Past nine."

"Past nine?" She sat up abruptly. "Why didn't you wake me up since *nau?* You know I have to be at work by eleven." She tossed the covers off her body and got out of bed.

"I'm sorry. I was being selfish. I wanted to spend time with you."

The frown on her face turned to a smile. "Awww, that's so sweet." She sauntered back to him, and with one knee on the bed and a leg on the ground, she brushed her lips against his. "I love you too babe. But you know how important it is that I get this contract." She worked at a real estate company and wanted a promotion badly.

"I know. I will make it up to you when you get back."

"How?" She had a twinkle in her eyes as she smiled at him.

He winked. "Just you wait and see."

Nene got off him and strode to the bathroom. Barely five minutes had gone by when she squealed and ran back to the bedroom. A pillow flew fast his way.

"Hey! It's a yes or no deal. Don't throw a pillow at me."

She screamed again and jumped on him. "I love you. I love you. I love you."

He laughed as she stared at the ring. It had cost him a lot but the look in her eyes assured him that he had made the right decision. Life was short, he felt, so he might as well start living it.

"Will you marry me?"

"Of course I will!" She pulled him to her and kissed him passionately.

"Aren't you supposed to be getting ready for work?" Not that he wanted her to leave. He loved the sudden attention she was giving him.

"My client can wait a little longer. Let me attend to my future husband first."

Oba smiled as her lips took his. In between celebration sex, he fought back memories of his Ibadan trip. As he suspected, a young woman was waiting for him at home. She was gorgeous with skin as sumptuous looking like a bowl of hot pap. But she wasn't his Nene. Far from it. His mother introduced her as his wife, leading to a heated argument. An argument that eventually drove him back to Lagos. Oba knew his mother loved him but she couldn't control who he wanted to love. It was the very woman in his arms. But despite his victory, why did he feel a heavy mass in his chest?

* * *

ELIANA

Eliana was busy whisking eggs that morning when a text message came in

25

from Kene, her ex. Amidst the usual pleasantries, he had asked for them to meet up. Eliana's heart thumped. Why would he think she would want to see him in the first place?

Love forgives. . .

I know, but he hurt me. It's hard to forgive him. I still feel the pain. Is it so bad if I keep my distance as well? We have nothing else to say to each other.

Seventy times seven.

Eliana squeezed her eyes shut. Sometimes, the whole love thing was inconvenient. Why couldn't she just avoid him forever? Why did she have to face him again? What did he even have to say to her? A phone call was enough.

But Eliana, you don't pick your calls.

She could almost feel God laughing at her. This was how her conversations with Him were, especially after the missionary trip. Talking to Him and getting a response. Sometimes, it came as a whisper or nudging. Other times, He spoke to her through scriptures she read.

Fine, God. I'll go. But please keep me calm. You know what I'm capable of.

* * *

ELIANA

"You look good."

"Thanks. I wish I could say the same about you. Are you okay?"

He took off his dark sunglasses to reveal those dreamy eyes she once loved, along with the long, curly lashes she wished she had. He had always teased her about them, offering to lend them to her.

"I'm fine. It's work that's making me stressed. What about you? Have you gotten a job now?"

"Not yet. I'm doing an Interior Design course though. I just might start my own business." She shrugged her shoulders like it wasn't a big deal. "But

I'm still praying about it."

"That's awesome babes. It's what you've always wanted. I'm happy for you."

"Thank you." She clenched her fist. "So, let's get down to business. Why did you want to see me?"

"You don't want something to eat or drink?"

"Nah, still full from breakfast."

"What did you eat?"

What do you care? "Pancakes."

"Nice! I remember those fluffy, vanilla pancakes you used to make back then." Laughing, he placed a hand on his tummy. "In fact, I have you to thank for this potbelly."

She responded with a polite smile, the only one she could muster.

"One second." He rose from his seat and headed to the service counter. About five minutes later, he returned with a tray of jollof-rice, chicken and a bottle of water. What followed next was silence. Thick, heavy and uncomfortable silence.

She watched as he moved his cutlery, picking up every grain in sight. His full mouth rotated in slow circles. With every second that passed, a new thought came, asking why she was there in the first place. Just as she was about to ask out loud, he spoke up, "So you're probably wondering what this is all about. Why I asked you to come." He could barely look her in the eye. "I just felt I owed you a serious apology for my mistake. I never meant to hurt you."

You mistakenly impregnated your colleague, right? Your mouth mistakenly hid the truth from me for two weeks? Your fingers mistakenly broke the news via text? She heard the grudges scream out loud and clear, but another side of her kept them calm. She was determined to move forward. "It's all in the past."

"If so, why don't you answer my calls?"

"Because I have nothing to say to you. To be honest, I was upset for the longest time but God helped me understand grudges weren't helping. They were weighing me down and I needed to let them go. So from the bottom of my heart, I forgive you."

"Thanks. I do appreciate that."

"How's she? Pregnancy and everything."

"She's fine. Always complaining of one thing or the other. It's either her feet are paining her, or she has back pain and needs a massage. It's tiring."

Eliana didn't say more. How could she feel sorry for him when *he* was the one who cheated on her? After all, he was merely reaping the fruit of his labour.

"Can I ask a question? Since we are here, we might as well just talk openly." He nodded. "Why did you cheat on me? How did it happen?" She paused. "Was she more attractive than me?"

Kene wiped his mouth with a serviette. "Kemi..." She used to love the way he called her that, with his subtle Igbo accent. "It just happened. Honestly. We were spending a lot of time together and one thing led to another. I wasn't bent on cheating, and no, it's not that I found her more attractive. I guess I was just horny."

When the full meaning of his words kicked in, she balled her hands to a fist to keep herself from dishing out a slap. "Really? I thought you agreed to be celibate with me?"

He laughed. "Kemi, I'm a guy. I'm moved by what I see and at that time, she moved me."

"She *moved* you?" Realizing her voice was raised she calmed down and said, "Question. If the devil offers you cold water in the desert for your soul, would you take it?"

"If I'm thirsty. . . maybe. See, you're taking it too far. It was a spur of the moment thing and it won't happen again."

Eliana shook her head, staring at him incredulously.

"You deserve happiness, Eliana Oluwakemi Awojobi." She raised a brow at the use of her full name. "You're an amazing woman and will make a good wife. Unfortunately, you won't be mine."

"Thanks. I admire you, you know. Your dad may have walked out on you, but here you are. You are ready to raise your child and be there for him or her. However, that doesn't mean you should marry someone who isn't God's will for you."

She glanced at her watch. It was getting late. She had to head back home to make sure her teenage brother hadn't burned the house down.

"I have to go. Dimeji's home alone."

"Ah! Dimeji my guy! Hope he's good. Has he passed level fourteen of that his game?"

"Do I know?" She rose to her feet. "Take care of yourself, Kene. All the best."

He smiled and said in a gentle semi-whisper, "And you too, Kemi. Thank you for agreeing to see me, and thanks for your advice. I just needed to clear the air between us so I don't have heaps of curses on my head. My Baby Mama's parents have done enough."

With nothing more to say, she smiled and went on her way. She was glad their relationship hadn't been anything more serious. And whatever love she had for him could gladly fade in peace.

She pulled out her phone on the bus and dialled Peju's number. She owed her updates.

Chapter 4

PEJU

It was official. Abdul was Peju's weakness. He was all she could think of even on a hot Sunday afternoon. At church earlier, the pastor had touched on God's gift of grace to His children and how it helped them overcome life. But she couldn't care less; the thought of Abdul, sitting front row in her mind.

Aberdeen was wonderful. He made sure to show her all its sights and sounds during their evenings together. They made out under the stars and spent nights cuddling in each other's arms. The urge for sex was real and deadly, but she held her own. He was understanding too, not wanting to rush things, and covering her with kisses instead. As for the shopping? She had two heavy suitcases to show for the shopping spree he took her on. They were full to the brim with designer clothes, perfumes, shoes, jewellery and chocolates.

That was love with Abdul. Fun. Exciting. Electric. The giddy feeling of knowing someone was thinking about you all the time. The deep knowing that you are loved and cared for. It was the best feeling ever.

Peju sighed. It had been so easy falling for him back when they were teenagers. There had been no worries or fears of the future. He was mature, and attentive to her needs, placing hers before his. Yes, he had his annoying moments but was generally a gentleman at heart.

It felt strange having him as her boss; it was something she was still trying to get used to. Sometimes it was distracting when there was a lot of work to get done and he invited her to his office just so he could steal a kiss or two. Apart from that, things were perfect. Magical almost.

She wondered if they could have a future together. After all, he was back for good. When he relocated to Canada, she didn't think she would see him again, despite his promises of returning. Titi, a former school friend, did the same and they hadn't spoken in years. Antonia was also out of the picture. But Abdul was back. He was with her again and maybe, just maybe they could have a *happily ever after.*

Maybe they could get married. That got her excited, the possibility. After her father died, she had felt so lost, as something had died within her. There was no one she could talk to about her problems. No one understood her or could comfort her.

No one?

Peju was struck with guilt. Okay, that wasn't exactly correct. How could she forget God? God had been there for her. His love had kept her going when times were hard. Together, they had picked up the pieces of her life and she was who she was because of Him.

"What do I do, Lord?" she asked, but no answer came. Again.

She knew if Abdul happened to propose, she would say yes. Yes, there was the daunting fact that he was a Muslim, but she loved him so much. She couldn't imagine her life without him.

"What if you want to marry more than one wife?" she had once asked him.

"The more the merrier."

She shoved an elbow into his ribs, causing him to wince from the pain.

"I was just joking jor. I'm not a one-man many wives guy. All that one is wahala. I'm okay with you."

"Are you sure?"

He pulled away from her side and stared into her eyes. "Do I look like I'm joking? You should know when we're talking seriously."

She made a face.

"Don't think about that one nau. Like I said I was just joking."

"What if tomorr-"

He placed a finger on her lips, then caressed her right cheek. "What if this. What if that. Peju! You worry too much. Don't worry about tomorrow. Today has enough worries."

He kissed her then, his arms going around her waist. His soft lips melted away her fears. He pulled back, rubbing her back with his palm. His loving eyes drove away her fears and worries. "I love you, Habeebah. Whatever tomorrow brings, we will face it together. Alright?"

She nodded, afraid to say how much she loved him. Everything just felt intense. And so she did the only thing she could. She showed him, with her body. Despite the pain as her first, it was a beautiful moment. Alone, in a dark corner of his parent's house, he made love to every part of her body, down to her toes. No questions. No regrets. Just love in its purest form.

Love is as strong as death; jealousy is as strong as the grave. Love bursts into flames and burns like a hot fire.

The words came quickly to her. It was one of the scriptures Eliana had shared when she was crazy about her then-boyfriend, Kene. Her hands flew to her chest and she could feel the heat. Was this what Eliana was talking about? Was this what Abdul's love was doing to her? It felt so intense. She was going to fight to make it work, no matter the cost.

Her phone rang. It was Femi. He had called multiple times but she had been so busy. Not to mention, she hadn't seen him in church as well.

Hope he's okay.

She picked her phone then and called him. It was the third time she called that he answered.

"Hey, Peju."

"Femi! Sorry, I missed your call. Didn't see you at church today. Hope you're okay."

"Yeah, I had a long day at the hospital so I ended up attending the second service. Thanks for checking up. Been trying to reach you for ages."

"I know. I've been busy." *Lies.* "Went to Aberdeen the other day for work."

"Wow. Sounds exciting. At least no mosquitoes."

She laughed and tucked a loose strand of hair behind her ear. "No mosquitoes."

"Awesome. Can we meet up for dinner later this evening? Hope that's okay."

"Er— sure." She didn't have a choice, making him wait the way she had. She was surprised he still cared as much.

"Great! I will pick you up at 7. Is that fine?"

"Sure."

"I can't wait to take you to this new restaurant I discovered. See you at 7."

An hour passed and Peju was dressed. For someone who had emptied retail shops abroad, it was tough choosing what to wear. She finally settled for an ankara top, jeans and red pumps to match. One of the many pumps Abdul bought her on their trip.

Speaking of Abdul, he would be so jealous if he knew she was going out with another guy. Telling him was not an option. At least not now.

She dabbed some perfume on the back of her ears and wrists. It was a fragrance Abdul had specifically picked out for her, from a *Selfridges* store on the High Street. She couldn't wait to spill the details of her date with Femi eventually. Maybe when he was annoying, she would share. She would let him know she had other men pining for her.

Yearning to hear his voice, Peju dialled his number.

"Habeebah!" he said, his voice upbeat.

"Hey hey. Where are you? What are you doing?"

"Just did laundry. Now I'm resting on my bed. What's up?"

Peju closed her eyes, imagining him shirtless on his bed. She opened her eyes to drive away the lewd thoughts. "I wanted to hear your voice. You're doing your laundry yourself? That's impressive. Maybe I'll drop by later on. Let's say around eight-thirty."

"Sounds good. See you then, let me get some rest for you."

As she ended the call, she felt like an excited school girl madly in love.

* * *

PEJU

"You are a beautiful woman Peju," Femi said softly over the candle-lit table. They had just finished an exquisite main course in a fine Italian restaurant in an elite Lekki neighbourhood. Femi assured her that dessert would blow her mind. *Tiramisu* he called it, with a delicious cocoa centre and coffee exterior.

She lifted her glass of non-alcoholic wine and took a sip. "Thank you. And you look good too. Well-rested."

"Really? I wish I could rest some more but I couldn't pass up the opportunity to see you. You're a sight for sore eyes."

She smiled at the compliment. It was going to be hard to say this was going to be their last date.

"So tell me more about this job of yours."

"Well, I work in RAFOL. We supply certain services to oil companies. I work as a P.A to the Managing Director who recently inherited the company from his late uncle. At work, there's always one appointment to make or cancel for my boss. Flights to book. Meetings to seat on and all that. Being called late at night to set some last-minute things up."

Peju gave an easy laugh and swept a strand of her hair aside. She remembered the night Abdul had called just because he couldn't sleep. She had expressed her grievances over it but after begging her, they spoke for close to two hours. Thankfully, the next day had been a public holiday.

"It's hectic but I love my job."

"That's nice. Sounds like a lot of work. I'm sure there must be perks as well."

Like travelling to Aberdeen at the last minute, she thought to herself.

"Yeah. What about you? You mentioned you became a doctor because helping people is what you love to do. You love the late hours and all that. How would you balance it all when you get married and have children?"

She almost pinched herself. *Why did I ask that question? What's my business with his life?*

"God first, family second, ministry and then work. I'm a family man. I would be sure to make out time for my wife and kids. Fortunately, my ministry and work are together. I counsel my patients and I ask God to

34

help me deal with them in a way that brings glory to Him and not to me. Irrespective of my work as a doctor, I remind myself that I'm only a vessel being used by God."

Peju found his words profound and somewhat challenging. What could she say about herself and if she was in the will of God?

"So how do you counsel your patients? I've been to one or two hospitals where the doctors refrain from talking to the patients about religion."

He gave an easy laugh. "I feel like I'm on the hot seat."

She raised her hands. "Feel free to refuse to answer."

"No, I will. After all, we're getting to know each other better. Right?"

She nodded, still trying to decide how to tell him they were just friends. Whatever was happening between them was never going to go past that level.

"Well, let's not look at it as me being a doctor or as you being a personal assistant or a lawyer, teacher or whatever - regardless of whatever field we find ourselves in. As Christians, we're all ambassadors of Christ. We should show forth the Light in our conversations, the way we dress and talk, showing the love of Christ to everyone. I know I run a risk of being queried, even though the hospital is my family's, but I do what I can." He laughed. "I feel like I'm preaching."

"No, go on. Go on..." She found his passion intriguing.

"Okay. Well, I offer them faith in being healed as long as they are ready to believe. There are some patients on their deathbeds who know nothing about Christ. I see that as an opportunity to talk to them and most of them end up being saved." He paused for a moment then said, "I have a boy who passed on last week. His parents' firstborn. It hurt, but there was nothing I could do. I'm thankful knowing he died in Christ."

She stared at him and her chest tightened at his eyes drowning in pain. "The boy... were you two close?"

"Yes, we were when I think of it. He shared a lot with me, about his life, his hopes, his dreams." He sighed. "That's in the past now."

"I'm sorry for your loss."

"Thanks." He laughed. "Okay, it's your turn. Let me ask you a couple of questions. You ready?"

She rubbed her hands together. "Sure!"

"What do you do when you're stressed?"

A little taken back by his question, she sat back on her seat and folded her arms. "Well, I turn off the TV, switch off the lights, pull the curtains with the fans turned on and rest on the tiled floor."

He raised an eyebrow and she covered her mouth with her right hand while laughing. "Crazy, I know but it's what works for me. I just want to shut out the noise and do anything but think."

"Interesting. Do you have any favourite childhood memories?"

She had a lot, mostly sweet. Her sweetest was with Abdul. There were also the few times her family could be called a family. "Yes, I do. When my dad was alive he used to take me to Ibadan to see my cousins. We would go once a year, during Easter, and it was always fun. We would eat Frejon with garri and fried stew with fish. Delicious."

"Nice. I have never eaten Frejon before."

"Seriously? You need to try it."

"Maybe you would make it for me someday? I can imagine how cute you looked as a little girl. I'm sure you were a beauty then. . . as you are now." She saw his eyes move to her lips. They quickly shifted away.

"Okay." She cleared her throat. "Femi, I think there's something you need to know. You are a great guy but what we are doing," she gestured at the both of them, "It's not something that's heading anywhere."

Femi's face fell.

"Let's just be friends. Again, you're a great guy. You're fun to hang out with, but I think it's best we stay friends."

"Does it have anything to do with my age?"

"No, not at all."

"Is there another guy in the picture?"

She paused, then nodded. "Yes."

He managed a small smile, his lips twitching. "Then I'm happy for you. Disappointed a bit, but happy you're happy. That's what matters."

Signalling for a waiter, he continued, "Okay, time for dessert."

"Nah, I think I'll pass. I'm getting a little tired." *And Abdul is waiting.*

"Are you sure?"

"Sounds tempting, but I'm good."

"Okay. Let me just sort out the bill then."

The rest of their evening was tense. Quiet. Uncomfortable. Femi barely looked in her direction the whole time. He was hurting and she knew it. She did that to him. *Nice guys like him aren't supposed to be hurt by good girls like me.* But here it was, happening. She will find a way to make it up to him somehow. She would come up with a plan. But right then, she had to rush to Abdul's and see what he was up to.

* * *

ABDUL

Abdul was lost in thought. Christmas was on its way, and he knew he would have little time to reflect, thanks to the constant meetings and the company's end of the year party. His lips curled up in a smile. He wanted to take Peju shopping for a dress and have her walk hand in hand with him. He wanted everyone to know she was his. All in due time.

His phone rang again and he assumed it was Peju till he saw the foreign caller ID.

"Good evening, Son. How are you? *As-salamu alaykum.*"

"*As-salamu alaykum,* Ma. I'm fine and you? How is Daddy? And Sherifat? And Biodun?"

"All fine. " She clucked her tongue. "It's too cold over here. I have been telling your father to let us have holiday in Nigeria this time around. I need some sun and hot akamu."

He laughed, knowing fully well his father would be stubborn about returning to the country. He loved the stress-free life. "Let's hope he agrees."

She snorted. "He has to, o *jere*. I have told him no more food for one week if he disagrees and on Christmas day, he would eat McDonald's." She whispered the next words. "I think he's gradually changing his mind."

He laughed. "Okay *o*." He rubbed his eyes tiredly and looked at the time. It was barely nine. He couldn't wait till Peju came around. Maybe he could coerce her into cooking for him.

"How's Peju?"

"She's fine." His mother was elated when he told her they were back together.

"That's good. I'm glad you two still love each other. I'm hoping for wedding bells next year."

Abdul smiled as the dream he had of her wearing a wedding dress came to mind. *"Insh'Allah."*

"Greet her for me. I called to see how you are faring. We will talk later. Your father is asleep and your sisters stepped out to see a movie."

"Okay, Ma. Talk to you later. Greetings to everyone."

He rolled out of bed and went down the stairs to take a bottle of water. Right then, the doorbell rang. He didn't have to ask who it was, flinging the door open with joy.

"Finally."

He pulled her into his arms and kissed her with desperate longing.

He gave her one last kiss and stepped back to stare into her eyes; glad that the love he felt could be seen.

"Thanks for coming," he said a second before his tummy grumbled.

Peju raised a brow at him. "You haven't eaten?"

"No. I was hoping you would make something for me."

She moved past him, and he had the pleasure of watching her swinging backside as she moved to the sofa and slumped her bag on it.

"Do I look like your cook?" She spun around to look at him. "Or your maid?"

"You would be my cook as soon as you marry me." He rubbed his stomach. "I'm very hungry and I think I have a headache too."

"You better have mouth sores as well with your lying tongue."

"Haba, is it your husband you're talking to like that? Better behave yourself. *Oya* go to the kitchen and prepare food for me before I change my mind."

With laughter in her eyes, she asked, "Change your mind about what?"

Abdul took the remote control and turned on the TV, settling down on a seat. "Make the food first and I will tell you."

"Hmm, so what do you want to eat?"

"Surprise me."

Shaking her head, she gave a slow hiss and plodded to the kitchen. He laughed to himself as he tuned to a football match. He hoped she would make *eba* and *efo-riro* for him. Two days ago, he bought ingredients to make the soup but couldn't find the time.

The thought of food triggered memories of Beverley, one of his Canadian casual flings. She was great in bed, but when it came to matters of the stomach, she stuck to what she could make - french toasts, eggs, pancakes and waffles. None of these could *hold body* like a typical Nigerian meal of *amala* and *gbegiri,* or *semovita* and *edikaikong* soup.

"Abdul!"

"Yeah? What's up?"

"Do you want *iru* in your soup?"

"Yes, love."

The match wasn't of much interest to him. The players' sprints across the field were all a blur. Instead of watching, he reflected on what his mother had said about wedding bells. In truth, what were they waiting for? He would marry her the next day if possible. He let the thought linger in his mind till dinner was served.

After a delicious meal of *efo-riro* and Poundo yam, Abdul took her hand and led her to the white loveseat in the living room. He sat down and pulled her down on his lap.

"You know I'm crazy about you," he said as he drew a line with his finger down her arm. "I'm your scapegoat."

"Awww. So sweet."

"What do you think if we got married next year?"

"Are you proposing?"

"Maybe."

"Then you better go back to the drawing board because this isn't romantic."

She pulled at his beard. "You should plan something nice and go down on one knee and ask for my hand in marriage. Not me sitting on your lap with you acting like a king."

"Am I not the king of your heart?"

"Cheesy much!" She stared into his eyes. "But always."

"Since I know what you want then I will plan towards it. Meanwhile, your lips are distracting me from thinking straight."

Peju threw her head back in laughter. "Are you complaining?"

"No. I should just kiss you now so my heart can stop pounding against my chest."

"Smooth operator. You have always had a way with words."

He smiled as she leaned close and kissed him. A moan escaped his lips as the kiss deepened. His arms moved to rub her back. "When are we taking the next step, Peju?" he murmured as he kissed her ear.

"After the wedding."

"Why not now?"

His question ended the moment abruptly. Peju stared at him with soft, yet piercing eyes. "Abdul, we have discussed this already."

"But you can always change your mind. I love you, you love me. We aren't testing waters. We are going to get married, so why can't we be together?"

She got off his lap. "How many people were you with when you left?"

"Two or three."

Her eyes widened. "Two or three? So you aren't even sure how many they are. For all I know, there could even be more. "

He licked his lips. "No. I was only with three people and they were all casual flings."

"Casual flings my ass!" Her eyes watered. "Abdul, you took what was sacred between us and shared it with everyone!"

"Peju -"

She held up her hand. "I'm going home."

"You can't leave like this. Let's settle the matter now."

Peju didn't answer as she picked up her bag and headed towards the front door. He followed suit. "Habeebah, listen to me."

She slapped his hand away as he touched her, before facing him with angry eyes. "I didn't go around sleeping with men while you were away. It didn't feel right. What is it with you guys just throwing around your thing with anyone in a skirt?"

Her pain hurt him. He tried holding her again but she shoved his hands away.

"I thought you were different, Abdul. I really did, but I guess I was wrong."

He pulled her against his chest and held her down. She struggled to break free. "I am different. I'm sorry I did what I did. I'm sorry I gave what was only yours to others."

She gave up the struggle.

"I'm sorry I hurt you." He pressed his lips on her forehead while he whispered how sorry he was.

"It's fine. It's expected you would move on."

"But I'm here now. And I love you." He raised her chin and leaned down to kiss her. "Don't ever doubt it."

Chapter 5

ELIANA

4th of December, 2015

So I cut my hair. My dad nearly killed me when he found out. He said I'm still under his roof and so I shouldn't believe I own myself. I thought Jesus owned me, but I guess I was wrong. #justkidding. But I get what he means. I'm still under his authority and as long as I'm in his house, he's my head. Pastor George explained this at a service. SoI apologized.

I like my new look. It makes me feel like I'm 21 and not 24. My mum - and partner in crime - agrees. In her own words, I look gorgeous. That's why I love her so much!

In other news, someone in my church asked me to attend his cousin's wedding with him. It's a funny first date (should I call it a date?) but I'm cool with it. I feel a nudge to do so, so I'll go with him. I'm hoping to drag Peju along.

I'll keep you updated on things.

"Who are you?" Eliana asked the tall, good looking man who dropped Peju off at her place. Nice build. Nice smile. Nice designer sunglasses too.

"Eliana!"

The fine man laughed. "Hi, Eliana. Peju has told me a lot about you. It's nice to finally meet you in person."

Eliana raised a brow, looked at Peju and back at him. "Well, I'm sorry but I've heard nothing about you."

"I'm sure you have," he said, his gaze fixed on Peju. Eliana didn't miss that gaze. It was piercing, intense, love drunk. "You just didn't connect it with me." He turned to her and extended his hand. "Abdul Layeni."

Eliana shook the hand reluctantly. Why had Peju not told her about this gorgeous creature of a man? "Eliana Awojobi. It's a pleasure." She crossed her arms against her chest. "So how did you guys meet exactly?"

"Back in school. I'm her boy—"

"Boss! He's my boss," Peju cut in. Eliana and Abdul turned to her, puzzled.

"Yes," he agreed and forced a smile, "I'm her boss."

"Oh. Why is your boss dropping you at my house?"

Peju cupped her elbow. "Eliana you're asking too many questions. He just did me a favour. Please, Sir, you can go. Don't mind my friend. Thank you very much for the lift."

Peju dragged Eliana into the house, not waiting to see Abdul enter his car and drive off.

"You're rude *sha*," Eliana said as they walked towards the house. "How can you just leave him like that?"

"He will survive. And you, don't be asking questions like that. It's wrong."

"Wrong how? I was concerned. It's not every day you see a boss go out of his way to drop your friend at your house. A very fine boss. How do you manage, staring at him every day?"

"Simple. I don't stare." They entered the living room and met Eliana's parents. Peju greeted them and they exchanged small talk before dismissing them. They needed to get ready for the wedding.

"You're such a killjoy," Eliana continued once they were in her bedroom. "What happened to the fun Peju I knew? You barely have time for me since you started that your new job. You hardly come to church. Even Bible Study *sef*, you don't come."

"You are nagging."

"And you are evading. Why do I feel like you're holding something back from me?" Eliana asked as she wore her earrings. Timilehin had sent a text that he was on his way and she didn't want to keep him waiting.

"It's all in your mind. Anyways, Femi called me back."

Eliana gave a girlish squeal. "That's awesome! So when is the next date?"

"Wait first and let me finish." She took a deep breath. "I told him I'm not interested in him."

Eliana's eyes widened and looked at her friend like she had lost her mind. "Why? Why would you do something like that? The guy is crazy about you."

Femi was a nice guy. A God-fearing man. He was caring to a fault and very considerate. She couldn't understand why her friend wasn't interested in him at all.

"But the thing is I'm not crazy about him. I can't see myself marrying him."

"And I was rooting for you guys *o*. I was already dreaming of my beautiful dress as your maid-of-honour. Bright yellow, take note. I was also thinking of powder blue and yellow for the wedding reception."

"Blue and yellow *ke*?" Peju smacked her lips together after applying red lipstick. She was standing in front of a dresser mirror, "Better remove such thoughts from your head."

"I'll try." She sighed. "Question. Did you pray about ending things?"

Peju laughed. "Madam, must I pray about everything? Hasn't God given us the sense to know who to marry?"

Eliana stared at her friend as she applied a blue eye-shadow and mascara. Something was going on in her friend's life. She could feel it. *Why is she defensive?* "Well, since you surrendered your life to Him, and asked Him to take control, it only makes sense that you allow Him to lead you in that aspect of your life. If you feel you can give Him other aspects of your life and not your choice of a husband, when trouble comes, then eventually you have to give it to Him."

"I've heard, Madam Pastor."

* * *

CHAPTER 5

OBA

"You did what?!"

Oba held back his phone from his ear as thick Yoruba insults blasted through. It was his mother. Timilehin walked into the room with a bottle of Coke in one hand and locally baked *Agege* bread in the other. Oba cringed as he watched Timilehin pour the coke into the bread. Years of watching him do so still didn't make it easy to bear.

"Mummy, calm down *nau*." He could hear his father in the background trying to placate her as well.

"*Kin fara bale?* Your son wants to marry that Igbo girl and you are telling me to relax? You aren't bothered?"

Oba heard his father say something but didn't quite get it. He put two and two together when his mother replied, "Even if she's a human being, some human beings in this world are wicked! *Olorun maje*! God forbid! Obatotosinloluwa Afolayan, *se on gbo mi*, if you bring that woman to my house I will send you two packing. I refuse to accept her as my daughter. That manner-less ingrate. I have told you now." A painful silence followed before she ended the call.

He closed his eyes in surrender. He was tired and yet, it was still morning.

"So *wetin* Mumsi talk?"

In response to his question, Oba shook a tired finger at Timilehin. His cousin could barely contain his laughter.

"My dad is cool with it. Mum, on the other hand, says Nene isn't good for me. That she lacks manners. I don't know where she gets all these ideas from. The girl gave her Ankara wrappers just the other day."

Why did his mother have to make everything so difficult? Nene had already shared the news with her family, and the world on Instagram. What if his mother followed through with her threats and didn't accept her as his wife? What would he do?

"Timi, Nene is perfect for me! She's beautiful. Gorgeous. Great in -" He was going to say bed but thought better of it and said, "The kitchen."

"Are you sure? The *efo* your Madam cooked made me purge for three days

45

straight." He bit into his almost finished Bread-Coction.

"That was her second time of cooking it *o*. Next time will be better."

"Which next time? *Abi* she *wan* make I die from food poisoning?"

Oba would have laughed at Timilehin's joke. But not today. Everything was falling apart. "She's an okay person. It doesn't get better than that."

"Guy, are you high? Since when do people marry wife because she's an okay person."

Oba snorted.

"If you want to follow God, follow Him a hundred per cent. Not all this one leg in, one leg out behaviour *abeg*. You're there collecting *nyash* anyhow." Timilehin stopped and turned to the wall clock. "Time *don* go. Are you still game for the wedding today?"

"Yeah."

Timilehin rose from his seat. "Okay, let me quickly change. I invited one babe *to* church. *Abeg*, we *go* pick her and her friend before we *reach* the wedding."

Oba nodded absent-mindedly. *Today can't get any worse than this.*

* * *

ELIANA

Eliana loved the décor of the hall. It was obvious a lot of money had been spent. Peach and coral. Each table had a tall vase of white flowers, with exquisite white and silver dishwares.

Everything was breathtakingly beautiful.

She couldn't wait to start her interior design business. As God would have it, two people had called her in the last two weeks to offer her gigs. They were small projects, but still opportunities to show what she could do.

Her daydreaming was cut short by a nudge on her side. She turned to

Peju who leaned close and extended her phone to her. "This is Titi. We were friends in secondary school." An ebony beauty smiled back at her in the picture, with serious cleavage on display. She also had a black belly-button stud, revealed by her crop top.

"She's a fine girl. Do you guys still talk?"

"No. Haven't heard from her in ages and I don't intend on connecting. People change a lot after school. And besides, I didn't have true friends back then." Peju adjusted herself on her seat.

Eliana placed her hand on her chest. "Like me *abi*?"

"What would you lovely ladies like to drink?" Timilehin asked, interrupting their teasing.

"Juice please," Eliana answered for the both of them.

"And food? Have you guys had a look at the menu?"

This time Peju spoke, sharing their meals of choice. After Timilehin left their table, his cousin in tow, she continued to scroll through her Instagram timeline on her phone. Eliana, on the other hand, curiously watched the two men leave. Timilehin, she knew from church, but it was her first time meeting his cousin, Oba. He seemed nice but had kept to himself during the drive to the reception. *He is probably really shy,* she concluded. She blushed at the memory of their eyes making contact in the car, and her having to look away. It was necessary before she left the wrong impression that she was checking him out. His cousin asked her out, after all.

At the wedding, she continued to watch them in silence. Timilehin was busy trying to cajole Oba into carrying a baby. Timilehin was a fun guy, fine too. How exactly he felt, only time would tell.

Ten minutes later, both men returned with servers carrying their orders. A lady followed. She was dressed in a black, halter neck dress that stopped abruptly at her thighs. Her complexion, an unnatural shade of yellow. She also had a handful of stares her way.

She greeted Timilehin who waved briefly.

"Babe," Oba said to her, before giving her a side hug. "Nene, these are Timilehin's church members. Eliana and Peju. Ladies, this is my fiancée, Nene Okafor."

Nene blinked. "Eliana? What kind of name is that?"

"Hebrew."

"Oh. Interesting" She said dryly. She turned her attention back to Oba, placing her hand on his shoulder. Eliana could have sworn it was a deliberate attempt to show off her dazzling engagement ring. Peju tapped her arm lightly and Eliana leaned close to hear her over what the MC was saying.

"Don't mind her. She's insecure."

Eliana laughed, but deep down she couldn't help but feel somewhat disappointed that he was in a relationship.

* * *

FEMI

I don't mean for us to be anything more than friends. You're a great guy. You're fun to hang out with, but I would rather we stay friends.

Femi angrily dropped his pen on the opened file and cleaned the sides of his mouth. It was a week since he had seen Peju. They barely saw each other at church. Was she avoiding him? Did she not want his friendship as well?

God, I thought she was the woman I would finally settle down with. Where did I go wrong?

No answer came to heart.

God, why are you being silent on this? I'm confused right now. Did I get it wrong?

I know the plans I think towards you.

Femi knew that to be true, yet there were times things hadn't gone the way they should and it made him wonder and doubt such plans.

Did God's plan include suffering? Quite frankly, he was tired of his share of heartbreaks.

"There's a lady who wants to see you." He almost jumped at the voice of the nurse he hadn't heard walking in.

"It's not a patient?"

"She is but she didn't request her file - only to see you." He could hear the curiosity in her voice. But he didn't give room for speculation.

"Send her in."

Within a minute his door opened once again and Femi looked up to see a woman smiling at him, dressed in an all-black fashionable hijab. He was taken aback by her appearance.

"Miss Ali?"

She nodded. "Yes, Dr Alakija. I almost thought you wouldn't recognize me dressed like this." She spread her hand over her outfit. "I guess you can say I have changed."

"Please have your seat."

She did so and released her bag from her shoulder.

"So what can I do for you today?"

"I have come to take you for lunch." He raised a brow and she rushed on to say. "It's the least I can do after how much you helped me."

He shook his head and waved his hand at her. "You don't have to take me for lunch. I'm just doing my job."

She pursed her lips and Femi hoped he hadn't offended her. That was the least he wanted to do. "Please let me. You may think it's unnecessary but it's just my way of saying thank you. God only knows what would have happened if I -," She paused and took a deep breath and looked down at her fingers, "If you hadn't caught it immediately. Good things haven't always been happening to me and for this to happen. I believe God has maybe heard my prayers for a change." She laughed and looked at him. "I'm sure you would think this silly or stupid but that's just -" She shook her head. "Never mind. It was probably a bad idea."

She rose from her seat.

"I will go with you." That earned him a shocked, but happy look from her. He raised a finger. "But on one condition."

"What?"

"What's your name?" Of course, he knew her full name since it was on her file but he asked just to break whatever nervousness she had going on.

She laughed. "Halimat. Halimat Ali."

They drove down to a fast-food restaurant not far from the hospital. It was after they had ordered their meals that Femi expressed his curiosity.

"You just wanted to thank me?"

She smiled. "Are we still going on about that? You don't get this much, do you?"

He shrugged as he bit into his chicken burger and relished the blend of flavours. " Well, a cheque or a gift is usually more predictable, but lunch? That's interesting."

"I'm glad to be the first."

"Thank you very much for the kind gesture."

"You're welcome."

Not wanting to stop the flow of conversation, he asked her to tell him more about herself.

Halimat cleared her throat. "Well, as you know I'm Halimat by name. I work as a chartered accountant in an auditing firm." She mentioned the name of the company; it was a highly prestigious one Femi knew of. "I schooled abroad for five years plus work experience and came back to do my National Youth Service in Bauchi. I came back to Lagos and started working here when I was done. That's pretty much it."

"Are you happy?" Femi had no idea why he asked that.

"Wow."

"You don't have to answer. I'm sorry I asked."

"No, it's fine. I want to." She smiled a little, then looked down at her full plate. "No. No, I'm not." She raised her head and looked back at him. "I've made a lot of mistakes in my life I wish I could change. But like ink, it's hard to wipe away. I've always been the good girl seeking for bad. Like a part of me feels life is too short to play nice. I need to have fun and live a little. My mother is sick and tired of my drama."

"Are you an only child?"

She shook her head. "No. I have two older sisters. They are the best.... I take it you're a Christian?"

Femi nodded.

"You're different from the ones I know."

"How so?"

"You seem joyful. At peace. And you are always this way every time we see. I think that's what drew me to you."

Okay?

The two talked for the next half hour about their lives and interests before parting ways. And while she was a nice distraction, Femi still couldn't get Peju Adams out of his head.

Chapter 6

PEJU

Peju was a nervous wreck. Her heart kept beating wildly, her palms a sweaty mess. She also kept rubbing her arms even in her mother's warm home.

I love you, you love me. We aren't testing waters. We are going to get married so why can't we be together? Abdul's statement kept replaying in her mind over and over again. And the idea was scarily becoming more appealing.

Last night, she saw herself in Abdul's arms. She was naked, happy and melting because of his kisses. Sadly, it was all a dream, but she didn't want it to be a dream. She wanted it to be her reality.

A part of her was jealous and angry at the thought of him being with another woman. But what right did she have to feel this way? He was in no way obligated to her when they had broken up, or to the romance, they had once shared.

She hadn't been in any serious relationship with anyone and had focused on her work, God and her mother. There had been little time for romance and to be honest, she wasn't interested in the men who approached her. It seemed God had saved her for this moment by bringing Abdul back into her life and wanted them together. If not, why would they happen to meet again? Why would she still have love in her heart for him after all these years?

Yes, their relationship was far from perfect. They quarrelled from time to time. Their last fight caused a tiny rift between them. Peju had to settle quickly but in the end, it had left her afraid.

"What are you thinking about?" Peju spun around from the window to see her mother carrying a plate of food towards her small dining table.

"Mummy, I asked if you needed help and now you have cooked the food." *Hopefully, that will change the topic.*

"You have forgotten this is my job. If I needed your help I would have asked for it." She placed the steaming plate of *jollof-rice* on the table and wiped her hands on a napkin. "How is your boyfriend? I thought you would come with him."

"He had to make a few stops on the way. He will be here soon." She took a slice of plantain, put it in her mouth and sat on a chair. "He's also hosting a few people from work later in the evening."

"Hmmm." Her mother sat adjacent to her. "Love looks good on you. See how you're shining."

Peju laughed. "That's true. Before I forget, I saw a photo of Titi, my friend from school. She was practically half-naked."

Her mother's eyes widened. "Really?"

Peju nodded.

"What about that your other friend?"

"Antonia? I don't know. I haven't heard from her."

"*E ya.* And you three were so close. It's sad how things end." With concern in her eyes, she continued, "You and Abdul should do quick and marry. Don't waste any time before your relationship ends again and another woman snatches him."

"He didn't get married when I wasn't with him. Why is it now he's here that he would marry someone else?"

Her mother clapped her hands together and hissed. "You talk like a novice." She pulled her right ear. "My dear, this is Nigeria. One woman can do *juju* for him and take him from you. Sit down there and be saying he won't marry someone else. Act fast!" She snapped her fingers. "Get pregnant if possible. You said he's rich now. *Ehen*, which woman doesn't like good thing?"

Peju was trying hard not to laugh at her mother's advice. Neither was she going to let it get to her. She trusted Abdul, and nothing could compete with what he felt for her.

She recalled having to apologise for introducing him to Eliana as her boss, and not her boyfriend. He felt she was playing games; she didn't see their love as the real deal. But she did, more than he would possibly know.

"It's not like that Abdul. Honestly. I just don't want her to know about us yet."

He immediately frowned. "Why? It makes no sense to me."

"I panicked. She has been trying to hook me up with a guy from church and I told her I'm not interested."

As if understanding suddenly dawned on him, he blinked. "You didn't want to tell her because I'm a Muslim?"

"Abdul don't -"

"No, it's the truth. You are afraid of what people would think." He shook his head, baffled. "Since when did you become this woman, Peju? Someone that's afraid of what people think?"

"I'm not afraid!" she snapped, annoyed that he was getting to the core of her worries. "I just don't want her wahala. That's all. It doesn't stop me from loving you or wanting to marry you. If you asked me right now I would say yes."

He raised his brow. His gaze questioning. "Are you sure?"

She nodded despite the gnawing feeling in her chest. She loved him. She really loved him. "Yes."

He stared at her for what seemed like several minutes and came close to her, enveloping her in his arms. "I believe you. But I won't ask you to marry me yet. Not now."

She was scared at that moment. Not because he wouldn't believe her or ask her hand in marriage, but because of the relief that had flowed through when he said he would ask her later. It wasn't that she didn't love him. No, far from it. Marriage was just very important to her, and to her, a wrong decision could mean spending the rest of her life with regrets. Peju didn't want hers to have the kind of ending her mother's had. It made her busy with activities just to fill up the loneliness in her life. *But things with Abdul will be different because he loves me.*

Satisfied with that thought, she spoke with her mum about other matters; making sure to steer clear from talk of Abdul and herself. Peju was halfway done with her food when he arrived, looking good in his wine native attire.

He also came bearing gifts.

"Ah, thank you, my son," her mother said. "If I had known you were bringing me a present, I would have prepared yours."

"*Haba* Mummy. It's not a problem." He took his seat beside Peju, gave her a side hug and squeezed her shoulder gently.

"It's what courtesy demands. I will send Peju to you," she said, leaving no room for arguments. "Meanwhile, I was just telling Peju how good she looks when she's in love. I'm glad you two still love each other after many years apart."

"Your daughter is an amazing woman and I'm fortunate to be with her." Abdul rubbed Peju's shoulders once more before taking her spoon and eating out of her food.

"You can finish it," Peju told him, as she watched him take spoon after spoon.

"No *o*! So you can cheat me of Mum's delicious cooking *abi*? Please bring mine for me. I'm very hungry."

Her mother laughed. "Don't worry, Peju. Eat your food. I will get his."

As soon as her mother was out of earshot, Peju questioned Abdul on his so-called hunger. "I thought you had food where you're coming from."

He took another spoonful, chewed and swallowed before answering, "I didn't eat there since I knew I was coming over. It won't be nice not to eat your mother's food *nau*. And besides, I have missed her cooking. I remember when you would bring her *Amala* and *gbegiri* for me in school."

Peju laughed. Her mother was so wrong. Abdul was crazy about her. Nothing and no one was going to take his love from her. She was willing to fight for him.

There was a whisper against her heart, and suddenly, she felt cold.

Even with Me?

***

FEMI

Femi kissed both sides of her face. She looked up at him and lovingly patted him on his. "Merry Christmas to you too, dear. You're too charming. Why no woman has snagged you still baffles me."

"*Abi o*! I wonder too." Osaz said, but he was all smiles. "Maybe it's the grey in your beard that's causing them to run."

Femi ignored him and gave a reply to Osaz's mother. "Mummy, God's timing is the best. How are you feeling now?"

"Much better. Thank you, my son."

At that moment, Oluchi, Osaz's wife, came out and crossed the room to hug Femi. For someone who gave birth to twins almost three months ago, she looked good. Some of his patients still carried their baby weight for months, blaming it on stress and not enough help amongst other excuses.

"Don't mind Osaz. Me, I'm on your side." Oluchi looked at her husband. "You don't know you can't just propose to any woman? When you found me, was it not God that led you? Or you think it was by your good looks that I married you?"

Osaz snorted. "Woman, leave that matter. Didn't you just admit I have good looks? At the end of the day, *shebi* you're in my house."

Femi laughed and shook his head at both of them. They were like this whenever he was with them, like Tom and Jerry in live-action.

"Where are the kids? I brought gifts for them." He raised the pink paper bags up for her to see.

"Awww, thanks Femi. They are sleeping."

"Have you gotten around to decorating their room yet?" He dropped the bags on their centre table and sat down on a couch. Osaz had mentioned trying to get the room ready but was too busy.

Oluchi brought over a tray with a glass and soft drinks. "Not yet. I have been trying to understand my schedule so I can get it done myself. Why? Do you have someone in mind?"

Femi thought of Eliana. She had mentioned running courses in Interior Design and he happened to see the beautiful designs she had made in the children's church. He knew she would be thrilled to land the job.

"Yes. She goes to my church and she's really good."

"And affordable?" Osaz asked.

"Yes, that too." He pulled out his phone from his jacket. "Osaz, I will send her number to you, so you two can talk."

Oluchi thanked him and left the living room to attend to matters in the kitchen. Osaz's mum, on the other hand, dashed off to check on the babies.

"Thanks for giving me time off," Osaz said. "Oluchi really appreciated me being around to take care of my mother and help out with the twins."

"Why don't you get a nanny?"

Osaz snorted. "I don't trust nannies. That's one thing my wife and I don't see eye to eye on. But enough about me. How's your babe? Has she finally agreed for you?"

Femi didn't want to talk about Peju. She was still on his mind and quite frankly, he was tired. He had handed everything over to God and was going to keep doing what he had to do. If she was happy with her new man, then fine, it was okay by him. He wasn't going to force himself, or keep feeling jealous.

"Can we not talk about this?"

Osaz raised a brow. "I'm guessing things didn't go as planned. It's fine. You know I'm here for you. What's the latest with you, besides that?"

Femi thought of Halimat Ali, his newfound friend who seemed as troubled as the sea on a rainy day. There were things about her he was yet to figure out. In little ways, she reminded him of Peju; having a tough exterior with a soft centre. She loved laughing and was caring when she wanted to be. He didn't know why Halimat came his way and opened up to him, but one thing he knew was God had His hand in it. The best he could do was keep her in his prayers and be a friend.

"Nothing much. Work, rest and church. That's pretty much the summary of my life at the moment." He wasn't ready to tell Osaz about her.

"It's all good. As long as you're fine." He paused. "I'm sorry if I've been pressuring you about marriage and kids lately. I just want you to be happy."

"Thanks for the concern. I'm happy, just not how you'd expect. A family doesn't determine my happiness. God does." He knew there were days he felt alone, but he was never lonely.

"Okay. I believe you." Osaz tapped Femi's thigh. "There's a movie you should watch. It's action-packed and I trust you would love it."

"Not as much as he would love to see these young ones," Oluchi said, walking slowly towards him with a pink double-stroller. He got up and met her halfway, squatting to see her daughters. "Hi lovelies. It's Uncle Femi, your favourite god-father in the world."

"Since you're their favourite, just pay for their room then," Osaz chipped in.

"Osaz!"

"What? It's a suggestion."

Femi paid little attention to them. He gave his finger to one of the kids and she grabbed it. Holding on tightly. *Lord, I won't mind a girl first.* "Is it just me or they are getting more beautiful as the days go by?"

Oluchi laughed. "Don't ask me. I'm biased."

"God bless you Osasere and Osayemwenre." Femi said. Someday, he would have his own kids. He just knew it. And whoever God chose to make that reality with was fine by him.

* * *

OBA'S MUM

Oba's mother stared at her son's baby photo dreamily. It seemed like yesterday when he came into her world. He was a peaceful baby, and never gave her trouble. How she missed those days. *Or am I being too hard on him?* she wondered. No. Just like any good mother, she wanted what was best for her son. And his current girlfriend wasn't it.

Why was he so bent on choosing her? Why couldn't it be like old times when she could tell him what to do and her words were final? Even the girl she had chosen for him had been thrown back in her face.

Mrs Afolayan kept the photograph aside. She stood up from her bed and walked over to the dressing table, picking up the expensive gold earrings her husband gave her on her birthday.

It wasn't that Nene wasn't beautiful. She was. But beauty wasn't as important. Could she take care of her son? Would she be a good mother to their children? Would she stand fast when the troubles of marriage came, and not run away? All those questions had the same answer in her mind. It was a simple "No".

"You look beautiful, dear."

She smiled, her heart leaping, as she stared back at her husband's reflection in the mirror. He was handsome in his cream *buba* and *sokoto*. "Thank you."

"I don't think you should give that out, Helen." He said, hinting at one of the gifts she placed on the bed. She knew he was referring to what Nene had sent to her through Oba. She had already gift wrapped it for a family member. They were having a dinner party, hosting her husband's brother and sisters.

"But if I'm not going to use them, why should I keep them?"

He walked up to her and stopped behind her. "If it's because the girl is Igbo, then you better find a better excuse." He took the chain from her hands and wore it on her neck for her. "Perfect."

Helen smiled in appreciation. Her husband was ever thoughtful. She had complained when he gave her the gold set, asking where she would wear them to since they were both retired and rarely attended functions.

"Even if you have to wear it for me in the house, then do so. You're worth it."

"Don't you want your son to enjoy what we have? Don't you want him to be happy?" he asked, breaking into her thoughts.

"Nkan te so ko da. Of course, I want him to be happy. But Kunle, that woman is not for him. She's not a proper Yoruba girl. No home training."

"Is Chioma a bad person?" he asked, referring to his younger brother's wife.

"No."

"Does she lack home training?"

She shook her head.

Kunle caressed her arms while peering at her in the mirror. "Give her a chance. If she's not God's will, then let it be scattered. If it is, pray for grace to love her." He kissed the side of her head and told her to hurry up, that his brother was on his way. And just like that, he had settled the matter.

Oh Lord, do that which You will. Hurry and perform it. If she's not Your will for Oba, then don't let them marry. Please. . .

* * *

ELIANA

Eliana didn't want to complain, but her frown said it all. She wasn't happy that her father sent her out on Christmas Day to buy drinks. Her mother added chicken to the list. She was hosting a few people from church for Christmas lunch and she wasn't sure she had enough chicken for everyone.

As if that wasn't enough, her brother was tagging along.

This isn't how I planned my day at all.

She held her shopping basket as she perused their wide section of chicken, hoping to pick a fat, juicy piece with plenty of meat. The kind her mother would be pleased with.

"Big Sis, can you get a drink for me? I'm thirsty."

"Better wait till we get to the house. I'm not wasting my money on your sugar rush," she said while still looking. The shop was crowded and Eliana didn't want anyone to grab what she wanted.

"But I'm really thirsty!"

Eliana let out an exasperated breath. "Go and take water. And get some drinks as well. Make sure you come back quickly so we can leave this place." She knew the queue to pay would waste time. Within a few minutes, she was satisfied with her choice. She picked it up and dropped it in her basket. She craned her neck to the drinks section and saw her brother reaching into a fridge.

So what has he been doing since?

"Eliana?"

She looked around and her heart skipped a beat. Her throat clogged when she saw Timilehin's cousin staring at her. She was pleasantly surprised to see him, and even more that he remembered her name.

"Hi, Oba." She gave a little wave. "Merry Christmas."

"Merry Christmas." He shifted left, letting a chubby woman through with her son. The woman glared at them before passing.

"The crowd here is just too much. Are you also doing Christmas shopping?" She gestured at his trolley, filled with all sorts of drinks and alcohol.

Does he drink? she thought to herself.

"Not exactly. There's a party a friend of mine is having and I'm helping out with the drinks. What about you?"

Eliana explained her predicament to him, ending it with a sigh.

He laughed. *"Pele.* It's one of those things. Family wouldn't be family if they didn't stress you out. Do you stay around?"

"Yes. Just down the road. You?"

"No. Are you guys done? Maybe I could give you guys a lift if you don't mind waiting a bit for me." he said, looking apologetic.

Eliana quickly weighed her options, knowing her preferred choice from the get-go.

"Please wait. It's Christmas. Let me show the love of Christ."

She laughed and nodded.

* * *

ELIANA

Things turned out differently after the drop-off. She invited him in to eat or drink something. That led to him playing a video game with her brother and discussing politics with her father. An hour quickly passed before he set out.

"Hope you aren't late for your party," she said as she escorted him to his car. They both walked slowly, with awkward hands in their pockets. "I didn't think it would be that long."

He glanced at his watch. "It's fine. The party is later in the evening but I have to get the drinks iced. I really had fun. Your mum's homemade shawarma was really good and it was nice meeting your family." He laughed softly and shook his head. "Your brother is a clown."

Eliana rolled her eyes. "You're telling me. He is the Chief Entertainer at home."

"He's fourteen right? Don't worry, he will outgrow that in due time."

She waved her hand. "Oh, I'm not worried." They were now at his car. "Thanks for dropping us and coming in. And Merry Christmas once again."

"You too dear." He got into his car, made a U-turn and drove off.

As expected, her mother was interested in who he was and how they met. The excitement came to a crashing halt when she found out he was engaged.

"He seems like a good boy," her father said. "Make sure you bring someone like that home. Not all those riff-raffs on the street. But anyway, I trust you."

Eliana smiled. She knew better than to trust solely on her instincts. After what happened with Kene, she had learnt to trust God when it came to relationships and other aspects of her life. She wouldn't deny she enjoyed Oba's company, and how funny and easy-going he was. He was the kind of guy she would love to get to know and maybe end up with. But she wasn't going to let her feelings run ahead of God, especially towards someone who was engaged. There was no way they could be together. Plus, she had her concerns about his alcohol drinking habits. Fingers crossed the drinks she saw were really for his friends, not him. Whatever the case was, he wasn't her problem. She wasn't going to spend time thinking about him before unholy thoughts flooded in.

Later that night, as she collapsed on her bed after tidying up the kitchen, she put down thoughts in her journal:

No matter what happens, whether I love a man or not, get married or not, my love for Christ isn't going to be shaken. I know nothing can be compared to my love for Him. It's amazing how much I have grown spiritually in the last few months, and how I have come to know Him. Even in the coming year, I want to grow more in love with Him.

Romans 8 came to mind. It was one of her favourite verses, with words on how inseparable she was from the love of Christ. Smiling, she wrote, *I have discovered God's awesome love for me and the knowledge of it makes my heart swell with love for Him. Sometimes I have shivers just thinking about it.*

Nothing can shake Your love for me. I would love and serve You with everything within me regardless of what the future brings. And I have a feeling it's going to be exciting.

* * *

PEJU

At past two in the morning, Peju snuggled close to Abdul, loving the feel of his naked skin against hers, and the smell of his cologne. She ran her palm across his hairless chest as he snored lightly.

She tried to console her guilty conscience, saying that this was what she wanted. The moment they had shared was better than she had ever dreamed, much better than they'd ever had, too.

It was obvious he was more experienced. He understood her curves and knew what buttons to touch at each point in time. The truth of him learning with other women came knocking, but she refused to let it ruin her day. The fact was she loved him, they were together, and that was all that mattered.

"Merry Christmas," she whispered once again, although Christmas was two hours gone. She kissed him on the lips, just like she did before their dinner party started. It had gone well and when it ended, they cuddled on the couch, talking. One thing led to another, and before she knew it, they were on their way to his bedroom.

"This is the best gift you could have given me. This and the gift hamper filled with my favourite things," he said, chuckling. "Thank you, Habeebah." He turned to his side to look into her eyes. "I love you."

"I love you too." *So much that it hurts.* "I'm sorry if I made it seem like I was ashamed of our relationship or the love we share. I'm not. In fact —" She gathered the sheets around her and stood on the bed, "I want to shout it out loud. I love you, Abdul Layeni!" He laughed, pulling her down into his arms.

"I don't doubt that you love me. The way you showed it tonight is proof enough."

Peju covered her face from embarrassment. "Please, don't say that."

He removed her hand gently. "What's that phrase again? Naked but not ashamed?"

She nodded.

"There shouldn't be any secrets between us. We are not just lovers but friends. We can share anything with each other. We can cry together. We can laugh together. But no lies. No secrets. No embarrassment. Deal?"

"Deal."

He shifted away from her. "Now to your Christmas present. I wanted to wait till next year, but then I think this is a perfect time."

Is he going to propose? Peju was ready to say yes. She suppressed her excitement and doubts as he opened a drawer by his bed and pulled out a small box. Yes! Her mother would be so happy. It was until he turned that she felt her bubble burst. It looked nothing like a ring box.

"Here's your present."

She took the rectangular box from him, raising a brow in curiosity and opened it. It was a car key. She looked up to find his eyes on her. He looked concerned and doubtful. Hence, she chose her words carefully.

"You bought me a car?" she said, careful to suppress the disappointment in her voice.

"Yes. Don't reject it. It's a Christmas gift. I can't stand the thought of you jumping buses. I want to take care of you, Peju. Let me."

Even though she told him not to, he had gone ahead to buy her a car. Peju had to mentally assure herself that he was trying to be sweet. He hadn't done it to show off his money or to make her feel incapable. He did it because he loved her. "Thank you, Abdul. I appreciate you for taking care of me. I have to confess something though. I don't know how to drive."

Abdul laughed as he drew her close to him. "That's not a problem. I will help you all the way. That's why I'm here."

Chapter 7

HALIMAT

Halimat dreaded the thought of her parents' New Year's party. Her whole family would be there, and while the urge to see her baby niece was tempting, she wasn't going to give in. She wasn't in the mood to indulge her family's piteous looks and their need to offer unsolicited advice.

At the spark of fireworks, she rolled her eyes; her heart calming to a normal pace. Knock-outs and loud music. That was pretty much what she had to put up with most of the day. As usual, everyone was hyped about the start of a new year, but for her, nothing was exciting about it. There was no change in her life. Nothing to celebrate about. So what was all the fuss for?

It was thick in the air - the hope for a fresh start, a new beginning. For some, they wanted marriage, and others, childbirth or promotions. Some believed their lives could change, the past easily forgotten. There was always the excitement of setting New Year resolutions and writing down goals to achieve, right until the next few weeks came rolling in, the plans forgotten or deemed impossible to do. Halimat snorted. It was all useless. The only change possible was ordained by God. At least, that was what she chose to believe. And God wasn't interested in her, so what was the point of hope.

She set aside her laptop and tip-toed her way to the bathroom. The tiles' coolness crept through her feet. She settled into a warm bath quickly to unwind. On most days, she loved her company but right now, staying home alone on the first day of the New Year made her feel lonely. Her other option was to drive down to a nearby pizza joint and get food. There, she would watch people from a corner and makeup stories of their lives. It was one of her many pastimes.

If one looked closely, one could tell if a person was happy or not. And in entirety, Halimat could say thirty percent of the people she came across were on the verge of depression. Unfortunately, she was in that category as well. Out of her bath, she fought back this truth as she got dressed and hurried out of her flat.

Are you happy?

Dr Alakija's question triggered something in her. Why he thought to ask was also a mystery. She lived a fun, exciting life to the outside. Her looks, on point, to match. But deep down in her was utter confusion. And she thought she had done a good job of covering it up.

The pizza place still had a couple of customers but Halimat didn't have to queue long to get her order. As she sat close to the window, she glanced at the few people there. On her left, a group of friends were hanging out and laughing at a seemingly funny joke. A guy and girl were holding hands in a corner, whispering to each other. The girl could barely contain herself, red-faced and flustered. Also, three noisy ladies were yapping off. There was so much tension in their space, and focus. *Hmm, Naija women. Most likely talking about men.*

Halimat laughed. She pulled out her phone to attend to Instagram posts in need of likes. All to while away time she wished she didn't have.

"Happy New Year to me," she murmured to herself.

* * *

OBA

He turned off the car ignition and welcomed the silence. "Babe, no doubt about it, your car has seen better days. You should consider selling it and getting another one." Like a child, Nene groaned, folded her arms and stomped her foot on the ground. "Hubby, why is this happening to me? We just started the new year for crying out loud. Do you know how stressful it will be for me to get public transport to work early in the morning?"

Oba stepped out of the car and wiped the sweat from his brow. He was in no mood for any more complaints. It was a hot Saturday afternoon and he wanted something cold to drink, and maybe some food as well.

Like that shawarma, I had at Eliana's house. "See, you're getting yourself worked up for nothing. We'll have to change the engine if it comes to the worst. In the meantime, take my car to work and I will sort myself out." He sighed. " Right now, I'm hungry. *Abeg,* let's get some food."

She strolled up to him and threw her hands around his neck, planting little kisses all over his face even with the sweat trickling down his face. "Thank you. Thank you. Thank you. You're the best soon-to-be-husband in the world! *Biko,* what do you want to eat? I haven't gone to the market for you though."

Say what?! "It's fine. Let's just go somewhere nice and get something to eat then you can go to the market." They did just that. After he was fully satisfied, he took her to the market, waited till she was done shopping then dropped her at home. He promised to drop the car off Sunday evening. On his way home, Oba recalled his last conversation with Timilehin.

"Yes! I forgot to tell you, I met Eliana's parents and her brother. They were nice."

"Met them where?"

"Their house. I bumped into her at the supermarket and took her home. She invited me in and that's how I met her family. She's a nice girl, Timilehin."

"I don't like how you went to her house. Couldn't you say no?"

Oba laughed. Was his cousin jealous? *"You know I'm engaged right? So you don't have anything to worry about."*

68

"I better not."

He laughed. Timilehin liked her; it was obvious. He just needed to make the next move. He didn't understand why his cousin felt the need to pray about it when he already liked her. It all seemed so unnecessary to him, but he thought to leave it at that.

Later in the evening, Oba was watching TV when his mother called. He hadn't spoken to her since December. She had refused to pick his calls. He eagerly answered, longing to hear her voice.

"Good evening Ma... Yes, I'm fine and you? And Dad?"

"Fine, fine. How's Nene?" she asked.

Oba was surprised his mother was asking after her. "She's fine. She's excited about the wedding." She was. Conversations on the wedding dress and bridal party gowns had started with the designer, down to the details. She wanted to sort out other things, but he kept stalling, hoping he'd someday get the go-ahead from his mother.

"Okay." He heard her sigh. "I want you to know you have my blessings to marry her."

He stood. "Really? What made you change your mind?"

"Your father spoke to me. Oba, you know I love you and only want what's best for you. If Nene -" he could sense his mother's hesitation, "If Nene is God's will for you, then who am I to oppose?"

He rubbed his head with a bare palm. Still in awe at what was happening. "Wow. Thank you, Ma. I appreciate it."

"You're welcome. Love is sweet, especially when you're with who God wants you to be with. It may not be smooth all the way but you will be confident you have God's approval. I hope you have that, Oba." There was a brief pause, as though to allow her words sink in. Then she said, "We would talk later. Enjoy the rest of your day."

"And you too, Ma."

The line went dead, leaving Oba dazed. Whatever his father had said to her, Oba had to thank him. He sat back down. His father was one of the few men of honour he knew. He was a man of integrity and his mother greatly respected him. Oba had seen that much growing up, seeing how they related with one another.

Would Nene respect me too in old age?

He didn't have an answer and it bothered him. And the concept of knowing God's will concerning marriage was still far-fetched. He believed it was a matter of personal choice. There couldn't be just one person God intended an individual to be with when there were billions of people in the world. And what if a person's spouse died? Did that mean they had no hope of ever remarrying?

What had Timilehin mentioned the other day?

"Guy, are you high? Since when do people marry wife because she's an okay person."

Oba knew there were a lot of things he did that were wrong but that didn't make him less of a good person. He paid his tithes, sometimes. He read his Bible every once in a while, as much as he could, but did that qualify him as a bad person? Why would it? Did it make him a candidate for hell?

***

PEJU

"Aren't we too old for sleepovers?" Peju took out clean bedding and handed them to Eliana to make the bed.

"Says who *abeg*?"

Peju remembered when she went to Ibadan to visit her cousins. They had sleepovers but not necessarily as fun as Eliana was making it sound. They were children and had to sleep whenever the adults told them to.

"Yeah, but when I was much younger. My dad used to take me to my cousin's place."

The bed made, Eliana sat down and picked up her phone. "You don't talk about your dad much. Why?"

Peju lifted her shoulders in a shrug. "There's nothing to talk about. He left my mum and me when I was twelve. He kept coming and going, but he had another woman on the side who never had kids for him. I don't know the full story but he died when I was twenty. That's all."

"Did you guys have a close relationship?"

"Kind of. He bought things for me. Took me out. Nothing really special."

"So you don't miss him then."

"Hmm, your questions plenty *o*. No, I don't miss him. He wasn't there for me to build a solid relationship with him. Anyways, I'm already used to not having a father figure in my life so I'm good."

Eliana got up and embraced her briefly. "And you have God."

A familiar feeling of guilt came knocking. It had been a constant visitor for a few days. "Yes, I have God. He's always been there for me, even in times I was too hurt to notice."

"You sound sad, Sis. Is anything wrong? You know you can talk to me."

Peju shook her head and stood from her bed. "There's nothing. I just have a slight headache." *Now you're getting used to lying as well?* "What do you want to eat? It's getting late." She took the dirty bed linen and pillowcases from the floor and tossed them in her laundry basket a few feet from the door. Then she got her phone from her jeans pocket to check for messages from Abdul. "I have fried turkey stew. We can boil rice or eat plantain with egg. I also have vanilla ice cream."

"Would you take painkillers?"

Peju raised a brow, confused and nursing disappointment at the same time. "For?" There was no message from Abdul.

"For the headache?"

"Oh! No, I will be fine. Have you decided on what to eat?"

Eliana looked like she wanted to ask something else but nodded and said, "Egg, plantain and turkey stew. Then we can have ice cream for dessert while we watch a romantic movie."

***

PEJU

His Glory Centre was brimming with first-timers, committed members, frequenters and once a year churchgoers who wanted to rejoice at making it to the new year. It was the first Sunday and the church was having a single festive service instead of their usual two. There was a lot of dancing and celebrating, and to that effect, a lot of women had taken extra care with their dressing and make-up.

Pastor George always made the call for single brothers and sisters to dance forward in the manner they would dance on their wedding day, after which he prayed for them. For the special day, Peju had donned on a burgundy *iro* and *buba* ensemble with a silver head-tie, while Eliana had gone for an off-shoulder yellow lace gown.

Yesterday, as they watched *The Duff*, a romantic comedy, Eliana had voiced out her thoughts on being in a relationship.

"You know, when I remember the story of Isaac and Rebekah in the Bible I smile. Do you know how she must have felt when Abraham's servant just came out of nowhere and told her family he's there to carry her to her husband's house? Rebekah may never have expected it, but she was ready. That's how I want mine to be like. It's another reminder that God has me in mind and I shouldn't be worried at all."

"Are you still hurt about Kene?"

Eliana shook her head and scooped her ice cream in her mouth. "At all. I've moved past that."

Peju thought it was a good time to inform Eliana of her relationship with Abdul but she had chickened out. Knowing Eliana, she would ask questions and make her feel more guilty. She would try to talk her out of the relationship. That couldn't happen.

"Hi, Peju."

Peju distanced herself from her thoughts and looked up to find Femi staring down at her, looking good in his suit. "Happy new year."

"Happy new year to you." She rose. "Thank God for His grace and mercy." She cringed inwardly, feeling like a hypocrite as she said those words. She didn't deserve His grace and mercy, not after what she had done. She could imagine God shaking His holy head at her, probably in disgust. The thought made her cringe.

"Yes, He's been good to us. You look good by the way. Your boyfriend is doing a great job taking care of you. I hope we get to see him soon."

"See who soon?" Eliana asked as she headed their way. She was holding a half-empty carton of mini juice packs for the Children's Church.

Peju shook her head, hoping Femi would get the message to stay quiet. Sadly he didn't understand.

"Peju's boyfriend," Femi said, turning his gaze to Eliana. "Have you met him?"

Eliana's eyes narrowed at him. "Peju has a boyfriend? Since when?"

Femi darted his eyes at Peju, understanding her prior actions. He looked back at Eliana and shook his head. "I er— I may be wrong but I just assumed she had a boyfriend."

"Peju, is it true? You have a boyfriend?"

What's the point of hiding? "Yes."

Eliana blinked twice. "Wow. How come you didn't tell me?"

Femi decided it was best he excused himself. He offered Peju an apologetic smile while leaving her to deal with Eliana's look of betrayal.

"Why didn't you tell me?"

Peju gestured for them to sit down. "I didn't want you to feel bad. You wanted me to go out with Femi and I wasn't interested. I know you want a relationship too —"

"And you felt I'd be jealous?" She shook her head in wonder. "Seriously? What kind of friend do you think I am, Peju? How can you think such a thing?"

Peju was frantic. She didn't mean for her to think that way. "No. I know you love me as a sister. It's just… " She sighed. "I'm sorry I didn't tell you sooner."

"So who's this guy that you're hiding from me?"

Here we go. "Remember my boss that dropped me off at your place? Abdul Layeni?" Eliana nodded. "He's my boyfriend. We've known each other since secondary school. We used to date. His family won the visa and they travelled out. He came back months ago, found me and told me about his late uncle's company and if I was interested in a job. We just started dating not long ago."

"Wait, so your boss is your boyfriend."

Peju nodded.

Eliana looked confused. "I still don't understand why you didn't trust me enough to tell me. What are you hiding?"

"Nothing."

"I've seen the guy so it's not like he's a dwarf or something."

Peju laughed.

Eliana narrowed her eyes. "Is he already married? Has kids?"

"No! And stop asking too many questions," Peju said, hoping to dissuade her from digging deeper.

"He's not a Christian?"

"What has that got to do with anything?"

"He's not a Christian? Peju! Doesn't the concept 'unequally yoked' mean anything to you?"

"That's for marriage."

"And your relationship isn't heading there?"

Peju sighed in defeat. "Yes, he's a Muslim. And I love him. *Shebi* you're a love fanatic, always talking about how amazing and beautiful it is to love and be loved. Eliana, he's an amazing guy once you get to know him. He's not bad. And he has no objections to me going to church if that's what you're concerned about."

Her friend shook her head in disbelief. "Peju, you're buying the lies you're telling yourself."

"Don't insult me. They aren't lies. Why don't you get to know him first before being judgemental?"

"I'm sorry if it looks like I'm judging you too. I'm not. I just need you to be sure you're making the right decision. Have you prayed about it?"

Peju rolled her eyes. She had seen that question coming. "What is it, Eliana? Every time, it's have you prayed about this, have you prayed about that. It's my choice. I get it, you're overreacting because of what happened between you and Kene. But guess what? I'm not you so back off."

Stop talking.

Peju ignored the soft warning. "You've suddenly turned to this over-spiritual girl who is afraid to make mistakes and is waiting for God to direct you on every small thing. My dear, God isn't going to come down from His throne with thunder clouds and tell you who to marry. So stop dreaming, my friend. Wake up and smell reality."

Finally. The load was off, and the relief? It felt good. Eliana stared at her, dazed and eyes welled up. She quickly wiped them with the back of her hand; her make-up smudged in the process.

Peju knew she had to apologise for hurting her but her lips remained shut. "I didn't know you felt that way. I'm sorry."

Apologise.

Again, Peju ignored the soft voice.

"I just felt it was better to —" Eliana pressed her lips together and shook her head. "You know what? Forget it. Let me quickly drop this at the church office and we can go back to your house."

Before Peju could say anything else, her friend hurried out of the church, her head hanging low.

***

ELIANA

Eliana brushed away the tears from her cheeks. *How could she say such hurtful things, God? Is she right? Am I short-changing myself from being in a relationship?*

Her answer came swiftly.

My plans for you are good all the time. No matter what may come My plans for you shall prevail. Rest in My Love.

She felt His peace settle in her heart and mind. *Thank you, God.* With eyes closed, she let out a slow, cooling breath. No, she wasn't making a mistake waiting on God.

But what about Peju? Her friend was in a relationship with a man who didn't believe in Jesus. What if they got married? What if they had kids

75

together?

God, what do I do? How do I help her when she doesn't want to listen to me?

Eliana had sensed something was wrong with Peju for a while now. She could never have connected it to her having a boyfriend - a Muslim one at that.

Lord, please. Speak to me.

"Eliana, are you ready?" Peju called out to her from the kitchen. "The food is ready."

"I'm coming!" She packed the rest of her things in Dimeji's old backpack and dropped it in the living room before joining Peju in the kitchen. They hadn't said a word to each other since the argument, even in her car.

"I made your favourite. Fried-rice with fried turkey." Peju scooped a large serving of rice on two different plates. "There's coleslaw in the fridge. You can help serve that."

Soon, they were seated at the dining table, eating in silence. Peju kept stealing glances at her before she finally blurted, "I'm sorry about what I said earlier on. I shouldn't have said all those things to you. I was just being defensive."

Eliana nodded. "I understand. You must like this guy."

Peju's eyes lit up immediately.

How did I miss this, Lord? How did I miss her newfound happiness? She just assumed since Femi wasn't in the picture, no other guy was.

"I do. Let me gist you about how we met." Eliana smiled as her friend started the story. She laughed a few times at how firm Peju had been back then. "That's how it all began. Truth is, I don't see myself with anyone else. That's why I need you to support me, Eliana. Not judge or criticise me."

Eliana swallowed hard.

"How do you want me to support you?"

"Meet up with him. And give me your blessing."

"You're a wonderful friend to me, Peju, and I love you as a sister. I've had your back on numerous occasions as you have had mine. I'm not trying to be vengeful or anything, but I can't support you in your relationship. I have no bad thoughts about Abdul because I don't even know him. But I cannot support your relationship. I pray God opens your eyes to see the truth." As Eliana spoke, the joy on her friend's face faltered.

"Are you sure you're not jealous?"

Am I? "No. I would be happier to see you in a relationship God approves of."

"Fine." Peju picked up her spoon and resumed eating. "Let's finish and leave so I can drop you at home. I still have to get my hair done for work tomorrow."

Eliana picked up her spoon too. On the outside, she was playing with grains. On the inside, she battled thoughts that questioned her relationship security.

Jealous? I'm not jealous. I can't be jealous... right?

Chapter 8

PEJU

"Let's go to the beach this weekend. Just the two of us," Abdul said, drawing circles on her arm with his finger. It was a Friday night and they were at his place, sprawled on his bed.

They were both tired after a long day of endless meetings. The compensation was knowing that all their hard work was paying off. The company's rise was steady and the future looked promising.

Peju yawned and closed her eyes. "Sounds good." She shifted away from his chest to rest her back on the bed. It ached from constantly sitting all day. She was in desperate need of a massage but couldn't relay her request to Abdul. If there was one thing she knew he was terrible at, it was giving massages. His long fingers did more harm than good.

"My mum called. She sends her love, my sisters too."

"Extend my love to them as well."

Peju really wasn't in the mood to talk. She just wanted to sleep for days on end. It was the only way she could stop dealing with her heart's heaviness. It came with a familiar sting of guilt and it wasn't going away. She wished she could vent to Eliana. It seemed like all they exchanged these days was "Hello" when they saw each other in church. Eliana hadn't called her too in a long time.

They had been friends for a couple of years and had been with each other through tough times. But her words that afternoon changed things. They stung, and Peju wasn't sure she'd forget them in a hurry.

"Are you still vexed?" His fingers were now playing with the mole on her earlobe.

She groaned. "Abdul, leave me alone *nau*. I'm tired and I need to sleep."

"You're being distant. I told you we were just friends —"

"*With benefits.*"

"Yes, with benefits but that was all."

Yeah, right. Peju opened her eyes, adjusting herself so she could see him. "And you're sure the baby isn't yours? What if she's lying? What if she doesn't want you to have anything to do with the baby?"

Abdul's recent breakdown of events with Beverley was also giving her a headache. He insisted they never really dated, that they were just good friends. But she knew better. There was also news of a baby in the picture. Beverly joked that it was his.

"I know Beverley."

She muttered under her breath, "Yeah, you know her."

"She wouldn't lie about something as important as that. I know the guy who got her pregnant. He was someone she liked but things didn't work out between them."

Unrequited love. Peju shuddered at the thought while Abdul pulled her close and rubbed her arm. He probably thought she was cold. The air conditioner was on full blast, a pleasant relief from last night's situation at her flat. The power supply was non-existent, and her neighbourhood mosquitoes resumed operations.

Abdul was still talking. "It hurt her, but she's okay."

"That's sad. How would she manage with the baby?"

"When we spoke, she seemed okay. Her sisters are helping out but sadly, her mother wants nothing to do with her."

"That's not fair," she said, feeling sad for her.

He brushed his lips against her forehead and rubbed her arm. "That's life."

Peju felt life was cruel in its way. Why did God have to discriminate over who one could spend life with?

Accept My teachings and learn from Me.

God, You're asking too much of me. I love him and I want to spend the rest of my life with him.

The burden that I ask you to accept is easy; the load I give you to carry is light.

How can falling out of love with Abdul be easy?

She shut out the voice and snuggled closer to Abdul. She didn't want to think of all the negatives. She didn't want to think of them being apart. What she wanted was to marry him. Was there any crime in that? Speaking of marriage, she wondered when he would officially propose. Then it hit her, *What if he's changed his mind?*

"Abdul, who is Jesus to you?" She wasn't sure where that question came from. But it had slipped out of her mouth already.

He paused briefly at her question. "A prophet."

"And not God's Son?"

"No. Why are you asking?" He resumed rubbing her arm.

"I'm just thinking, we have different beliefs. What are your thoughts on possible clashes? What if I want our kids to go to church with me, for example? Would you object to that?"

"I don't have a problem with that. God should be a big deal to them. I don't want them not knowing who He is."

"But you just don't believe Jesus is God's Son."

He sighed and turned to stare into her eyes. "Here's what I believe. God is divine. Some people believe Jesus, a human, is God's son. Even saying it sounds weird."

Peju raised a brow.

"But we can agree to disagree, okay? I won't force you to become a Muslim if that's what you're concerned about. I know how dicey these things can be. I respect your belief and you respect mine. That's all we need to make it work. At the end of the day, we are serving God. That is all that matters."

She smiled and nodded in agreement, but the heaviness remained. She desperately wanted to believe what he said. To have a strong conviction like him. But she couldn't.

* * *

OBA

Oba observed Nene as she added extra sugar to her garri and stirred it in quick, anti-clockwise motions. While his eyes were fixed on her, his mind wasn't. All he could think about were the words uttered.

"I'm sorry what did you just say?"

"Don't you think it would be better if we didn't have children? This world is something else and I don't think raising children here is the best."

Oba glanced at Timilehin, who sat across the kitchen table, as he raised a confused brow. "So why did your Mum give birth to you?"

"The way people reason back then is not the same way they think now. Besides, Oba and I have careers, and we have to grow in that line too."

Timilehin continued, "And so having children will slow you down? What about Oba? What if he wants to have children immediately?"

She took a spoonful of her cold garri and swallowed before answering. "Oba and I will talk about it." His parents had met with Nene's a week ago. They had finally chosen a date and it had been a long day of visiting her family and checking various event halls for the wedding reception. It was going to be the talk of town according to Nene, so everything had to be perfect. A particular hall was dismissed for not having enough chandeliers.

They stopped over at Timilehin's to take a quick break before continuing their rounds.

"*Oya* let's talk now because what you're saying is new to me."

Timilehin took that as his cue. He rose from his seat and went outside, giving them privacy.

"We have never discussed when we'll have kids. We can get pregnant after two years of marriage and have them with four years spacing."

Oba stared as though he was seeing her for the first time. He was stunned that she had everything figured out and left him out of the program. It wasn't just her future they were talking about, but his as well.

"When were you going to inform me of this arrangement?"

She slightly shrugged her shoulders. "Baby, it's not a big deal. I didn't think we needed to raise a discussion on it. It's not as if you like children."

It's not as if I like children ke? Is this babe joking? He stood.

"The plan you have in your mind, the one you made without my input, delete it."

Nene looked up at him, frowning. "Oba, when do you want us to have children? Immediately we get married?"

"I'm not saying that! The point is you can't make decisions on such matters on your own. We are going to be husband and wife and we should decide on it together. You aren't the man in this relationship. I am."

She laughed and that infuriated him the more. "Is this about being a man? Did I bruise your ego? Okay, I'm sorry but you aren't going to carry the baby, are you? You aren't going to be stuck with baby fat and end up with your body disfigured. I am. So I think I own the deciding factor in this."

Once again, she surprised him. Oba opened his mouth to speak but knew if he did, it would make matters worse. Instead, he turned around and walked out of the house. Her voice called out in the distance, asking where he was going. He saw Timilehin outside sitting on a wooden bench, legs crossed at the knees and tapping away on his phone.

"How far? You guys *don* settle the *mata?*" Timilehin asked once Oba sat next to him.

"How can she think I wouldn't want children?" He pointed at Timilehin's apartment. "And she's saying she has the deciding factor because she would carry the baby. Isn't that stupid?"

Timilehin rubbed his chest as if it was on fire. "You guys are getting married and need to figure out how to thrash out issues. You can't storm out of the house all the time."

"Please, I don't need your sermon," Oba said, though he knew his cousin was making perfect sense.

"*No be* sermon. Na *koko*. Didn't you guys talk about this when you were courting?"

Oba shook his head.

"So what then? How many times you will have sex in a day?"

Oba didn't answer. He knew they had never really discussed much when they were dating.

"I'm not trying to be harsh, but these are things you guys should have spoken about. How many kids do you want? When would you want to have kids? If the kids come earlier than planned what do you want to do?"

Oba sighed for possibly the tenth time that day. "So it's too late to ask?"

"It's never too late till you say I do." Then in a lowered voice, he said, "You need to be sure it's her you want to spend your life with. Better late than sorry." His cousin tapped his phone to life and laughed at something on the screen.

"This babe is making me trip for her the more."

"Who?"

"Eliana. We are chatting about LGBT and the craziness of our world. At least your fiancée is right about one thing - this world is getting crazier by the second."

"How is she?"

"She's cool."

Oba nodded. He was expecting Timilehin to say something else but he didn't. *Did she ask about me?* Wait. Why did he want her to ask? His cousin had his eyes on her. And two, he was getting married.

"Go back into the house and talk to Nene," Timilehin cut in, disrupting his line of thoughts.

"I'm not in the mood. I feel I might say something I would regret. She didn't even come after me *sef* so we can talk. The girl is proud."

Timilehin took his eyes off his phone to stare at Oba. "*Na* today you take know?" They both laughed, but deep down Oba knew he had some serious thinking to do.

* * *

HALIMAT

His alarm went off. Lunch break was over and it was time to get back to work. He was organised like that. Halimat wished he didn't have to go just yet. She enjoyed chatting with him.

"Do you ever get bored with your job?" she asked before picking up her glass of iced tea from the table. The restaurant was half-empty with most customers coming in to order take-out and be on their way.

Femi shook his head. "No. You rarely get bored when you are doing what you love to do."

Halimat made a face. "And you love seeing sick people?"

"Capital no. I'm happy to see people recover. Many come thinking they will never get better. Some, suicidal and depressed. I don't just treat malaria or typhoid."

"I see what you're doing. You're trying to relate this to a church thing? But no one who isn't sick ever goes to the hospital. Aren't Christians supposed to be perfect?"

"Jesus said it isn't the healthy that need to see a doctor, but the sick. He didn't come to help good people but those who are bad or sick, to change their lives. In other words, get better."

Halimat caught that. She tucked the sentence aside to reflect on later. "How did you become the proud owner of such a prestigious hospital?"

"My father owned it. He's dead now. My mother had cancer and passed on not too long after."

I'm sorry to hear that." Though she wasn't too thrilled about certain members of her family she didn't wish them dead. "So, it's a family practice then?"

"Yes." He glanced at his watch and looked at her again. "I'm sorry to cut this short but I have to get back to work. There's a patient I've been scheduled to see this afternoon."

She spread her arms. "On this beautiful Saturday? Don't you ever rest? Take a break, watch a movie?"

"If your question is if I know how to have fun, trust me I do."

Halimat raised a brow at him. She didn't believe him.

"Okay. That sounds like a challenge. I'm free Sunday after church. We can meet back at the hospital and I would show you how I get to have a good time. Deal?"

She knew better than to miss out on his offer. "Deal."

After Dr Alakija took his leave, she stayed back to order small chops and a huge glass of Chapman. She could imagine him telling her to watch her sugar level.

A sigh escaped her lips. Her elder sister, Esther, had called last night to check up on her. They hadn't spoken for long.

"You know we are worried about you. We thought you would show at the house for the New year party." Esther sighed, *"Why are you being difficult? You know that's just how Mummy is. She treats us all the same but you don't see Miriam and me running away."*

"That's a lie and you know it. She doesn't treat us the same and you're too much of a coward to talk to her," Halimat had snapped back.

"We all miss you. Even she misses you. Come back home."

Halimat still didn't believe her. Her mother just felt bad that, as a Christian leader in her church, it seemed that her family was dysfunctional. And that would make her look bad in the eyes of the congregation and the elders of her church.

She took a long sip of her drink, relishing the sweet taste.

For a long time, she had tolerated her mother talking down on her. Criticizing her every move and making her out to be the black sheep of the family. She knew if she went home, her mother and sisters would start with their tirade speeches about how she should change, and look at her with sad eyes. . . Pity. As if there was something she was missing and she was in the wrong.

She laughed at a thought. *Maybe they're the ones who need to be pitied. Instead of looking at me like I'm the devil, maybe they should examine themselves first.*

Halimat remembered the day her mother saw her dressed in a hijab. She had gaped at her with shock. Halimat almost thought she would have a heart attack. It had hurt Halimat, but not enough to change her mind. Her mother was following a religion practised by hypocrites.

Halimat hadn't always felt this way. At first, she had been torn between her parents' different religious backgrounds. Her mother was a Christian, her father was a Muslim.

As she grew older though, she noticed her father was always calm and practical. Mrs Ali, on the other hand, made frequent visits to church as much she did the bathroom but it still didn't stop her from always being judgemental. She was the complete opposite of Dr Alakija, which was slightly strange. The confidence. The joy. He looked like a person that, no matter what came his way he wouldn't be unnerved. He also didn't seem to have a judgemental bone in his body. So why wasn't her mother the same?

* * *

ELIANA
10th of February, 2016

My love life: It's currently four days to Valentine's day. And I'd be lying if I said I'm not sad being all alone. Last year, I had Kene to keep me company. No. I'm not going to reminisce and get depressed. Not at all. I'm taking myself out. I'll see a movie, buy takeaway food and come home to read a nice novel.

Things with Peju: I hate that we aren't talking. Is it wrong to stand up for what you believe in, even if it might cost you something great? I'm confused! And I still don't think talking to her bf is the way to go.

Business plans: It is picking up gradually. I did a job for Uncle Femi's friends and they loved it! They also promised a referral. Gosh, I'm so happy. I shared pictures of the before and after on my Instagram page and had close to 70 likes and a few comments commending me. I've thought of three names for my company and would have to choose one -Signature Décor, Signatory Décor or Creative Instincts.

In a nutshell: Guess what? Life is good despite the ups and downs. God still finds a way to make you smile even if your life is not 100% perfect.

Lol. Can it ever be perfect?

"Is everything okay?" Eliana's mother asked. The two ladies were in the kitchen cleaning dishes and packing leftovers into storage bowls.

"Is it that obvious?"

"No, but I'm your mother and I know when something's wrong. You always prefer to keep to yourself. So what's the problem?"

Eliana didn't want to bring up Peju's boyfriend. She didn't want her mother seeing Peju in another light.

"I'm taking Bible study today so I'm trying to get ready." It was true. She was a little nervous as it was the first study she would be taking.

"Oh great. What's the topic?"

Eliana shifted her gaze from the bowl in her hands and directed it to her mother, "Is Jesus enough?"

Her mother crossed her arms over her chest, leaning on the sink. "Wow. That's an interesting topic. Why did you settle on that?"

"I don't know. It just struck me one day. Is God enough for me despite the hard times? Is He enough for me when I don't get all I think I want? Is He enough that I don't fall into a relationship that displeases Him just because I don't want to remain single."

"Hmm, deep questions. Even I have to ponder on them."

Eliana laughed. "That's good."

"I thought you would want to preach on love since Valentine's day is just around the corner." There was a high-stool close to the kitchen door. Her mother moved to it and sat down. "Tell me more about this topic."

"Talking about love would be cliché. Everyone would expect that but I believe this topic would address the issue of love as well. You know the passage that talks about Jesus being the bread of life?" Mrs Awojobi nodded. "It says if we come to Him we would never go hungry and if we believe in Him we would never thirst. Hunger and thirst. Those are the two most important things any human being requires. But Jesus was telling this to people that were more concerned about what they could get from Him and not Him alone. It made me look inwards and ask if I love God enough to want Him alone?"

Eliana wiped her hands with a napkin before moving closer to her mother.

"Do I love Him more than the glamorous things of life? And then there's marriage as well. Mummy, there are so many people out there who want to get married because they feel a spouse would complete them and make them happy. But they forget, and probably don't know, that God alone can complete them. That marriage is more of God transforming them into better people, and lasting joy and happiness can only be found in Christ. And if I do get married, would Jesus still be enough or would I base my satisfaction on my husband and children." Eliana shrugged. "I used to feel that way too but God has been working on me and teaching me a lot. Well," She smiled, "Those are some of my points."

"I'm at a loss for words."

"I was the same way when I studied. God led me to some amazing scriptures."

Eliana's mother tilted her head to the side with a thoughtful look. "You know I'm proud of you, and I bless God that you turned out the way you did. It's not every mother that can confidently say their daughter is sold out to God or is living a godly life. But again, I must say, I hope you don't plan to become a nun anytime soon."

"*Haba.* I want to get married, but I'm not going to be desperate and agree to marry anyone that comes my way."

Judge not, that ye be not judged.

Eliana inwardly cringed. *Am I judging Peju? God, you know my inward parts. Search me. Please, correct me if I'm doing wrong.*

"God will not allow just any man come and marry you. You will marry the best of the best in Jesus name, Amen."

"Amen."

"Are you sure nothing is wrong with you?"

Eliana grinned and bent to hug her mother. "I'm fine. And if I need to share anything, I will"

"Alright. How's Peju *sef*? It's been a while we saw her. Hope she's fine."

"She's good. Just busy with work and life." And she left it at that, ending their conversation abruptly.

Later that evening, Eliana was scrolling through received texts on her mobile phone. The first of many was from her newfound friend, Timilehin. He was funny - very funny - and made her laugh often. They seemed to talk a lot, with Timilehin dropping serious hints of his interest in her.

Despite this, she couldn't stop her mind from wandering to Oba. He was so different from his cousin. Timilehin was nice, thoughtful and serious about his faith. But she didn't find him attractive for some reason. He was more like wood with roughened edges to her, with his beard and big, black lips, that needed sandpaper to be smoothened. Oba, on the other hand, seemed more refined. He was cool, calm and collected. He was also soft-spoken, unlike Timilehin whose voice and personality was loud enough to wake the dead.

Eliana laughed at the thought of it.

Snap out of it, Eliana. He's off-limits and you know it, she told herself.

Eliana closed her eyes, trying to shut out the thoughts and mental comparisons. Each time she spoke with Timilehin, she made sure not to ask after him, to kill whatever feelings she may have. She wasn't sure, but if Timilehin was God's will for her - then so be it. But one thing was sure. She had better cast aside whatever funny feelings she had for Oba. He wasn't hers.

* * *

ABDUL

Abdul didn't wait till Valentine's Day to surprise Peju. He was smarter than that, knowing fully well she would be on the lookout. And besides, he wanted to blow her away with something unexpected and out of the ordinary. A Valentine's Day surprise was none of these things. He had already picked out the ring - a sterling silver option with a nice emerald stone. The moment he laid his eyes on it the year before, he knew she would love it.

On the big day, just a few days before Valentine's, it took a lot of planning on his part to get her out of the house to buy food and pick up his laundry. Two days prior, he had given out most of the food to his very grateful security man. Abdul also used the opportunity to encourage her to drive on her own since he drove to and from work most days.

Three hours later, he got out his phone from his pocket when she arrived. He took a deep breath. No doubt about it, he was nervous. He heard the door open some minutes later.

"Gosh! It's so sunny outside. My throat is parched and I —"

A loud thud accompanied her gasp. Her shopping bags had crashed on the floor while her hands went to her mouth. From the corner of the room, Abdul zoomed in to catch tears running down her cheeks. Soulful R&B music filled the room, and candles lit up the place.

Peju stood still for a couple of minutes as her eyes scanned the room with the different picture frames, the white balloons he promised he would never blow up again without a pump, and the rose petals on the floor. "Oh my God," she muttered and her eyes finally found his. "Abdul?"

"Yes, love." He started walking towards her slowly. "You deserve the best and I'm glad you like it. I have loved you from the first day we met, and you are without a doubt the woman of my dreams. You are the woman I want to spend the rest of my life with and be the mother of my children. You make me want to be a better man, one that has all of your heart. I love you like *kilode!*" She laughed and brushed a tear from her eyes. "Will you marry me?"

He was standing before her now, slowly going down on bended knee. The ring emerged from his back pocket, and she let out a small scream with tears in her eyes. She nodded as she stretched her hand out, and he put the ring on her finger.

It fit perfectly.

Abdul had gone through his old photographs of two of them back in school. He had blown eight of them up in black and white, lined them on the walls and hung pink, white, blue and green balloons up in different parts of the living room. He also had a bottle of wine cooling in the fridge.

He stopped recording and rose to his feet. She pulled him by the shirt and stood on tiptoes so she could kiss him. They were like that for a few minutes, kissing and enjoying being close, enjoying the euphoria of the moment. Minutes later, he stepped back a little dazed.

"Wow." He ran a thumb across his lips, which he was sure had to be pink at the moment. "Maybe I should propose every day."

She shoved him gently before saying, "I was beginning to think you weren't going to ask me to marry you again after what happened."

"What?" He shook his head. "Never going to happen. You and I are stuck together forever."

Peju laughed and brushed away the tears with the back of her hand as she looked around the room. "I can't believe you did all this for me."

"I know right?" He stared at one of the photos. He could still remember the day clearly as if it was yesterday. They had finished final year exams that day and were being silly. She wasn't that much of a make-up girl but had drawn eyebrows for him and rubbed pink lip-gloss on his lips. Young and in love, he allowed her, just for the fun of it. The photographer had looked at them like they were insane. Next to this photo was another interesting one. She was dressed in a short white dress on the beach, walking towards the water. It was the night of their graduation. The night when their goodbyes seemed inevitable.

Back in reality, she was still his. He pulled her into his arms and held on close. Nothing was going to keep them apart now.

"I keep telling you you're worth it and more. When would you like to get married?"

"As soon as possible."

* * *

PEJU

Finally, Peju's dream had come true. She was going to become Mrs Layeni! It felt strange having a heavy piece of metal around her wedding finger, but it was gorgeous to look at. She was thrilled that Abdul would do something so amazing. Then again, recalling their trip to Aberdeen, he proved he had great taste again and again in the way he spoiled her.

In high spirits, they both spent the next few days spreading the good news to friends and family. His friends and family. Most of Peju's were in her church. Eliana included, and she already knew what their response would be. Her mother's excitement made up for everyone else's though. She was ecstatic, jumping into *aso-ebi* planning mode after her jubilation. She insisted on Peju getting pregnant to lock-down Abdul, to which Peju silently declined.

Abdul's mother had also called to congratulate her with his father and sisters. Sherifat and Biodun couldn't wait to come down for the wedding, hoping to be part of the bridal party. Unfortunately, university exams were coming up, but the wedding was going to be towards the end of the year which was fine with all of them.

Amidst all the excitement, there was still the unspoken question of where they would get married. There was her church, His Glory Centre, which she wasn't 100% sure would officiate the wedding. Her mother offered hers as a better alternative, but Peju decided to confirm with Pastor John first. He was an Associate Pastor in church and she always saw him as approachable. She guessed it had something to do with his age; he was much younger than Senior Pastor George.

A phone call was set up to kick-start discussions.

* * *

PEJU

"Hey, Sister Peju. How are you?" he responded after she introduced herself to him.

"I'm fine and you?" She twirled one of her loose braids around her finger. Abdul had stepped out for a meeting so she was free to talk without fear of him listening in on her conversation.

"Very well. What can I do for you?"

"Erm-" The words were stuck in her throat. "I recently got engaged and I would like to know the procedure for arranging the wedding."

"That's great news! Congratulations. Okay so you and your fiancé will have counselling sessions, and either Pastor George or I will appoint someone to take it. But first, we would love to see this favoured man who wants to take our sister from us. Or does he worship at His Glory Centre?"

"No."

"Okay. What church does he attend?"

Peju blinked. "H—he," She cleared her throat. "Sorry. He doesn't have a church." She hoped he wouldn't inquire more but knew he would.

"Oh, okay." He paused. "Is he a Christian?"

All of a sudden her throat felt dry. "No." There was a brief pause and she bit her lip. She could sense the next question.

"Hmm. Why is your fiancé not a Christian?"

"Er- it's nothing. He's a nice guy, Pastor John."

"Hold on. Maybe you don't understand my question. Does he believe in Christ? Is he born again?"

"Yes, he believes in Jesus but not as we do." Peju closed her eyes. *That sounds silly.*

She heard him sigh. "Can we meet one-on-one? This isn't a conversation to have over the phone."

Why? Peju rubbed her forehead; her head was throbbing all of a sudden. "Yes, we can. What time would be okay for you?" They agreed to meet Saturday morning at the church office.

"Please Sir, I would appreciate it if you kept this between us."

"Sure, I will. See you then."

The call ended and the slight headache waned. She wondered if Pastor John would side with Eliana and disapprove of her marriage. What if he said he wasn't going to perform the ceremony?

She brushed the thought away. She wasn't going to let that ruin her mood. Whatever he said, she would at least listen to, but there was nothing he could say that could change her mind. She was going to become Mrs Layeni, and that was final.

* * *

OBA

"Are you trying to get me pregnant?" Nene threw the question at him after they were spent. She dropped by last night after work with intention of going through wedding plans. It was three months away and she was knee-deep in them. It didn't bother him much, as long as she left him out of certain things that were of no importance to him. One thing led to another and they ended up in bed. "You keep giving different excuses why you can't wear a condom."

He scoffed. "Why would I want to get you pregnant? So my mother can

94

finish me *abi?*" His mother would think it was his reason for wanting to get married and fault him for it. She could also change her mind about accepting Nene despite having met her parents.

She eyed him curiously. "Ever since we had that discussion at Timilehin's, you've been acting funny."

"I don't know what you are talking about." Oba looked away from her suspicious gaze and adjusted himself on the bed. He pulled her close to him and pressed his lips against her forehead. "Let's have another round before you head out." He kissed her again, this time on an eyelid, his hand rubbing her back in soft, circular motions.

"Oba, if I get pregnant, I'm getting an abortion. Like, I won't waste time."

He drew back and searched her eyes for humour. Nothing. "You're serious? Is it that repulsive to have my baby?" He shifted away from her, disappointed at his failed plan.

"Of course I want to have your baby. I love you." She reached out to touch his cheek but he brushed her hand away.

If she truly loved him, like she was claiming to, wouldn't she be willing to make sacrifices? Oba didn't believe a word. "But what you said earlier sounded like a threat."

Nene sat up, holding the covers close to her chest. Her hair tousled, dark circles under her eyes. "You're blowing this out of proportion. Honestly. Why all this talk about pregnancy and babies all of a sudden? What has Timilehin been filling your head with?"

"Timilehin has nothing to do with this. You're the one talking like a woman I barely know."

"Me?" She threw the covers off her and got out of the bed. He resisted getting distracted by her body and dragging her back to him. This was a serious issue on their table that needed to be thrashed once and for all. "You are the one making a big deal out of something we never discussed!" She pulled on her black pantsuit after wearing her underwear. "What's the problem? Are you scared of getting married to me? Are you afraid of me being able to have children? Don't worry I know I can."

Oba's eyes narrowed. "What does that mean?"

"Just leave me alone." Her blouse on, she grabbed her bag from the bedside and brushed her long, curly weave with frantic, heavy strokes.

"Aren't you going to have a bath?"

She dumped her brush back in her bag. "I will do that at home. Thanks. See you and your selfish self later." Before he could say anything else, she stormed out of his bedroom.

He heard the door slam shut minutes later.

Oba let out a breath, his chest tight and tensed. *What is happening?* Everything had been going on smoothly till this pregnancy argument came up. It was exhausting and quite frankly, he was fed up. He dropped his head back in surrender, as he put his thoughts together. Minutes later, he decided to call her at the end of the day to apologise. She was right. He *was* being selfish.

He wasn't going to carry the baby after all. It was her body. They would settle things like adults and move on from this. Oba yawned. He closed his eyes and drifted off to sleep. Everything was going to be alright. He was sure of this.

* * *

ABDUL

Coffee and Cream was a close second to Abdul's favourite place in Lagos. It reminded him of his neighbourhood *Starbucks* back in Toronto. At the moment, it was full of customers but thankfully, they had gotten a table for three.

Abdul was expecting a friend. His best-man. With his tray of coffee and cinnamon rolls, he made his way back to the table. Twenty minutes passed by before his phone rang. "You're here? I *dey* come. Okay, okay." He ended the call. "He's coming in now."

Peju gave a thumbs-up as she gulped her water.

He saw his friend come in through the glass doors and raised his hand to get his attention. His friend smiled and walked straight to their table.

"Idris!" Abdul got up.

"A-b-d international!" Abdul saw Peju raise a brow at the moniker. The two men shook hands and patted each other's backs. It had been a couple of months since he saw his university friend.

"How you *dey*?"

"Guy, I'm good. Just chilling. What about you? I believe this pretty damsel is your woman." Idris swung his eyes at Peju and winked before returning his gaze.

"Yes *o*. Idris, this is Peju Adams. The love of my life. Peju, this is Idris Azeez my best friend."

The two exchanged warm waves.

"This guy was a heartbreaker back in school. His mouth was too sweet and had the ladies coming back for more. That was until he met the love of his life who showed him pepper. He got married two years ago and now has a baby girl."

"Nice to meet you, Mr Azeez."

"Same here, Peju. I've heard a lot about you. Abdul always spoke about a girl that he dated in secondary school. You have one great man here."

"Yes, I know." She smiled at Abdul, but he noticed her eyes were saying something different. *Hope she's okay.* She was yet to tell him how her meeting went.

"But he's also lucky to have a woman like you from all he's told me."

"And I'm also lucky to have him." She reached out and rubbed his arm affectionately.

Idris whistled. "So when is the big day?"

"We are thinking sometime in August," Abdul answered.

"Nice! Guy, I'll be the best best-man ever."

"Like you have a choice."

The two men went on with wedding plan details. Peju chipped in from time to time but was mostly on her phone. And that bothered Abdul a lot. He knew her well enough to know she was worried about something. He was concerned but kept up his conversation with his friend until they parted ways.

Peju excused herself to the bedroom once they got to his place, expressing complaints about being tired. Abdul watched her as she went to his bedroom.

* * *

ELIANA

It had been a long, productive day for Eliana. She pondered on this as she applied finishing touches to her latest idea board. Her new client had said she wanted a cosy bedroom that was simple, yet stylish, with the colours purple and orange used. Eliana felt the colours were a little extreme but she was eager to test her skills and see what she could come up with. She had bought home design magazines and browsed the pages for concepts that fit her client's taste and budget. She also went to different furniture, fabric and home décor stores to search for materials.

She was about to cut out a piece of fabric when from the corner of her eye, she noticed her phone light up. She reached out for it, smiling at the caller ID.

"Hi, Timilehin."

"Hey. What's up? How's the design stuff going?"

She balanced her phone against her ear as she cut out a piece of orange fabric. "It's going well. I'm working on an idea board to show my client."

"Hmm, what's an idea board?"

She laughed at his confused tone. "Sorry, it's just a board with arranged fabrics and design concepts on display for clients."

"Like a vision board?"

Eliana dropped the scissors and held her phone. "Yes. Something like that. But enough about me, dear. How are you?"

He told her he just called to hear her voice. Sweet. It was one of the many he'd said in their frequent phone conversations. He usually did most of the calling. She preferred chatting on WhatsApp.

"That's very kind of you. Thank you."

"So really, how are you? Have you heard from your friend yet?"

He had asked about Peju a couple of times, and when Eliana didn't have much to say, he asked if everything was okay between them. She had answered but not gone into full details. "No." Even though she had sent Peju messages and called, Peju kept being evasive. "I guess she doesn't want to talk to me."

"Can I ask what happened? And if you don't want to talk about it, it's okay."

Eliana lowered her head to look at her yellow coated toenails. She didn't think it would be wrong to talk to him about it. It wasn't like he was going to tell anyone else. He wasn't that kind of person, and she could use some advice.

"We don't see eye to eye on a particular issue." She took a deep breath. "She's going out with a Muslim. She wants my support in her relationship and wants me to see the guy. But I told her I couldn't support her because it goes against what I believe in. Did I do wrong?"

"Oh . . ."

"Yup."

"That's why she's not talking to you?"

"I think so."

"I don't think you were wrong in making your stance known. It must have been tough."

Eliana raised her head and sighed. "Hmm, very."

"*Pele.* I can imagine."

"And it's not like she doesn't know it's wrong. She's a Christian."

"Hmm. Don't be quick to judge her."

"I'm not judging her." God had said the same thing to her the other day.

And now she realized why. She had always found it hard to understand why some Christians, who knew right from wrong, still went ahead to do wrong.

She echoed her thoughts to him.

"I think we Christians forget we aren't perfect. And that's why it's easy to point fingers at others. You may have the ability to stand fast in one area while your brother or sister is struggling with that same thing. It doesn't make you a super-Christian. The Bible says he who thinks he stands should take heed lest he falls. We should lift each other in prayers because it would be so easy to judge instead. Trust me, I've been there and learnt the hard way."

Eliana laid her back on the bed and took his words in. "I hear you. And honestly, I think I've been judging her subconsciously. I will keep praying for her, but do you think I should meet her boyfriend?"

"Yeah, there's no problem with meeting the guy. Peju is still your friend after all. She needs to be surrounded by loved ones who will be a voice of reason."

He has a point. "Thank you so much, Timilehin. I appreciate this. You've helped me a lot."

"It's my pleasure. Let me let you get back to work."

"Thanks. Bye."

She felt so much better. Now, she had a clearer understanding of what she needed to do for her friend. With this in mind, Eliana decided to call her. But there was only one problem. *I just hope she picks up the phone.*

* * *

PEJU

All-day, Peju had kept up appearances that all was well. But deep within was a raging battle with her emotions. It didn't help matters that she didn't feel good either. She pulled off her trousers, wishing to slump in bed and sleep off her troubles. Abdul walked into the room just as she sat on the bed.

"You know, you didn't tell me about what happened with your Pastor. Did it go well?"

Peju nodded. "There's nothing much to say. He was happy for me." She took off her shoes and wriggled her toes against the soft, wool rug.

"And you don't want to tell me details of your conversation?"

"It's not important." She smiled with eyes lit up; her voice peppy and fun. "But anyway, guess what? I decided where I would like us to get married. I'm thinking we use a hotel."

Abdul blinked twice. "A hotel?"

"Yes! And don't look at me like I've lost my mind or something."

He laughed and came to sit next to her on the bed. "I'm just surprised. I thought you wanted to get married at a church with your friends and family."

"It doesn't matter where I get married but *who* I get married to, and as long as it's you, I'm fine."

They can keep their rules and ideas to themselves.

"So why the change of plans?"

She shrugged. "Nothing. I just want something romantic. Something unusual. Something memorable. "

He smiled, pulled her close and brushed his lips against her forehead. "One of the most memorable days of my life was when you said yes to being my girlfriend." He took her hand in his, rubbing the back of her palm with his thumb. "I love you very much, Peju. Thanks for agreeing to marry me."

"Well, thanks for asking me," Peju murmured against his chest. She took a steady breath and closed her eyes as tears raced down her cheeks.

"So let's talk at length and don't hold back, okay? Why do you want to get married to Abdul?"

"Because I love him, I've known him since secondary school, and he's a good man."

Pastor John leaned forward and placed his arms on his desk, clasping his fingers. "Is that all?"

Peju wondered what else was there to add. She already said she loved him. Wasn't that the most important thing. Wasn't that why people got married?

She shook her head. "No. There's nothing else."

"Okay. Why do you love him?"

She smiled. "He makes me happy. He loves me as no man has. He's kind and considerate of my needs. He cares a lot about me. The list goes on."

He nodded. "Those are good reasons. Truth be told, not all men can attest to having such lovely attributes, but... " Peju detested the word and prepared herself for what he was going to say, "that doesn't mean he's right for you."

He continued, his voice calm and soothing. "The Bible says do not be unequally yoked with unbelievers for what fellowship hath righteousness with unrighteousness? What fellowship has light with darkness? How can a believer be a partner with an unbeliever? It's what the Bible says, not me. I can tell you love this guy a lot, but I'm not going to lie to you and say it's okay to be with Abdul. It's not."

He said nothing more at that moment, allowing his words to sink in as they reached out to her soul. A frazzled Peju tried hard to keep her emotions at bay. "So are you saying I can't marry him? And this is although he's a good man who doesn't smoke or drink or do anything wrong. Just because he doesn't believe in Jesus? He believes in God. Isn't that enough?"

He looked at her with piercing eyes. "Sadly, no. What about your children? Would they be Muslims or Christians? Would he allow you and the children to go to church? What if he wakes up one day and decides to force you to become a Muslim? What would you do?"

She sniffled. "He's not like that. And why are you focusing only on the negatives? There are positive sides to this as well."

"Which are?"

Peju opened her mouth to speak but no words came to mind. She couldn't defend her point. She pressed her lips together and allowed the tears to flow down her cheeks.

"Why would God do this to me? Doesn't He know how much I love him? How much he loves me?"

He smiled a little. "Does Abdul love you the way Christ would want him to?"

"The Bible still talks about an unbelieving spouse marrying a believing husband - it means they can get married."

"In that context, it means a woman or man who, along with their spouse, wasn't born-again when she or he got married but later became so. They shouldn't leave their spouse with plans of getting married to a Christian."

The rest of their conversation played on in her head. She fought hard against it as she wrapped her arms around Abdul and took in his scent. This was the love of her life. She didn't want to let him go. She couldn't. Pastor John, Eliana, or anyone else could never understand.

"Babe, your phone is ringing." She felt him move to get her phone behind her. "Eliana is calling you."

"Leave it. I don't feel like talking right now. I just want to be with you."

She heard a thud as he tossed her phone on the bed. "Are you sure everything is okay?"

Peju closed her eyes. She couldn't afford to leave, considering she had a feeling she was pregnant. "Everything is perfect."

Chapter 9

ELIANA

His Glory Centre had a singles program scheduled for Saturday morning, and Eliana had made up her mind to attend in spite of her busy work schedule. She told herself it wasn't because Timilehin's cousin was going to be there. She wanted to learn, to grow in the things of God. So when a part of her jumped for joy on sighting him, she blushed. It was amazing, how his eyes searched around the hall until they found hers. He gave a slow smile and walked towards where she sat.

"Hi Oba," she greeted shyly. It was the second time she was seeing him in native attire and once again, he looked good. "This one that you came to our church today. . ."

He laughed. "Timilehin invited me. He said you guys were hosting a youth program on marriage and all."

She nodded and asked why his girlfriend wasn't with him. It was a chance to remind herself he was taken. "Work," he said bluntly.

"That's sad. I'm sure you will enjoy today's session. Pastor John is amazing."

"So I heard. Timilehin won't let me hear word again because of him. He's single, right?"

Eliana took in the scent of his cologne. *Musk. French vanilla musk.* "Yes, and between you and I, nearly half of the girls in church are dying to be 'the one'." She almost smacked herself on the head. *Why did I say that? He would think I'm one of those girls.*

"Except you." It wasn't a question but a statement.

She cocked her head to the side and raised a brow at him. "What makes you think so?"

"Well, I assume you're not that kind of girl. I could be wrong. But you don't come across as someone like that."

She tried not to smile. *Oh my God, he knows me. He knows me! But he's engaged, Eliana, so control yourself! Act cool.* "So what kind of person do I come across as?"

"A kind and gentle woman. Someone with listening ears who won't want to hurt anyone intentionally."

He took his hands out of his pocket and folded his arms.

"You can tell all of this even though you haven't known me for long?"

"It's quite clear for all to see."

She cleared her throat. "Well, he's getting married soon."

"Pity. He missed out on a nice woman."

Eliana looked away from him, smiling to herself. The program was about to start, and Timilehin was standing in as an usher, leaving her to sit with Oba. Worship began and she stood to her feet; feeling his eyes on her. She squeezed her eyes shut, concentrating on the song, losing herself in it. Basking in the presence of her Maker. Loving up on Him.

She didn't care that Oba was beside her and probably watching her. At least she tried not to. With hands raised, she sang her heart out and worshipped God. Knowing the lyrics by heart. He was her lover. Sometimes, she liked to think of her worship going up to him like the aroma of *egusi* soup. That as she sang the words, they formed scented smoke drifting up to heaven. She worshipped God, soaked up Pastor John's session and had a great time.

Femi approached her at the end of the service and she excused herself from Oba to meet him.

"How's Peju?" Femi asked after they exchanged pleasantries. "She hasn't been answering my calls. It feels like she's secluding herself from everyone."

Eliana couldn't explain her friend's situation to him. Frankly, she wished the man standing in front of her was with her friend instead of Abdul. But sadly, there was nothing she could do about it. "I really don't know. She hasn't been picking my calls as well."

"And she hasn't been coming to church. Could it be her job?"

Maybe it's because she's running away from the truth. "I'm not too sure."

"Don't you think we should visit her? What if something happened to her?"

Eliana's heart ached for him. Despite Peju's rejection, he was still concerned about her. "I planned on going to see her today after the program."

"Should I go with you?"

She shook her head. She wanted to see her friend alone.

He pursed his lips. Disappointed. "Alright. Please, get in touch with me. Let me know what happens."

She nodded. "I will."

He looked like he would say more but thanked her and went on his way. Eliana couldn't help but feel sorry for him. She couldn't imagine how he must feel. She spun around and headed back to her seat, deep in thought, unaware that Oba had been watching her the whole time.

"Is everything okay?" he asked

"Yeah, I have to rush somewhere."

"Would you like me to give you a lift?"

"No, don't worry about me. I'll be fine. See you later." With that, she hurried out of the church.

* * *

HALIMAT

She got a call that her father was ill. That was the only thing that could bring her to her parents' house four months later. There were other cars parked in their large compound. Mostly luxury cars, with two looking very familiar. Her sisters', they were around too.

Taking a deep breath, Halimat got out of the car and strolled to the main entrance with slow, heavy steps. She stared around in the meantime, admiring the blooming flowers in her mother's garden.

The house itself hadn't changed. It was still the same cream-coloured bungalow she'd left behind. Yet, with each step she took to the entrance, her heart raced faster.

Halimat knocked on the door, prepared for the worst. The door creaked open, a smallish woman with mahogany-coloured skin behind it. She opened up her arms, inviting an embrace.

"I'm so happy to see you," the lady said. She pulled her in close, holding on for longer than a minute.

Halimat wasn't moved. She couldn't say the same.

"You look beautiful. Thank God you aren't wearing that hijab again." She whispered in her ear and it took everything for Halimat not to push her and leave the house.

"Esther, where's Daddy?"

"He's in his bedroom." She shifted aside. "Come inside."

The scent of sandalwood and ginger welcomed her as she walked in. It was her mother's favourite home fragrance oil. In view was the baby she'd longed to see. Smiling, Halimat made her way to her other sister, Miriam. She greeted her and lifted Jasmine, their niece, out of her hands.

"Jazzy, how are you?" she cooed as Baby Jasmine stared at her. Halimat rubbed her nose against hers. "How are you?"

"So you are here?" Halimat recognized the voice and the edge in it. The disappointment and hatred. She noticed Miriam's face turn from a smile to a slight frown, but she said nothing.

As usual.

Halimat swung around to faced her mother. She looked older, with deep wrinkles on her face. She was also worried, and slightly unkempt.

"Good afternoon Mummy. How are you?"

"Oh, so you care?" she said, scowling.

"Mummy..." Esther warned.

"What? I'm just surprised she's asking after me. She doesn't call. She doesn't come to see how we are doing, but she opens her mouth to ask how

I am? Isn't that hypocrisy?"

Halimat remained quiet and fixed her gaze on smiling Jasmine. She wasn't going to lose her cool, not in front of this beautiful baby.

"Mum, please let's not do this," Miriam spoke up this time. "Daddy isn't feeling too well and we can't start fighting."

"What exactly happened?" Halimat directed her question at her elder sister.

"Mummy said he complained of chest pain and not long after, he collapsed. He was rushed to the hospital." Esther's voice broke and her hand flew to her mouth as she paused briefly to compose herself. "He had a minor stroke. His left arm is temporarily paralysed."

God, please . . .

"But he's going to be okay?"

Esther nodded. "He just needs to take things easy and avoid stress."

Halimat nodded. It was obvious who the source of his stress was with her constant complaints and troubles. "Is he awake? Can I see him?"

"Why are you asking? Go and see Daddy." Miriam took her daughter from her arms. Halimat took her leave and headed down the hall. She could feel her mother's piercing eyes on her back with every passing step.

There was a lump in her throat when she saw her father looking frail in bed. This wasn't the man she called her hero. That man would carry her on his shoulder as a child. He would run around with her and her sisters in their family playground like a little child. Now, he looked weak.

"Hi Daddy," she said softly.

His eyes fluttered open, a crooked smile given from the side of his mouth. "My b-baby g-g-gurl. How are y-you?" She could barely make out his words.

"I'm fine Daddy. How are you feeling?"

He opened his mouth to speak but winced in pain.

"Daddy, don't talk. Just relax. I'll do all the talking." She clasped her hands together. "Where do I start from? I'm good. My job is okay as well. I'm not travelling as much as I used to. I have a new friend. His name is Femi and he's a good person. He's also a Christian." She saw the look of surprise on his face and tried to laugh. "Yes, that's strange. He's different. I talk to him and the way he talks about God is beautiful. He makes me want to know more. Who knows?" She shrugged. "Maybe he's a different kind of Christian. Unlike *her*."

His brows drew together and she knew he was chastising her for what she had said. But it was the truth. Why wasn't anyone ready to acknowledge it? "I know. I'm sorry. I'm sorry about everything that happened. I'm sorry about the hijab. I only wore it to annoy her. I knew her church friends would be around and I purposely wore it to humiliate her. I know it was wrong of me. But I couldn't take it anymore. I'm tired of her hurtful words."

He blinked. She hoped it was to tell her he understood.

She held her father's right hand and brought it close to her cheek. "I love you, Daddy. Please, get better. I need you here to walk me down the aisle when I get married." The tears flowed freely. "I need you here with me. Please get well soon." Please don't *leave me with her.*

Mr Ali smiled and tapped her hand. He nodded, and that was all the encouragement she needed. She left him after spending an extra ten minutes and headed to the living-room. Her sisters had left, and her mum was seated on a grey, velvet armchair looking out the window; her lips moving.

Praying?

As far as Halimat could remember, that was where she loved to seat. Her mother must have heard her footsteps because she turned to her with a wearied look.

"I'm going now. Hope you are okay and don't need anything."

"I'm fine. Your sisters were kind enough to buy a few things from the market and cook. There's nothing for you to do."

Wow, thanks, Mum. "Okay. I will call and try to be here tomorrow to see h-"

"He's okay. There's no need for you to *waste* your time coming here. Your sisters are enough for us."

"Well, he's my father and I have every right to be here. I'll come tomorrow whether you like it or not." With that Halimat exited the room. Once in her car, she expelled a breath and tried to calm down as another wave of tears rushed to her eyes. *Why does she hate me so much? What did I do to her?* She had been asking herself those questions since she was a teenager. When she noticed the preferential treatment her mother gave her sisters. But over the years she had still not found the answer.

She reached out for her phone in her back pocket and dialled Femi's number. She let out a sigh of relief when he picked on the third ring. "Hi, Femi." She sniffed. "Are you busy?"

"Not really. Just have to see two more patients. What's up?"

"I need to speak to you."

"Are you okay?"

Her heart melted at his concern. Why couldn't her mother love her that way?

"No." She sniffled. "Can we meet up?"

He told her he was heading out but would join her at their usual fast-food joint in an hour. She didn't drive away immediately when she ended the call. She sat there a little longer and cried.

***

PEJU

Peju had guessed she was pregnant, but deep down had hoped she was wrong. The test results in her hands confirmed her assumptions. She had gone to a clinic not far from her house and had the test done.

She wasn't sure how to feel. Happy? Worried? Upset? She had no clue. It was also strange how it happened. After all, they used condoms most of the time.

I guess it's true what they say. Once is enough.

She sighed. *What am I going to do?* She could have an abortion. No. She frowned. That was a terrible thought. Why would it even come to mind? She could simply tell Abdul so they could hurry up the wedding. Then another disturbing thought came to mind.

What if Abdul didn't want to have a baby now? What if *he* asked for an abortion? Peju shook her head as if that would let the silly thoughts fly away

110

and chided herself.

Why would she think Abdul would want an abortion? He loved children and would be a great father.

All through last week, she had kept more to herself, leaving Abdul to feel left out and bothered by her recent behaviour. Her conversation with Pastor John kept playing in her head, and the heavy pangs of guilt in her chest were getting harder to bear.

A knock on her door snapped her out of her reverie. She ignored it but whoever it was, was persistent and kept knocking. Then she heard Eliana's voice and rolled her eyes. What did she want? Peju rose from her bed and wore her housecoat, taking her time to walk to the front door and open it.

Eliana stood there, dressed up in one of the Ankara peplum gowns she loved to wear. Peju assumed she was either going to or heading from church. *Where else would she go?*

Her friend smiled a little. "Hi."

"Hi," Peju replied, dryly.

"Can I come in?"

No. Peju stepped aside and allowed her in. They moved to the living room and sat down. "I hope you don't plan on staying long. I have an appointment to keep."

Peju saw the pained look on her friend's face and felt a little bad. Only a little. "I wanted to check up on you."

"Hmm. Well, as you can see," she spread her arms wide, "I'm fantastic."

Eliana played with her phone. Her friend had something to say but was having a hard time getting it out. Peju had no intention of helping her. Instead, she picked on the tiny hairs at the back of her neck. There were other issues on her mind.

Eliana broke the uncomfortable silence seconds later.

"I'm sorry about what happened, about what I said. I know you needed me then as your friend, not a counsellor, or someone who would look down on you. I'm sorry and I hope you'll forgive me."

Peju stared at her friend. "You know what you did was painful. I only asked for you to meet him. I wanted you to get to know him a little and see for yourself what an awesome guy he is. Instead, you told me because you're a Christian, you can't get involved. That hurt."

Eliana looked down, ashamed to make eye contact. "I know."

Peju wasn't done. She had to get everything off her chest if they were going to be friends again. "It made me feel like I didn't matter to you. You neglected me and ostracised me because you felt I wasn't good enough to be with you or to be your friend." Peju gave a humourless laugh. "I felt like a leper, like those in the Bible sent out of town."

"I understand." Eliana looked up then and Peju saw the tears glistening in her eyes. "And I'm sorry. This opened my eyes to the fact that I'm anything but perfect. If at all, I thought I had it all going, this has taught me to think otherwise. It was never my intention to make you feel the way you did. I'm here now as a friend. Will you accept me?"

Peju bit her lip as if she was contemplating but then smiled and nodded. She got up and went over to Eliana to hug her. Her friend hugged her back. "I forgive you. And I've missed you."

"Me too."

Peju pulled back. "I know you may not agree with me but you have to accept that this is my choice to make. My life. My decisions. Okay?"

Her friend nodded. "I've heard. So tell me what's been happening with you. Femi has been worried as well."

"I'm engaged." She raised her hand to show off her engagement ring.

Eliana's eyes widened as she took Peju's hand and brought it close for her perusal. "Congratulations! When?"

"Like three weeks ago."

"Awww, this is so beautiful. When do I get to meet your Prince Charming?"

"We can fix a day. I will call you to let you know. How's your business?" She asked, eager to change the topic.

Eliana said it was fine and she currently had a client that demanded a lot from her but she was ready for the challenge. "Have you set a date for the wedding?"

"August, but not sure of the date yet." She didn't want to mention that she spoke to Pastor John about the wedding and what he had said. She got up.

"I didn't even offer you anything. What would you like to eat? Where are you coming from sef?"

"There was a program at church. I want that your yummy Jollof-rice."

Peju raised a brow at her as they walked to the kitchen. "I *don* hear." She knew about the singles program they were having at church but didn't want to go. She felt people may look down on her. Not that Pastor John would betray her trust, but she didn't feel comfortable. She had deliberately left out telling Eliana about her pregnancy. She wasn't ready to tell anyone about it without deciding what she was going to do. And most importantly she wanted to tell Abdul first.

***

ABDUL

Abdul parked in a haste and hurried into the store to get a cup of hot chocolate and croissants. His mind was on his car and where he had just parked it, but thankfully, it was a weekend and traffic officials weren't working in that area. But then this was Nigeria; it was better to be safe than sorry.

Now he was hurrying back to his car.

"Watch where you're going!" A lady shot at him.

He apologised and shifted his eyes from his car to the woman he bumped into. There was a tiny brown stain on her white blouse and she pinched it to lessen the damage.

"I'm sorry. I wasn't looking at where I was going," he admitted.

When she finally looked up something struck him. She looked vaguely familiar. "It's fine."

He turned to leave but changed his mind. He spun around just in time as she moved to a free table. It didn't seem she recognised him, so maybe he was wrong. If she had seen him before she would have said so. Nevertheless, Abdul walked up to her. "I'm sorry to disturb you, but you look familiar.

113

Have we met before?"

"Oh really? You mean you purposely poured the *hot* drink on me just so you can talk to me?" The lady asked in an irritated tone. "What next? You want my phone number?"

His brows drew together. *Okay? That's rude.* "Trust me. I'm not interested." Abdul concluded she wasn't in a good mood and had probably cried a great deal since her eyes were a bit red.

"So what do you want?"

"Did you go to —" He mentioned the name of his secondary school.

She blinked then and the frown dissolved. "Yes."

"I did as well. I'm Abdul Layeni. I can't place a name to the face."

Her eyes widened. "Abdul? As in Abdul, Peju's boyfriend?"

"Yes! Wait.. are you Antonia?"

She didn't reply, but instead got up and gave him a side-hug.

"Honestly, I didn't know it was you. I had to force myself to ask and face the embarrassment if I was mistaken," he said laughing as she pulled back from him. "You look good."

"So do you. Don't mind me, I'm just going through some things now. When did you get back from Canada? Or was it America?"

Abdul affirmed the former. "And you? Heard you went abroad to study."

"Yeah. The UK." She folded her arms. "Do you still hear from Peju?"

"Not only that. We are getting married in a couple of months." Antonia let out a small scream at what he said, attracting onlookers. "I'm so happy for you guys. Wow! That's awesome. I can't wait to see her." She brought out her phone from her bag. "Can I have her number?"

He gave her along with his. "I'm sorry I have to run. It was great seeing you."

"Same here."

He promised to keep in touch and hurried out of the building. As he drove home, he couldn't believe he had just bumped into Antonia. She was very different from how he remembered her in school. Back then, she had multiple pimples on her face and was skinny. But now. She was stunning.

Back in school, he always sensed she had a crush on him, but she had denied it when confronted. That was in the past anyway, so he swept the thought to the side.

He couldn't wait to tell Peju.

Chapter 10

ELIANA

27th of March, 2016

What I've Been Up to Lately

1. *Interior design jobs have been pouring in like crazy. Yay!*
2. *My Bible Study time has been suffering. Boo!*
3. *Peju and I are talking again *phew!**
4. *Peju's man and I have talked. He's cool BUT Muslim.*
5. *I found out Kene's married to his baby mama. I liked all 15 photos on his FB and he acknowledged receipt. Honestly, the only reason why I went out with him in the first place was because of my emotions. I let them get the best of me, with his fine boy looks and personality. I knew he wasn't fully sold out to Christ because there were some funny traits he had. I thought he would change and it would happen through me when he saw my own lifestyle. So when he cheated, it broke me. I admit I made wrong choices but it opened my eyes about my selfish desire to want him more for myself than for God. I don't know if I'm making any sense. Lol. Can't seem to properly articulate my thoughts.*

And it seems it's happening all over again with Oba. Except that he's already taken. I'm liking ANOTHER WOMAN'S HUSBAND!

I practically ran away from him last time. I had to take control of myself. I have settled it in my mind and heart that NOTHING can happen between us. NOTHING!

6. The name of my company is . . . Cr8tive Splash Decors! :) I'm already working on my company cards and invoice.

7. Timilehin, Oba's cousin, asked me to be his girlfriend The plot that is my life thickens.

***

At the hospital, Femi heard the sound of babies crying from a distance but tuned it out. Right now, his thoughts needed his full attention. He needed to figure out why he was still thinking of Peju.

He thought he was over her. The news of her engagement was supposed to have completely deleted any iota of feelings he had for her. But all it did was make him uncomfortable and have a burden for her in his heart.

When Eliana had gotten back to him on how Peju was, she had also revealed her friend's engagement. It baffled him, that she would willingly be involved in an interfaith marriage. It also made him question himself. Maybe he was wrong all along; keeping her on a high pedestal when really she was far from it.

Why would she do that? He tossed his pen on the table.

"I don't understand what's going on, God. She's engaged. What's the point? I'm done loving her. I'm moving on," he spoke to himself in the confines of his office that Friday morning as he got ready to see patients.

His door suddenly opened.

"Knock knock." Oluchi said, peeping into his office. "I hope I'm not disturbing. I heard Osaz's already in surgery, and the nurses told me you weren't with any patient so I decided to drop by. Hope that's fine."

"It's very fine." Femi rose and watched her pull the baby stroller in. The twins were sound asleep and he noticed their tear-stained faces.

"Immunization?" he queried, then remembering the babies he heard crying earlier on.

"Yes *o*. I had to pacify them with milk."

They both settled down at the sitting area of his office, adjacent of each other. "You mean you bribed them."

"Bribe, pacify. . . as long as they stop. It's just -" she glanced at her watch, "eleven in the morning and I'm already tired. Can you imagine?"

Femi laughed. "I can understand. How's your mother-in-law by the way? Osaz mentioned she's back home." One of the twins opened her eyes. After seeing her mother, she drifted back to sleep. Femi thought that was the cutest thing he'd seen in a while. It also triggered the best news he'd heard this year. His sister had called a few days ago to tell him she was pregnant.

"She's fine, taking things easy. I will try my best to call and visit when less busy."

"How would you manage since your husband doesn't want a help?"

Oluchi snorted. "What's my own? Osaz is a joker. Maybe he should stay home alone with two kids and see how it feels like. I love my kids, but I'm struggling to keep up with the day-to day madness. I will get one of those nannies that come and go. He has no choice but to agree. Unless he wants to come home one day and see his wife has run mad."

They both laughed.

"How are you Femi? Really."

He gave her an amused look. "I'm fine. Why? Did your husband say otherwise?"

"No. I'm the one asking. You don't look too good."

Femi let out a breath, thinking if he could open up to her. "There's this woman I liked and felt God was leading me to, but she's getting married to another man. Not just any other man but someone who isn't a Christian." He massaged his temples. "I just can't understand. I've known this woman for two years now and deep in my heart I feel, I mean, I *know*, God has kept me till this moment to be with her. Now it seems like she isn't for me."

"She isn't for you, or she's not interested in you?"

"Not interested."

CHAPTER 10

"Okay. Well, that's huge. Are you sure your emotions aren't leading you astray?"

He raised a brow at her. She raised her hands. "Okay. I know after all these years you wouldn't just rush off to marry someone that isn't God's will for you. Sorry, I asked but I just wanted to be sure. Did you talk to her about it?"

"No. I made it clear what I wanted from her and she downrightly told me she was not interested in any other relationship than friendship. And even that has been impossible since she's avoiding me."

She angled her head. "What has God said about this?"

Femi scratched the back of his head. "I don't know. The need to pray for her is heavy on my heart. But I no longer want to wait or be her second choice. I have made up my mind to move forward."

Oluchi nodded slowly and he knew she was putting together her choice of words. "You could pray for her. It won't take anything from you. But be sure the reason you're moving on isn't out of spite, but it's God giving you the go-ahead. I don't want you to have any regrets."

He sighed. "Yeah, thanks." She was right, although he felt he had already made up his mind.

***

PEJU

It was the first of April and everything appeared to be going so fast. Peju placed the bowl of jollof-rice on the dining table and strolled back to the kitchen to get the fried chicken and salad she prepared. The last couple of weekends were long and tiring with checking various halls and event centres for the wedding. They had finally settled on *Oriental Hotel's Grand Ballroom* for the reception. The main wedding would hold at the *Terrace Sky Garden*. Both were going to be elegant and beautiful.

Peju pressed her fingers against her forehead and breathed out. She needed some breathing space from all the movement. Or maybe it was the pregnancy that was troubling her. She hadn't told Abdul yet and more than

119

once, she had caught him staring at her weirdly.

As if he suspected something.

What if he does?

It didn't matter. She planned on breaking the news to him after their guest left. Antonia was a guest. It didn't matter if they were somewhat close friends back in secondary school or that Antonia once frequented her house and they would gist for hours - Antonia doing most of the talking. What mattered was that their friendship ended years ago. It was clear that she had a secret crush on Peju's boyfriend. She had denied it, but Peju's instincts never let her down. Whatever the case, old things had passed away.

That was what Peju chose to believe.

When Abdul mentioned crossing her path, Peju couldn't shake off the jealousy and insecurities of years ago working their way back. She wasn't keen on his idea of having her over for dinner but adopted the adage of keeping your enemy close.

"It's really good to see you, Peju," Antonia said, for the second time that evening. Peju's lips curled up to a smile. "Same here. It's been what? Eleven years?" She was still amazed at how different her old friend looked. Gone was the skinny girl with a flat chest and acne heads on her face.

"Yeah, eleven years." She forked some salad into her mouth and finished chewing before her next words. "It's amazing how time goes by so fast. I was telling Titi the other day how I ran into Abdul."

Abdul smiled and sunk his teeth into a chicken thigh.

"You're still in touch with Titi?" She recalled seeing her pictures on Instagram. Reluctantly, she had followed her and sent a direct message later that day. No response was received.

Antonia nodded. "Once in a while. She's currently working in Dubai as a geologist, and is happily married."

Titi is married?

"She was psyched when I told her about you and Abdul."

Peju blinked. "Wow. That's good. When did she get married?"

"Two years ago." Antonia wiped the sides of her mouth. "The food was delicious! You really took after your Mum. I wish I knew how to cook like this. I'm more of a junk food addict."

And you aren't fat? "Thank you."

"You eat junk food but aren't fat," Abdul stated as though he read Peju's mind. "That's good genes. I remember when you were so thin in school."

Antonia laughed. "*Abeg.* Thank goodness I added a little weight when I travelled. I was afraid I wouldn't be fat, but when I saw some obese people over there, I just mellowed."

Abdul laughed. "Humans. The grass is always greener on the other side with us."

"True." Antonia turned her gaze back to Peju. "So what have you been up to? Work and all? When is the wedding? How can I help? Gosh, I really can't believe you guys are getting married!" She placed a finger on her chin, revealing an unpainted manicured fingernail. "I remember when you guys started dating and how Peju was being so stiff. We practically had to cajole her to finally go out with you, Abdul."

"Ha-ha, I also remember. Trust me, she's not that stiff anymore." He winked at Peju and she rolled her eyes at him.

"Don't mind him, please. In response to your questions, I work with Abdul as his personal assistant. The wedding is in August. There's really nothing you can do for now. If I need any help I would let you know. We already have an event planner working on it."

Antonia nodded and said she would love to help out if Peju needed it.

"Thank you. So, what do you do?"

"Nothing exciting. I work with numbers. Accounting stuff."

After their dinner, they had cake and ice cream over their conversation. Two hours later, the dishes were cleared, courtesy of Abdul, giving Peju time to have a quick shower and settle in bed while working on how to break the news. She constantly told herself there was nothing to worry about.

"She could be your maid-of-honour," Abdul said when he finally strolled into the room.

Peju frowned. "Who?"

"Antonia."

What?! She threw a pillow at him but missed.

"You guys are friends."

"We *used* to be friends. We're no longer close, so why would I want her to be my chief bridesmaid?"

Especially when she had the hots for you.

"For one, she is a long time friend and was aware when we started going out." He picked the pillow from the floor and tossed it back on the bed. He began unbuttoning his shirt. "Number two, she would give a beautiful speech about how we met and how annoying you were, and everyone would laugh. Besides, you said Eliana wouldn't be free to do it. Antonia is God-sent."

Peju shifted her eyes from his bare chest. She came up with an excuse for why Eliana couldn't make it. She didn't want to put her friend in a difficult situation. Eliana would probably be afraid to hurt her feelings again. It was best she didn't ask.

"Are you considering it?" he asked when she remained quiet for some minutes, lost in thought.

"I'll think about it."

Abdul had a twinkle in his eye as he took off his trouser and dumped it on the floor. She groaned inwardly. She had told him numerous times to stop leaving his things on the floor. If Peju said something, he would think she was nagging. *I guess this is how my life would be like henceforth.*

"For a job well done this evening, you deserve a reward."

She shook her head, having a vague idea of what he was referring to. "Nope, not interested."

"*Ahan*, why? A labourer is deserving of her wages."

"This *labourer* will pass." Of recent, she had found herself uninterested in sex. Even kissing bothered her.

Peju turned on her side but that didn't stop him from coming close and wrapping his arm around her waist. "Baby, just a quickie."

So it's not even for me sef. "No. I'm tired." She faked a yawn. "And tomorrow is a long day." She had to see the fashion designer making her dress and discuss amendments. Then, there was her outfit for the traditional wedding to sort out too. Just the thought of everything was already making her tired.

He let out a deep breath. "Are we good? Is there a reason why you're giving me a cold shoulder?"

She took note of his concerned tone and turned to face him with a smile on her face. "Yes, we are. I think it's because -"

"What?" His eyes searching hers. His brows were drawn up, concern written on his face. "Because of what?"

Peju swallowed hard and mumbled, "Because I'm pregnant."

He didn't say anything for a moment. "Oh really? Good for you." He moved away from her and laid back on the mattress.

She felt her heart sink. "What's that supposed to mean?"

"It means congratulations that you're pregnant."

"You don't want the baby?"

"I don't know."

Peju was surprised at how nonchalant he sounded. Like he wasn't the least bit bothered that she was having his baby. She felt the tears rush to her eyes. What was she going to do? "So you want me to have an abortion?"

"Whatever you want to do, babe."

She sucked in a breath as the tears flowed down her cheeks. Anger wasn't long in coming. She threw the covers off her and wore her slippers. She sniffed and talked as she pulled out her carrier bag from the wardrobe. "You are a terrible human being, Abdul! God punish you! I can't believe I wanted to get married to you."

"Where do you think you're going to?" he asked.

She didn't answer but kept throwing clothes into her bag. How could she be such an idiot to believe in him? It was rubbish! She was about shoving her blouse when he held her arms and she pushed him away. "Don't touch me!"

"*Ahan* Peju. Aren't you taking this too far?"

Too far? She wiped the tears and spun around to look at him and poked him on the chest. "I made a mistake thinking you were the guy for me. You don't care about me or our baby! You just opened my eyes to the truth." Peju tried getting the ring off but it wouldn't budge.

"Wait Peju. . . *shebi* it's April fool you're doing?"

"Which stupid April fool!"

His eyes widened and he grinned widely. "You are? Really? You're not playing, right? No April fool nonsense?"

"No. I'm six weeks pregnant!" She practically screamed at him.

He laughed, looking dazed at the same time, causing her to stare at him in confusion. He pulled her close and pressed his lips against her forehead. "Wow! Baby, I'm sorry. I actually thought you were joking. I'm so sorry baby." He hugged her close. "I guessed as much. No wonder you have been feeling tired and complaining of headaches and stuff." He kissed her lips. "You know what this means right?"

"What?" she asked, trying to stay composed while chiding herself for thinking the worst.

"No more stressing out and we would have to move the wedding date upwards."

"But what about your mum and dad? Your sisters?"

Abdul waved his hand like it wasn't a big deal. He tossed her bag on the floor and led her back to lie down ."I'll sort it out. If we can move it fine, if not it's okay."

"I'm going back home this weekend."

"Why? You know you can just move in."

Peju gave him a look. "No. I need to take care of a few things at home. It's been over a week I was there and I need to clean and get a change of clothes. Besides," she kissed his pouted lips. "You can always come and visit me."

"I've heard. Just don't do anything stressful and hurt my baby." He placed his palm on her slightly flat stomach. "Daddy's here. I already love you crazily. Grow well o, don't be stubborn like your Mummy."

She flicked his ear in reproval.

"Don't disturb your Mummy too."

Peju laughed and placed her palm on top of his. "Did you disturb your Mum?"

"My mother never stopped telling me. She said I made up for it when I came out handsome and smart."

She laughed, knowing she was going to have a lovely family, but despite the euphoria of the moment, she still felt something gnawing at her heart.

* * *

OBA

Oba drove over to the Okafors's residence. Things were strained between them for over a month. They spoke of other things, but not the elephant in the room. He had paid attention to a couple of things the Pastor John guy had said. It was important discussing certain things while courting to help their relationship and marriage. It was also important to observe how the person behaved in certain situations. Another thing he mentioned was marrying a woman who respects you. Oba had a hard time seeing Nene completely in that light when it came to their present issue. She was bent on having things her way.

"My in-law!" Mrs Okafor, Nene's mother, welcomed him as she opened the door. She could pass off as Nene's elder sister though she was plump.

"Good evening ma."

"The evening is indeed good! How are you, my son?" He walked in, and she motioned for him to have his seat while waiting for Nene. Mr Okafor was out.

"Very well Ma. "

Nene came down at that moment, looking beautiful in a short red dress, her hair cascading down her shoulders and back. The memory of when they met at an eatery late at night came to him. Her fair glowing skin caught his attention as soon as he walked in. Her hair was glistening with oil and he assumed she just had her hair done. Oba had to admit to himself he sort of fell in love that night and was heavily attracted to her and her curves. There were a few people in the queue and he offered to pay for her meal. He hadn't bargained for what happened next.

"No, thank you." She said, eyeing him. "Did you hear me say I'm broke or don't have money?"

The female cashier had looked away, with lips pressed firmly to hold back her laughter. Oba, pretending to be unfazed by her demeaning tone, said he didn't assume a beautiful woman like her to be broke but he just wanted to be of help and her disapproval wasn't a problem to him. He called out his order, and didn't give her another look but could feel her eyes on him. When he was done he expected she had left, only to find her having car troubles outside.

The rest was history. He wouldn't deny he knew about her slight attitude problems and sharp mouth. After all, they had been together for almost three years and were getting married soon. Also, he couldn't help but compare her to Eliana. Speaking of Eliana, He wondered why she had left the way she did. Had he offended her with his compliments? Timilehin said all was well but Oba knew something had changed between them.

"I'm set." She hung her bag strap on her shoulder.

Mrs Okafor said something in Igbo to Nene and she shrugged replying, "He likes it like that."

Her mother clapped her hands together. "Okay, have a nice time *o*."

On their way to the restaurant, Oba asked her what her Mum said.

"She thinks my dress is too short and I told her you like it that way. She said I will attract unwanted attention."

He laughed.

A colleague had spoken highly about the Chinese restaurant and he thought to give it a try. It had just the right ambience needed for their conversation. The dim light and private seating area were just right. They ordered plates of samosas and spring rolls with sweet and sour spare ribs as starters before the main meal.

"We have been pretending all is well when it isn't. We need to come to an agreement about when to have kids and what we would do if the children come earlier than planned. I'm sorry if it seemed I was pressuring you, I guess you can say a part of me didn't like you dictating the terms of our marriage and expecting me to just follow. Babe," He took her hands in his. "I'm your husband to be. We make decisions together."

"I'm sorry as well. We just never really spoke about it so I made plans that suited me. I also don't like how this issue is causing *wahala* between us."

"Me too."

"But I need you to understand that it's my body that would be disfigured. Not yours. It's me that would endure all the crazy pain of labour. Not you. It's also me that might have to suffer for it career-wise. Not you. You want to have kids early but I don't. That's why I did what I did."

Oba's brows drew together in confusion. "Did what?"

She signalled for a waiter and ordered a glass of wine then excused herself to use the toilet, leaving Oba perplexed. It took another ten minutes before she came back to meet her drink waiting for her and she took a gulp of it.

Which one is all this drama? He wondered but waited for her to get her bearings.

Nene took a deep breath. "I had an abortion." She grabbed her glass and took another huge gulp of wine while Oba suddenly felt sick to his stomach, hoping she would say *April's fool.*

Chapter 11

OBA

Oba blinked hard and tried not to jump to conclusions at the bombshell she dropped. She had signalled the waiter over once again and was about to order another glass of wine when Oba quietly warned him to stay back. He addressed Nene after the waiter, annoyed at the manner at which he was spoken to, walked away.

"I don't get. You had an abortion? Was that before we started dating?"

She flipped her hair backwards and sat back. "It was a mistake. Well, back then it *was* a mistake but I don't regret it now."

"I still don't under-"

"Remember the second time we went to your parents' place last year and I was complaining of tummy pains and blamed it on cramps?"

He nodded, dreading what she would say next.

"I lied. It wasn't cramps. I just had an abortion. I was scared of what would happen if I decided to keep the baby. I wasn't ready to be a mother and care for a child, and couldn't imagine putting off my career. You hadn't proposed yet and I wasn't sure you wanted to marry me, especially with the way your mother was treating me. I thought you were a Mummy's boy and would do as she wanted. So where would that leave me? As a single mum struggling to care for her child while trying to balance work as well. Or worse, a woman with no job trying to start over again."

He still couldn't believe what he was hearing. "And so you aborted my baby?"

"It wasn't a baby yet!" she snapped. He felt her saliva graze his upper lip. "I did it quickly."

Oba swallowed hard, feeling the tears at the corner of his eyes. "How far gone were you?"

Nene licked her red-stained lips and looked away from him as she said, "Eight weeks."

He clasped his hands at the back of his head and bowed his head on the table for a few minutes, then looked back at her. "So why are you telling me this now? The damage has already been done."

She shrugged. "I guess the pressure of getting pregnant and talk of babies made me feel guilty." She leaned in, resting her hands on the table and fixing her gaze on his. "When I did it, I thought it was the best decision for both of us."

"And you couldn't tell me? Why would you think I would date you for years without considering marriage?"

Nene rolled her eyes. "Like you don't know you can change your mind. I've heard of couples who didn't head to the altar even after six years of dating. I was looking out for myself."

Oba shook his head in amazement. "You were being selfish."

She didn't say anything to that but stared down at the vanilla scented candles he had requested be placed on his table.

"Who are you?" He stared at her, baffled. Not believing she was the same woman he had asked to marry him. How could she be so cold-hearted to kill the baby? Their baby. He could have been a father now. Would he have been ready? He wouldn't know now since it never happened. She had stolen that opportunity from him.

"A woman. Scared. A little insecure. Determined to do what she had to for her life. I admit I made a mistake Oba and I'm sorry."

"But you don't regret it?"

She looked down, and that answer was enough. He signalled for a waiter who hurried to their table. The bill was sorted and he told Nene to get her things. Not waiting for her, he walked out of the restaurant and straight to the parking lot to get his car. He tried his best to maintain his calm as he drove her home in silence.

Nene tried starting up a conversation but it was of no use. He wasn't interested in talking. If he spoke, he knew the words would end things between them for good. So when they got to her place, he waited for her to get out of his car then said, "We shouldn't see each other for a while. I need some time to think. Let the wedding preparations be suspended. I'll call you."

"Oba, I'm sorry."

He gave a single nod. "Me too."

He drove off into the darkness, the nightmares from his past welcoming him.

* * *

ELIANA

The weather was changing. It was cold and getting dark with the clouds gathering in the sky and the wind blowing. The rainy season had since begun and it wasn't a bother to her. She liked it when it rained but mostly when she was home and could cosy up with a hot cup of chocolate and a great novel. It had been a while she had time to read a good book.

Even her father complained, she was hardly ever at home and they didn't have family time any longer. Eliana had wondered what he was referring to. They never had any. Dinner was taken at different times. Her father liked to eat at the dining table when he got home from work and the rest of them had already eaten. So what did he expect?

"From now on, we will be having dinner as a family on Saturdays and Sundays." Her father announced in anger last Friday night after he seized Dimeji's video game. Ha had knocked down his father's bowl of soup while rushing from the

toilet to continue his game.

Eliana hadn't understood why she also had to be punished for her younger brother's mistake. "But Daddy, I have to be in church for a children's church meeting or I might have work to do that day."

"What time is that?"

She swallowed hard. "Church? It's four till six in the evening."'

"We eat dinner at seven-thirty," he said with finality.

Her mother gave her a look as Eliana opened her mouth to protest, saying it was no time to negotiate with him. The soup Dimeji had poured away was the last with assorted meat and the eba was half-eaten.

Eliana shut her mouth while her mother pacified him by making concoction rice immediately.

Dimeji was in a sour mood, missing his companion. He whined that he had nothing else to do and had pleaded with their father to release his video game. That didn't go well, earning him two sets of tongue-lashing. Since then, he had resigned himself to being preoccupied with his phone. Lightning flashed and a crackling sound of thunder soon followed. Comfy under her duvet, she snuggled close to her pillow. She heard a woman shouting at a child to stop sweeping and enter the house.

Thank God I've ironed.

She was hanging out with Timilehin later in the afternoon and hoped the rain would have lessened by then. She wondered where he would take her to. *Somewhere romantic?* Eliana shook her head. *No, he's not that kind of person.* She had always seen him as an everyday kind of guy, the typical Nigerian man that liked to be catered to and needed a high dose of respect. He had asked where she would like to go to and she had said wherever he wanted.

He told her he was up for the challenge.

Flopping on her back, she gazed out the window; watching the branches on the palm tree flay and the beads of the rain line up on her window. A yawn escaped her lips. It was three hours before her date with Timilehin and taking a short nap wasn't a bad idea. The weather was just right for it. She closed her eyes and drifted off to sleep, dreaming of what life would be with Timilehin as more than a friend.

* * *

HALIMAT

Halimat cleared the dishes and carried them to the kitchen. The power supply had just gone off and the kitchen was cold with the heavy downpour of rain. She couldn't close the windows because it would make it too dark to see. Her mother had complained of the same thing on countless occasions but was yet to come up with a solution.

With a sigh, she went to clear the other dishes in the sink.

Her father was getting better by the day. His speech was now comprehensible and he was able to give a full smile. She was grateful to God for that, never wanting to ever imagine if he got worse and died.

The sounds of her sisters' laughter made their way from the living room to her ears, and Halimat smiled. Her childhood hadn't been all that bad. When the rain was just starting, they would run out and play a little until their mother yelled at them to come back into the house.

At the end of the day, Halimat would be the one to receive the whipping because she was the dirtiest of them all.

"Oh, you're still here."

Halimat looked up from the plate to see her mother standing at the door. She thought it unnecessary to reply.

Her mother walked further in and opened the fridge, peeped in and closed it. "It's good that you're doing house chores now. You aren't lazy again *abi?*" Mrs Ali laughed. "I guess you have seen all your friends are married and you are all alone so you want to up your game."

Halimat was shaking and didn't know from what - the cold or anger at her mother's words.

"I don't think I was ever lazy."

"Are you calling me a liar?"

"No, Ma."

"You had better not. You think I don't remember when I would send you out to get something from the market and you would frown your face and be defiant."

"I think every child has that streak in them one time or another."

"Will you shut up?" she snapped, her voice raised. The chatter coming from the living room had ceased. "You are in *my* house. Don't you dare talk back at me! I didn't ask you to come here. I don't need your help. I have other daughters that are far useful to me. They have given me grandchildren. They have husbands and are doing well. Maybe the reason you haven't married all this while is that you're a lesbian!"

"Mummy!" Esther screamed.

Halimat swallowed hard, determined to speak her mind, damning the consequences. "I've always wondered why you hated me. You go prancing around, saying you're a Christian but your behaviour says another."

She hadn't seen the slap coming but had half expected it.

The light was restored, yet Halimat couldn't see anyone because of her blurred vision. Still, Halimat didn't back down. "You don't want to hear the truth. It's because of you I am the way I am. It's because of you I see Christianity as a bunch of lies and all the love talk is bull! It's because of you! You think I'm a hypocrite but I'm just being real. So if you care to slap me again, do so. Maybe it would make you feel good but it would never change the truth of who you are. *You are* the hypocrite."

Halimat brushed the tears away as she walked out of the kitchen only to see her father standing in the hallway. He had heard every word. She took hurried steps to him and he hugged her as she cried against his chest.

"It's okay, dear."

"You are always taking her side. Every time she does wrong you take her side!" her mother said.

Is that it? Is that the reason why she has held a grudge against me all this while?

"You have always shown her more love than us all."

"That's not true!" Halimat faced her. "Daddy loves my sisters and me equally. He scolds us just the same. What are you saying?" Her father squeezed her shoulder, a sign she had said too much.

"Folasade, how can you be jealous of your daughter?" her father asked, his eyes on his wife.

What?

Jasmine's cry broke the silence and her mother walked out on them just as Esther hurried off to get her daughter. Miriam walked in the direction of their mother and Halimat turned to face her father again, desperate to understand what he meant.

"Daddy, what do you mean? Why did you say Mum is jealous? Is she jealous of me?" Nothing made sense.

"It's a long story. A story for another day."

"But I -"

"Go home, dear. Let the anger clear and come back tomorrow. We'll talk then. Okay?"

No. But she didn't want to argue with her father. She couldn't afford to stress him out. And so she nodded, "Okay, I'll come back."

* * *

ELIANA

As the time drew near and she gave herself a once-over in her standing mirror, she was a little excited about going out with him. Timilehin was sort of mysterious to her. He was different from other guys she had dated in the past but she didn't know him well enough to say he preferred something to the other. Was he a movie person or a cartoon freak?

She had not expected him to take her to an art gallery at Lekki.

"You're impressed, right?"

"Yes, I am. Usually, it's either the cinema or the beach or a restaurant." She looked at the painting before her, admiring the beauty and splash of colours.

He laughed. "I was going to take you to Lekki Conservation Centre but the rain just messed everything up. Thank God for that."

"*Abi.*" She looked back at the painting, praising God for inspiring someone with the exquisite idea. It was a painting of an African woman with dishevelled, black hair staring at her reflection in a mirror. Eliana didn't know what the artist was trying to portray, but it reminded her of what it felt like to read the Bible and see how God saw His children. They were initially broken with sin but in God's eyes, they were washed clean with Christ's blood as soon as they gave their lives to Christ and transformed in His eyes.

"Hallelujah," Timilehin said when she expressed her thoughts to him.

She suddenly felt embarrassed.

"What are you thinking about?" he asked, after noticing her withdraw a little.

Eliana hesitated a bit then said, "Maybe you feel I'm being overly religious by bringing God into this since we aren't in church."

He laughed. "Why would I think that? Wasn't it God who made the flowers with their different colours? No doubt, God's an artist."

She smiled back. She was glad she could be open with him. She was free to be herself. They looked around more before heading to a small restaurant at Surulere.

"What do you do for a living?" Eliana asked him over french fries, grilled chicken and salad. So far, their time together had been wonderful. Gradually, they were getting to know each other better and discovered they had a few things in common. They had spoken about movies and were fans of Marvel Movies. They both loved to read a different genre of books, of which their favourite book and verse in the Bible happened to be Song of Solomon. Then they broached the topic of Church and how a lot of people were interested in Pastor John's future wife, spreading rumours that she wasn't a Christian and was probably a prostitute. It was amazing how easy it was to judge people from their outward appearance or just based on what others had said. Eliana knew she had once been in those shoes.

"I work as an IT guy in an insurance company."

"Nice. Do you like it?"

Timilehin shrugged and chewed on a piece of chicken. "That bad, huh?"

He laughed. "It's okay. Not my dream job but I'm making do with it. I want to go into business someday."

"What kind of business?"

"Transport. I'm just gathering money and praying I blow up quick so I can start." He cleaned his fingers with a paper napkin. "What about you? Are you enjoying Interior Design?"

She nodded and took a sip of her Chapman. The ice had almost melted and the drink had lost its original flavour. "I love it! Love it so much! Going to the Art Gallery made me inspired with an African theme for a client."

"This babe you are hot *o*!"

Eliana laughed but was cut short from replying when he excused himself to answer his phone.

"Guy, this better be impor-" He frowned. "What? *Na* so she talk?" He sighed. "Okay, I *go* reach your side before I go house." He ended the call and expelled a breath.

"What happened? Is everything okay?"

He dropped his phone back on the table. "It's my cousin. He's a bit down and would like me to see him."

"Is he sick?"

Timilehin shook his head. "I don't have the full details yet, but it has nothing to do with physical sickness."

"Would you like to leave now?"

He shook his head. "No, you aren't even through with your food. I will call an Uber as soon as you're done. I would take you home then go to his place."

She returned to her food and spoke a little more, but Eliana could tell Timilehin was worried. They were both concerned about the same person.

One probably more than the other.

***

OBA

A brain and nervous system were formed. The heart was beating. Small hands and legs were active. Oba covered his face with his hands and didn't hold back the tears. *His baby was dead.*

God, why?

He couldn't help himself; doing research online, checking what his son or daughter was like at eight weeks before being killed. Killed without being given a chance at life or to be whomever.

It wasn't cramps. I just wasn't ready to be a mother and care for a child. I just couldn't imagine putting off my career. You hadn't proposed yet and I wasn't sure you wanted to marry me.

Oba squeezed his eyes shut to drown out her voice and the agony. He had been a father and hadn't known. *Imagine, she didn't think it was important for me to know about it.* He slammed his fist on the armrest of his chair.

Not long after that, Timilehin arrived.

"What happened?" he asked as soon he opened the door. Oba already had his back turned to him and was making his way back to his seat.

"Enter and shut the door after you."

"Talk *jor*. Over the phone, you sounded drunk. Are you?"

"Do you smell alcohol on me?" He collapsed on the couch and rubbed his eyes; he had barely slept a wink in the last twenty-four hours. "I'm just tired."

Timilehin took his seat opposite him. *"Oya* follow me talk. *Wetin* happen?"

Oba narrated the whole ordeal to him, leaving nothing out. After he was done, his cousin simply shook his head, stunned speechless. He collapsed back on his chair and gave a low whistle. "That one na big *gobe.*" He ran his hand over his head. "I'm sorry bro. I can imagine how badly you feel."

Oba laughed, though nothing was funny. "What's worse is she feels okay with her decision. Like she had every right to do it and doesn't regret not telling me. I can't believe how cold she is."

"I don't know what to say. What do you want to do?"

"Simple." He picked his phone from the coffee table beside him and dialled her number. It rang several times before she finally picked. He could tell he had interrupted her sleep from the grogginess of her voice. It further infuriated him that she could sleep peacefully after what she did. It gave him the guts to go ahead with his plan. "Nene, the wedding is off. I will inform your parents in the morning. Take care."

He ended the call.

"What did you just do?" Timilehin gaped at him.

Oba switched off his phone and dropped it on his lap. "I called off the wedding."

"Just like that? And over the phone? *Haba nau.*"

"It's done already."

But even doing that didn't take the pain away. What Nene had done to him was to blame, as well as an event from his past. It was a secret he had kept between himself and someone else for many years.

Chapter 12

OBA

A few days later, Oba's mother called to confirm a few wedding details. She was in for a surprise when her son started talking. "What do you mean the wedding is on hold?"

He threw his head back and let out an exasperated sigh. Deep down, he knew his mother was probably beaming with joy at the news. *So why is she forming concerned?* "It's nothing."

"You put your wedding plans on hold, and you say it's nothing? Something *must* have happened."

Oba rubbed the back of his neck. If he told her about the abortion, it would put an end to her questions but he wasn't going to give in. He wanted that piece of information kept to himself. "I've finally heeded to your advice and ended things. That's all."

"I don't believe you but I won't argue with you. Think about this very well and let me know your decision before the end of the week."

"It's a little too late for that. I met with her parents last night."

"This boy *o*!" She muttered a few things in Yoruba, on why he was bent on shaming her. "What did you tell them?"

"Don't worry. I'll tell you everything soon. But right now, I have to go, Ma. I'm at work."

"Please get back to me soon. I won't go ahead with my plans without you keeping me posted. Okay?"

"Yes, Ma. Have a nice day."

"You too my dear. I love you and know that whatever decision you make, I will support you."

Oba nodded. "Thank you ma."

He reclined back on his chair and stared at his computer screen but was not entirely interested in it. He thought back to the moment he uttered the words 'No wedding' to her parents.

Nene's mother was still dressed in her George wrapper and lace, looking beautiful after her society party. Her face fell. "What are you talking about?"

Nene's father just stared at him.

"Nene and I have decided it's best we went our separate ways." Oba didn't bother looking at Nene who sat at a corner, legs crossed and fuming.

"I -"

"Mummy, don't mind him. He's pulling your legs. He and I are just having issues now. We will resolve it."

Mrs Okafor, who had turned to Nene while she spoke, fixed her gaze on him once again. "Two of you have problems? And so? All couples have problems, that doesn't mean they should walk out of their marriage or break an engagement. When you're in love, there is nothing that can't be forgiven."

"Oba, what did Nene do?" Nene's father asked quietly, his facial expression blank.

Oba glanced at Nene, his look asking if he should spill details or she would.

"Daddy, it's between the two of us." Nene said, her eyes silently pleading for him to keep quiet.

"But now that he's involved your mother and me, it includes us. So what happened? Why have you decided not to marry again?"

"Sir, Nene and I just can't agree on certain matters. We don't seem to see eye to eye."

The old man raised his grey brows. "And you didn't realize that before you both decided to get married?" He wiped the sides of his mouth. "What is wrong with you young people these days? Do you think marriage is like dating where you enter today and leave the next? That's why we hear of couples getting divorced after five months of marriage. Like Nene's mother said, in marriage, you can't walkout. God won't like it and I will rain hell on you Oba if you hurt my daughter." He picked up his newspaper. Done with his side of the conversation. "The both of you should go out now and resolve this so-called issue."

"Sir -"

"Yes, Daddy." Nene cut him off. "We will talk." She got up and stepped into the kitchen that led to their backyard. Oba stood to his feet and went out as well, telling himself to remain calm. As he was about to close the door behind him, he heard Mrs Okafor speak to her husband in Igbo.

"Oba, we should talk." Nene said, sober.

"What was that all about?" he replied once out of earshot. He was trying hard to keep his anger in check; his voice lowered to keep her parents from being an audience to his fury. "I already told you I don't want to get married. Is that too difficult for you to understand?"

"I understand you're vexed at me, but let's not throw away the good thing we have because of a mistake that happened years ago."

He almost laughed at what she said. "A mistake? Are you freaking kidding me? Do you call killing my child a mistake? Something you willingly did?"

She folded her hands and rubbed her arms. It was cold outside and she had on a tank top and a knee-length skirt. "I told you I'm sorry. I'm sorry. Try and understand that I had no choice."

"That's bullshit! You had a choice!"

"Choice over my career and my plans. Tell me, were you ready to be a father?"

"That's not the point," he said through clenched teeth.

Nene shook her head in disbelief. "Then what is the point? You are being unfair. Think about it, if you were in my shoes what would you have done?"

"Spoken to you about it."

She nodded. "Easier said than done. Okay. But I love you, Oba. Doesn't that mean anything to you?"

"I need time. You can't expect me to forget everything just like that."

"Okay, how much time are we talking about?"

He raked his fingers through his hair. He was in desperate need of a haircut. "Maybe a week. I would get back to you."

"What about the wedding? Can we keep preparing? Or you still don't want to get married to me. . ."

When he said nothing, Nene came close to him, gazing into his eyes. She hesitated a little then placed a palm on his cheek. "Don't give up on us, Oba. Please."

Oba expelled a breath and closed his eyes, enjoying the cool silence of his office. He kept asking himself if he was overreacting. She had apologised, so why was he being such a pain in the ass? He had given her the go-ahead to keep planning but not make any new plans without letting him know. Timilehin also didn't want him to make any rash decisions but to think properly about it. *If you choose not to marry her, you have to be ready to bear the consequences. Think very well.* Truth be told, he wasn't ready to be a father, but he also wouldn't have supported her having an abortion.

God, help me. I need to make the right decision.

He knew he cared about her. But he doubted if he was still in love with her after this mess.

* * *

PEJU

There was always this dull feeling whenever the power supply went. The atmosphere felt boring and depressing. Empty. Just like herself. She couldn't explain the emptiness. For the last couple of weeks, it felt like she had a deep, black hole within her that kept growing with each passing day. The guilt was gone and she wasn't confident God was still with her, having strayed from Him a long while back.

Was He still interested in her?

Had He departed from her?

Leave and be separate. Touch nothing unclean, and I will accept you. I will be your father, and you will be my daughter.

Come out of where? What's unclean? Abdul?

142

"Earth to Peju."

Peju glanced up from her magazine and looked at her friend. "Sorry, were you saying something?"

"What are you thinking about?"

"Nothing important. Just been feeling a bit dull these days."

"Why? Is it the wedding? Or you're stressed?"

"I'm pregnant." Peju blurted out.

Eliana's eyes widened. "*Ehn?*"

"Six weeks pregnant," Peju added.

"Is that why you guys are getting married?"

"No. I just found out a while back. We are getting married because we love each other." Peju smiled. "I can't imagine my life without him."

"But can you imagine your life without God?" Peju shuddered at the mere thought of it. Was that why she felt so sad? Was God drifting away from her?

"Does Abdul want the baby?"

"He does. He's excited and is already thinking of baby names. The other day, he made oats and diced bananas, with strawberries and apple slices." Eliana smiled. "He sat with me till I finished it all, saying his baby had to be healthy."

Her friend's lips curled up in a flat smile. Peju didn't need to be told Eliana was disappointed. She tucked the pain away.

"That's cool. Congratulations on the baby. As long as you are happy."

"Yeah. It was unplanned but I'm happy."

Eliana nodded. "How's your relationship with God? I don't see you at church anymore. I ask and you say you're busy with work, wedding prep and all. I'm concerned because I don't want you to drift from God. I don't want you to feel empty."

Peju's eyes snapped back at her. How did she know her inner turmoil? "I didn't say I was empty."

"I didn't say so either." Eliana leaned forward, placing her hands on her knees. "I know what it's like to be far from God, especially when it's you that puts the distance. You feel down like something is missing in your life." She placed her palm on her chest. "I've been there when I was with Kene. I loved him but at the back of my mind and in my heart, I knew our relationship was wrong. I ran from my quiet time with God because I didn't want to hear Him tell me no. No about my relationship. That Kene wasn't His will for me."

"Is Timilehin God's will for you?" Peju asked, desperately wanting to brush aside the truth in her friend's words.

"I'm not sure yet but he ticks all the boxes. At first, I thought going out with him would be weird." She covered her mouth and laughed.

"Weird how?"

Eliana shrugged. "I don't know. Like he's the same guy I see, and he's a fellow Christian brother."

Peju laughed. "I hear you, Sister Eliana."

"Whatever. You *sha* get what I'm saying. But he surprised me. I had a lovely time." Eliana narrated the whole evening up till when he had left to see his cousin." Peju caught on to her friend's worried look.

"What's the matter? Why are you looking like that?"

"I think I like Oba but I'm fighting my feelings because he's getting married."

"Awww, sorry dear. I'm sure it's hard for you to see Timilehin and think of him as well. Do you think it's a wise thing to keep seeing him?"

"Timilehin isn't a problem. It's my emotions, and God is helping me. I would deal with them. It's just a crush."

Peju gave her a thumbs up. "Strong girl. Okay, I want to ask something. Was Kene your first love?"

Eliana made a face. "Sort of. I was crazy about him. Why?"

"Nothing." Peju lifted her legs and tucked them under. "It hurts a lot to think about letting go of the person you love."

"I know. You remember how I was back then, crying and wanting to be alone. Going on a hunger strike," Eliana said, laughing. "That was when you gave me the diary. Anyways, it gets better with time. God helped me out. He held my hand and walked me through the pain." She smiled. "Kene is married now."

Peju's brows drew together. "Ouch."

"Ouch *ke?*" Eliana snorted. "No o. I'm okay. I advised him against it but he made his decision which is okay by me."

"I can't imagine life without Abdul. I love him so much." She watched Eliana return the bottle after taking a sip.

"Do you love Abdul enough not to want him to go to hell?"

Peju's heart skipped a beat. *Hell?* "*Ahan*, what kind of question is that? Why would I want him to go to hell?"

"He isn't a Christian, Peju." her friend replied softly. "If he doesn't believe in Christ, he will end up there. That's what the Bible says. I don't want to make you feel sad or bad but I need you to realize how serious this is. You are misrepresenting God and Christianity."

She shook her head, dropping her feet to the ground as though ready to run. "I don't want to talk about this."

"Pe-"

"I said I don't want to talk about it!"

"Okay, I'm sorry."

Peju excused herself, took hurried steps to her room and sat on the bed after locking the door. The need to be alone was pressing her. Her heart pounding in anger at what Eliana had said, and also out of fear. She had never thought of Abdul ending up in hell. Or about being a false representative of Jesus. She felt the tears at the corner of her eyes and blinked them back. No, God couldn't expect her to give up on Abdul. He was her first love. Her only love. The father of her unborn child. No. She sniffed back the snot making its way down her nose and wiped her teary eyes.

God wouldn't be so cruel to ask that of her. She refused to accept that. She was going to marry Abdul by all means and everyone would be happy.

* * *

FEMI

The nurse placed the open file on the table. Femi read its content as if studying it intently. "I can see here that you love chocolates." He looked up then. "Am I right?"

The five-year-old girl nodded slowly. "Yes, but how did you find out?" she asked and raised her chin to look at his file.

He smiled. "I know all I need to know about you, sweetheart. It's my job. Let me tell you what I'll do." He closed the file and leaned forward. "I'll make sure to get you two," he gestured with his fingers, "chocolates the next time you're here. Okay?"

She grinned and nodded her head in excitement. "Okay!"

Still smiling, he sat back up. "Nurse Eniola, please take this lovely patient to have her shot done."

The pretty nurse nodded and held the small girl's hand as they exited his office. Femi guessed the nurse was in her early twenties. He made a mental note to ask how she was finding the work environment since she started working there. Word around was that she was effective at her job and was genuinely pleasant at all times, regardless of the situation. He was yet to have a proper chat with her, having left hiring to Osaz.

Femi shifted his gaze back on the little girl's mother who had worried lines on her forehead. "It's all going to be fine. The treatment is working effectively and since tomorrow's the last day of the injections, you do not need to worry." He paused. "So stop."

She nodded and smiled a little. "Thank you so much Doctor Alakija. It's been a rough week. If anything happened to Tola," she shook her head, "my husband's family would blame me." She stared at the door. "I don't know what I would do." She laughed and returned her gaze to him. "Yes, I know I shouldn't be afraid and put my trust in God. But it's hard. I've lost three babies to spontaneous miscarriages in the past. One stillborn. My mother-in-law calls me a witch to my face." She looked down at her hands in her lap. "Sometimes, I wonder where God is when all of this is happening. He opens my womb to conceive and then lets my child die? I can't seem to understand."

He nodded. He understood her underlying pain. How painful it could be to lose a baby at the early stages of pregnancy and have people give the usual encouragement that one could always get pregnant again. His sister had been there before, her pregnancy progressing nicely. But the truth was he didn't know what answer to give.

"God's ways aren't ours. His thoughts aren't as well. I can't say I know why it happens. It could be a spiritual issue or the devil having a stronghold over the person. But I know for a fact God's plans for us are good and not evil. We may never understand why certain things happen, but we are assured God is in control and won't ever forsake us."

Femi's answer seemed to appease her. Her daughter came back into the office accompanied by the nurse. Mother and child left after saying their goodbyes.

"Eniola, hold on."

She glanced at him over her shoulder. Her hand was still on the door handle. "Yes sir?"

"Please, have a seat." She walked back and sat opposite him. "How are you? How are you finding it here?"

"It's been wonderful thus far. I love the environment and the ethics of the hospital."

Femi nodded. "Great. The work hours aren't stressful?"

She shook her head. "Not at all, sir. It's very okay."

"That's good to know." Femi clasped his hands and rested them on his abdomen. "I've been so busy that I couldn't interview you weeks back. Tell me a bit about yourself."

She blinked and looked away from him, obviously she was a little nervous and he found the action cute on her.

"Er -" She took a deep breath and returned her gaze to him. "My name is Eniola Oyebade. I studied Nursing at the University of Lagos. I'm the firstborn of my parents, both alive and kicking. I'm a Christian and I love my job."

"Great. Why did you decide to be a nurse?"

She smiled. "Because I love taking care of people. My mum always says it's like God gifted me with a truck full of kindness and compassion because of my tender heart." She laughed and he took note of dimples on both sides of her cheek. "I've always known this was what I wanted to do so I focused straight-up."

"That's beautiful. I admire your determination."

She looked down, suddenly shy. "Thank you, Sir."

"Okay. With time, we would get to know each other better. If you have any questions or concerns about anything, my door is always open."

"Thank you, Sir." Eniola stood and left his office.

He expelled a breath and rested his head on his desk. Lately, thoughts of Peju were gradually becoming a distant memory. But he never ceased to pray for her. He hoped she would come to church and he could talk to her. He tried to make sense of why she wanted to get married to the guy.

Is she pregnant?

No. He shook his head. It couldn't be. Peju wouldn't lower her standards. Did he even know her standards?

Whatever she did, it was because she loved her fiancé. That was the only plausible reason.

God, that's the reason right? She's in love with him.

He groaned. *It would be best if I moved on. Life would be easier on me.* The story of Moses came to mind when Moses asked God to go with him and the Israelites as they embarked on their journey.

Femi knew God was talking to him then, telling him it wasn't time, and Femi wondered when exactly that time would come. He raised his head and took out his phone, placing a phone call to Halimat. The last time they spoke, she told him she was going to see her father. Femi understood in part why she was in his life and he hoped to help out in any way he could.

* * *

HALIMAT

"Your mum loved all those old school jams," Halimat's father said to her after she ended her call with Femi. She listened to the music playing on their sound system. "She used to be so full of life despite her insecurities."

Halimat had taken her dad to the hospital and on their way back, they had stopped over at an ice cream store. It was his treat, but she knew he also wanted them to talk in private. She hadn't been able to rest with constant thoughts of what her dad had said the last time they were together.

"What made her change?"

"I guess her life took a new turn after she started going to church and becoming serious with God. One day, she came home and packed away all her *Kool and the Gang* records. She said the music was unedifying."

Halimat scooped a small portion of vanilla ice cream in her mouth. It was her second cup of ice cream within thirty minutes. "How did you feel about everything?"

"I took it as one of her numerous phases or mood swings, leaving her to do what she wanted. There was no harm as long as she didn't involve me in it. Of course, we had our differences but nothing we couldn't resolve with time. Anyway, things changed after she gave birth to you. You came out beautiful. Different. Not like your elder sisters. You took my fair complexion and not your mother's chocolate skin. Your hair wasn't brown but dark like mine." He smiled and stared above her head as if reliving the memory of her birth. "I loved you immediately. Your mother blamed me for loving you more than the others. She felt there was suddenly competition between the both of you for my attention and affection. She also believed I spent more time with you than your sisters."

"So Mum blames me for something I had no control over? Something I never did?" She asked, slack-jawed. She racked her brain, trying to think if there was ever a time her dad put all his attention on her and never included Esther and Miriam. There was none. At least none that she could remember.

Her father heaved a sigh. "I don't want you to hold any grudges against her. She's still your mother. Maybe I'm the one truly at fault. Maybe I did something wrong. But I've always felt I showed all three of you, equal love."

Halimat shook her head. "I don't think you did anything wrong. Esther and Miriam don't hold anything against you."

"I know but," He sighed and rubbed his head. "deep down they may feel the same way."

"I doubt it. So she harboured bitterness towards me all along." Halimat was still dazed at the news. How could a mother be jealous of her daughter? Wasn't she supposed to cheer her on and pray for the best? Halimat recalled all the painful memories of her mother beating her, insulting her, maltreating her. And all because of what? "I don't know how to take this. What am I supposed to do?"

"Love her."

She found her father's answer amusing and sat back. Her ice cream was pushed to the side. If Doctor Alakija were here, he would admonish her for stress eating. "Love someone who doesn't love me?"

"She loves you but her insecurities get in the way."

"Daddy, why are you defending her?" she responded, angry at her father for taking her mother's side. "Why are you still with her?"

He smiled and looked into her eyes. "Because she's my wife. I made a vow to love her. A vow to be committed to her in the good or bad times."

Halimat turned from him and brushed the tears from her eyes. She sniffed. "Did you think her faith, or being a Christian, had anything to do with it?" Even as she asked she already knew the answer. Doctor Alakija was a good example.

"No. Your mum had her insecurities even before she went to church but she hid it very well. She didn't want to be seen as a weakling. I have no problem with church or God or Jesus. Funny enough, I listen to all those preachers on TBN or DayStar and I'm getting to understand a few things little by little. But for your mum, it's just who she is. You can't change a person unless they are willing to. Unless they come to terms with their flaws."

"Daddy, you're too good for her."

Her father laughed.

Halimat said nothing after that, but her father had given her a lot to think about.

Chapter 13

OBA

Plans for the wedding were underway, with Nene anxious to get things done quickly. Meanwhile, Oba was finally coming to terms with his past. It had happened before, the sorrow of abortion. But the present pain was far worse. The wounds hadn't healed completely then, and now, it felt like someone had pierced him at that same spot with a dagger.

Nene had reminded him of something he had hoped to forget. She thought he didn't want kids. But she didn't know why any time he saw a child, he felt a sting of guilt.

The voice of the pastor jarred him from his thoughts, and he looked up to see an older man standing at the pulpit, with a mic in hand. Oba had practically dragged him out of the house to attend church with him.

"Where are you? That's the message the Lord laid in my heart to share with you this morning. Let us pray." The pastor bowed his head and closed his eyes. He uttered a few words and the congregation said an *Amen*. He opened his eyes and smiled down at everyone. "Today, I just feel a little uncomfortable standing here at the altar talking to you." He signalled for two of the ushers standing in front to lift the glass podium down the stairs to be at the same level as everyone else. "This is better." He opened his IPad. "Let's turn our Bibles to Genesis 3 from verse eight till thirteen."

The pastor shifted from the podium and walked amid everyone. "Have you ever imagined what it would be like to have God take a stroll with you and chat? I'm sure a lot of you would bombard Him with questions and tell Him all your problems - which of course isn't bad, but just imagine you and God are gisting. And not just once in a while but every single day." He stopped and placed his hand on his waist. "Isn't that amazing?"

"Yes, Pastor!" Oba jolted as the woman beside him shouted. He refrained from glaring at her. She was already making him uncomfortable with her fat arms pressing against his side.

"Now, Adam and Eve enjoyed this privilege of having God fellowship with them until one day when they fell and God had to ask a question He may never have asked before, 'Where are you?'. Today, God is asking you where you are."

The pastor continued to mention how people who were once in close fellowship with God stayed away from Him once they sinned. He listed several factors that caused people to run from God and Oba could pick out two or three things that had kept him away. The top reason was that he never forgave himself for consenting to an abortion that happened years ago. He had never remained the same afterwards. Timilehin didn't even know about it.

"There are so many lessons to get from that passage and I would share a few of them with you. Adam and Eve were married but had God involved in their marriage. When the problem arose God was aware and proffered a solution, and we can see that when He dressed the both of them. If you don't have God involved in your marriage don't expect Him to intercede when the times get tough.

"Why are you hiding from God? The psalmist David asked where he could go to get away from His Spirit? If he could go up to the heavens, God is there. If he could lie down in the grave, God is there. Even if he had hope in the darkness covering him, he knew the darkness wasn't dark to God. Darkness and light are the same to Him. So don't bother hiding your sins from God. The book of Romans says if we confess our sins, He is faithful and just to forgive us. God knew Adam and Eve had sinned and yet, He came to the garden. Likewise, Jesus saw the depth of sin in the world and came to die for you and me. Today, God is asking where you are. He's ready to forgive you. What are you waiting for?"

Oba felt like he had been hit in the gut. How could God forgive him? He didn't know why he bothered coming. He had lied to himself that he was over what happened in the past with his ex. When she had gotten pregnant and they had both decided she aborted the baby. It had torn at his heart when it happened, but he had kept the pain at bay. The guilt had been terrible for both of them. They had both gone their separate ways, but Oba had never really gotten over it. He just simply swore that the incident would never repeat itself.

And now Nene had repeated history for him, without his knowing.

He closed his eyes and let out a breath. How was he supposed to forget? How was he supposed to forgive someone who didn't even doubt her actions? How could he trust her not to repeat them once they got married?

He wished he could answer those questions.

And can God forgive me for what I did? Oba closed his eyes. He didn't think so.

"There is no sin too great for God," the pastor countered, as though he had heard Oba's thoughts.

Come to Me.

Oba's eyes snapped open and he looked around to see if someone had spoken to him. Those sitting either side of him had their heads bowed and eyes closed. He heard someone speaking in a language he didn't understand. He licked his lips, his heart racing. The pastor said it again, calling for those who wanted to come back to God and surrender their lives to Him. A woman began singing, the lyrics of a song reaching down to the deepest part of his soul.

Come out of hiding, You're safe here with Me...

Still singing but with a lowered voice, the pastor spoke once more. "I love this song so much. God is telling me someone is battling with a decision to finally come home to Him. God wants you to come home. Don't hold back. Don't fight it. Like the lyrics of the song, God is telling you, you're almost home now. Please don't quit. You're almost home to me. You're almost home to me."

Oba felt like he couldn't breathe, like there was a huge mass of covering over him and he needed to get out quick. A ceaseless prodding to go forward. With the lump in his throat and tears at the back of his eyes, he stood to his feet.

***

PEJU

Peju ran out of the church, hand to her stomach. The sun was blazing hot. Once out, she finally willed herself to breathe. She bent over, the sun scorching her back. She felt like throwing up. Flapping her hand in rapid motions, she fanned herself. What was wrong with her? She had never felt this way before when coming to church. Maybe it was the pregnancy.

Why did I allow Eliana talk me to into coming to church? I should have stayed home and rested.

But then she knew that to be far from it. It was Pastor George's message that got to her. It spoke to her on so many levels. A female usher who had followed her outside, and observed her at a distance, walked over and asked if she was okay.

Peju forced a smile and nodded at her.

"I'm fine, thank you."

She didn't look convinced. "Are you sure?"

"Yes, I'm fine. Just needed some fresh air, that's all." Peju smiled wider. "Thank you very much." The usher nodded and headed back to the church without a backward glance. Strutting carefully back to the church in her dangerously high, blue stilettos and looking beautiful in a lovely combination of a khaki knee-length skirt, a white shirt and navy-blue blazer.

Peju sighed and stood up straight, a lot calmer. She was ten weeks pregnant and starting to show. For that reason, she had worn a loose blouse and a pencil skirt with an elastic band.

"Peju?"

Oh no. She froze still, recognizing the voice. She turned around slowly and gave her best smile. "Femi, good morning!"

"Good morning."

When last had she seen him? He looked concerned. Had he also noticed her running out of church? He looked trimmer like he had lost some weight. He was still good-looking though, she couldn't deny that.

"How are you?"

Peju shrugged. "I'm fine. It's been a long time. You look good. How's work?"

Why am I talking so much?

"I'm good. Work is fine. What about you? How's your boyfriend?"

"He's fine as well."

He nodded. "I've been trying to call you. I ask after you all the time from Eliana." His eyes strayed to her hand on her tummy and she dropped it immediately. "I've been worried about you. You don't come to church much. You refuse to pick my calls."

"There's no need for you to be worried. As you can see, I'm okay. Sorry for not picking your calls. I have a lot of things going on."

Femi shoved his hands into his pockets and his lips curled up to a smile. "Right. Congratulations. I heard about your engagement."

Peju looked away from him then, feeling uncomfortable. This was a man who wanted to date and ultimately marry her. "Thank you."

"I know how tasking preparing for a wedding can be. It's best you take it easy and not stress yourself much. I was wondering, can I take you out for lunch after service? I'm not trying to take you from your man. I just want us to talk."

She raised a brow. "Talk about what?"

"Just catch up on each other and life. Remember we are friends."

"Sure," She nodded, "okay."

"Thanks. We'll talk more after the service. Let's go in now before people start to wonder what's going on."

***

ABDUL

Abdul got off the phone with his mother and sisters. His father had spoken to him in less than a minute, but the others were eager to know progress with wedding plans. It was settled. The colours for the traditional wedding were peach, coral and powder blue while the wedding colours were ivory and rose pink. The invitation cards had been printed and distributed to necessary parties. The cakes were taken care of. The gifts to be presented at the traditional wedding, as well as the *alagas* anchoring the event, were also settled. He was glad it was only once he had to get married. He couldn't imagine going through the stress all over again.

To pass the time, he decided to scroll through his WhatsApp messages. He was expecting Peju after her church service, but she seemed to be running late. They were supposed to attend a friend's child's naming ceremony together. He sent a text to her, checked through his messages and then spotted Antonia's WhatsApp picture - a glass of water with slices of lemons. She wrote, "Give yourself a spa treatment with the lemons life offers you."

He smiled to himself and sent her a message. It took a couple of minutes before she responded with a smile. It didn't take long before he found the idea of chatting back and forth tasking and he called her.

"Hi, you!" She sounded chirpy.

"Sorry, I got tired of typing."

She laughed. "It's fine. It gets like that from time to time. When does Peju get back from church?"

Abdul glanced at the wall clock. "She's supposed to be back by now. Maybe they had a long service."

"Oh okay. I was thinking of coming over to pick my dress since I couldn't get it from the tailor's last week."

"I think the dresses are at her place. You should call her."

"Yikes! Okay, I would." He heard a click sound in the background and figured she was working.

"Thanks again for agreeing to be the maid-of-honour. Peju appreciates it."

"You guys should stop thanking me. High school sweethearts finally tying the knot. That's the highlight of my year and to think it's all because of my juvenile matchmaking skills." She teased.

Abdul laughed and shifted the phone to the other side of his ear. "Yeah, right."

"You need to thank me very well. You owe me a big bowl of ice cream with chocolates."

"Better take it easy on the sugar."

"Haha!"

"So what's up with you? Should we start ordering your wedding *aso-ebi*?"

Antonia snorted. "For where? I can't bother myself with romance at the moment. Lots on my mind."

"Hmm, okay. And your dad? You mentioned he wasn't feeling too well the last time we spoke."

"He's better now. Thanks for asking. Enough about me. Tell me, are you excited about the wedding?"

"Over excitement *dey* do me *sef*!" They both laughed. "But really, I can't wait to finally call her my wife. I'm totally in love with that girl with all her stubbornness and *wahala*. I love her like crazy."

She sniffed. "That's so romantic. You guys give me hope of love. I feel love is sort of overrated."

Abdul frowned. "Why?"

"I don't know. I've had my fair share of experiences. Maybe love is yet to reach my side. I have been dealt with the other side of the coin. Even in my own family."

He raised his brow. "What happened?"

"Well . . ." He could feel her hesitation over the phone. "It's a long story. All you need to know is I'm moving forward with my life."

He didn't press any further. They rounded up their conversation and ended the call a few minutes later, with promises to keep in touch and enjoy the rest of the day.

***

FEMI

Femi took his jacket off and flopped it on the back of the chair. He unbuttoned the cuffs and folded his sleeves. The restaurant was packed with people, and from their attires, he guessed they were all coming from their church services. Peju had invited Eliana but she had hurried home, making an excuse of having things to do. But he was pleased she hadn't come. He wanted some alone time with Peju; who knew . . . maybe this would be the last time they had to spend together.

Especially with the way she kept her distance from him.

"What would you like to eat?" he asked her.

"Salad and chicken is fine, with a cold bottle of water."

"Are you watching your weight?" he teased and was sad he did when he noted how self-conscious she became.

"Yeah, for my wedding dress."

He nodded, feeling like a fool. He excused himself and hurried off to join the queue to get their food. He was back within twenty minutes and apologised.

She smiled, the uneasiness from earlier on gone. *Is it me or she seems more vulnerable?* "It's not your fault. Thank you."

They conversed as they ate.

"Their food here is really good. How did you find this place?" she asked as she ate a piece of chicken, chewing slowly as though relishing the taste.

"A friend and I discovered it weeks ago. Now, we come here once a while."

"That's good. A girlfriend?"

He gazed at her to see if there was any sign of jealousy. No. She was just vaguely interested. "No, just a friend. So what's his name? Tell me about him."

Femi saw the curious look she gave him. He added, "We may not be in a relationship but I care about you. You could take me to be your big brother if that would make it easier for you to talk to me."

She tilted her head to the side as if considering it, then said, "Okay. What do you want to know?"

Everything. "What you're willing to share?"

"Well, his name is Abdul Layeni. He's a great guy and cares about me. He

159

loves me. We've known each other since secondary school. We dated for a while till his family won the lottery and left the country. He came back one day, and lo and behold, he offers me a job to be his assistant but I knew there was more to it. Long story short, we are getting married."

He had watched her closely as she spoke. He noted she left out he was a Muslim and he wasn't going to inquire about it. She was happy with this man and whatever arrangement they had. This mystery man held her heart. The sad fact that she would never be his woman hurt but he didn't give himself up to that emotion. "I'm happy for you. I wish you all the happiness in the world."

"Thank you."

"When is the wedding?"

"Twentieth of August."

"Hope I'm invited."

"Of course, I will get the invite across to you."

As he drove home an hour later, he played a gospel song by Steffany Gretzinger, *Letting Go*. She was quickly becoming his favourite gospel artiste. The choir had performed one of her songs that morning in church. Femi hummed to the song, as the lyrics had a calming effect on his emotions. The words meant a lot to him, and he took that to mean one thing; it was time to let go. It was time to get over his feelings for Peju he had carried for the last year and a half. He was going to let go and hold on to God.

He felt a nudge in his heart but he shook his head.

"I can't take it anymore, Lord. I'm done."

***

PEJU

The parlour smelt of chicken when she walked in. She dropped her bag on the table in the waiting room and walked further in. Abdul was sound asleep on the couch. She smiled and tiptoed to him. She bent low and brushed her lips against his softly.

160

He woke up.

"Hey, you." She said.

"How was church?"

"Fine. How did you spend your morning?"

He took his feet off the couch and dropped them on the floor. "Rested. Spoke with my family and made something to eat. Nothing serious. I assume you haven't eaten so let me get something for you." He tried to stand up but she stopped him.

"I went out with Femi, a friend from church and we had lunch."

He frowned. "Isn't that the guy who wanted to go out with you?"

She nodded. She had told Abdul about him and he had been a little jealous. Peju had enjoyed teasing him about it for a short while.

"I need to meet this Femi guy. He better watch himself *o*. This one that he's taking my two babies out. Hope you flashed your ring in his face very well so he would see you're not on the market."

Peju laughed and went to sit next to him. "He knows that. Anyways, what did you cook? I smell chicken and curry."

"I made rice and chicken sauce, and diced some tomatoes and lettuce for you to eat it with." He placed his arm around her shoulders. "What did you eat? Hope it's something healthy."

She told him.

"Good girl! You know you can't take cinnamon, parsley, or large doses of Vitamin C because it can lead to miscarriage."

She rolled her eyes. "Yes, Dr Abdul." He pulled her close and kissed the side of her head. He then suggested she go upstairs to their room and rest a little before they headed out for the party. She didn't hesitate to invite him as well, suddenly having the urge to be with him. It had been too long. She kissed him and he got the message. They made love and snuggled in each other's arms as sleep clothed them.

When she woke up, she could hear water running in the bathroom. Abdul's side of the bed was also empty. She tried to sit up but gasped when she felt a sharp pain in her abdomen.

Peju flung the covers off her only to discover she was bleeding.

***

ELIANA

May, 8th 2016

Love Note to God: I'm here again like every other day to meet with You. To talk to You. To hear from You. I love the sweet pleasure I experience whenever I'm with You. That romance I feel in Your presence. I know something is missing when I don't have time out with You that always leaves me refreshed. Today, I praise You. Even in worship, my soul makes that contact with You when it realizes it's in the presence of its Maker. Even if it doesn't feel like I would gear it up to praise You.

Birthday loading!: Thank You, Jesus. My birthday is coming up in ten days and I'm praising God every day till then. I don't know what I want to do yet. Maybe I'll visit an orphanage or take myself out to the cinemas. Not too sure. Timilehin is hinting at taking me out but I'm not sure yet and I told him my reasons. I'm not certain where our relationship is heading to and I don't want to get ahead of myself. And I'm not in a hurry to be in a relationship, when the time is right, I believe everything would sort itself out.

Today, Oba gave his life to Christ. Timilehin told me and he was so happy for his cousin. I'm equally happy for Oba. We haven't spoken since February but Timilehin tells me he asks after me from time to time. Timilehin says Pastor John is going to follow him up and disciple him. There's something inside me that screams 'finally!'. But he's still engaged, though Timilehin also mentioned they are having little issues. I pray all works out for his good.

Chapter 14

PEJU

There's no heartbeat. Your baby is dead. Peju eyes fluttered open. The words had been swimming in her head over and over again as she drifted in and out of consciousness. She didn't know how she had survived the news. The remorse on the doctor's face as she said it tore at Peju's heart. How could her baby be dead? What had she done wrong? What sin had been so great for her baby to die?

"Doctor, are you sure? Maybe the monitor is wrong," Abdul asked, the agony in his voice not hidden.

"I'm sorry Mr Layeni. There's no heartbeat. We checked twice."

"Why did it happen?"

"From all indications, it was a silent miscarriage. Unfortunately, these things happen and there are no reasons for their cause. I'm sorry for your loss. There are three options I can suggest for her to complete the miscarriage. It's either we let it naturally take its course, we offer her some drugs to aid the process or we perform a D&C."

Peju shook her head. "I don't want surgery." She felt Abdul squeeze her hand, telling her everything was going to be alright. Willing to be strong for both of them.

"Which option is best?"

"I would suggest the operation. Your wife would recover quickly and the bleeding would be less and ease her of any distress. The sooner it's over, the quicker the

163

both of you can recover."

"So - there will be no damage to her womb?"

"Not at all. She can have more children. We would monitor her after the surgery and give her some painkillers to take home. There will be minor bleeding for two weeks, thereafter she should be back to normal but you can bring her back for follow-up if it makes you more comfortable. She must have complete rest when she gets home.

Peju bit her lip as tears gathered in her eyes.

"I will let two of you decide." The doctor stepped out of the room, leaving them alone with the pain and emptiness.

It had been three days since her baby was gone. She didn't get to know if it was a boy or girl. She mourned for the baby she might have had. Maybe he would have been tall like Abdul or she would have had Peju's caramel skin tone. Her mother had suspected the baby to be a boy because she was free from morning sickness, saying while pregnant with her she had numerous morning sickness episodes. Peju hadn't believed that to be true because she knew of women who had boys and horrible nausea while at her former place of work.

Either way, there was no baby.

Peju groaned and lifted her hand to her eyes, rubbing them with drained hands. The room had a floral scent and she was grateful it didn't smell of strong antiseptic.

Her eyes moved to where her mother slept. Abdul had been in the hospital the day of the surgery and had only gone home last night to freshen up and check on things at the office before returning to see her. Eliana had also come to visit.

Her throat felt parched, so she reached for the bottle of water on the bedside table.

"You should ask for help."

Peju jumped at the sound of her mother. Her hand flew to her chest as she breathed hard. "I didn't want to disturb your sleep." Her mother filled up the foam cup with water. "Thank you, Ma." She took a sip, then two until she downed the half-cup of water. The doctor had given her the go-ahead to eat and take fluids when there were no complications during the operation.

"How are you feeling?"

Peju nodded. "I'm fine. When can I go home?"

"The doctor said she would come by this morning, and if everything is okay, you will be discharged. I have a job this afternoon and I have spoken with Abdul. He said he would handle your transfer to his house." Her voice dropped. "My daughter, all will be well. Miscarriages happen and sometimes, we can't point a finger at what caused it. Be strong. You and Abdul will have more children."

Peju forced a smile and nodded. "Thank you, Mum."

"I will make goat and fish pepper soup for you to get your strength back. Is there anything else you would like?"

"No Ma." Peju just wanted to be alone. Why was everybody's consolation speech that she would have other children? She was sick and tired of it. Didn't they understand she had already formed a bond with the baby? That she was already talking to her baby from time to time? She couldn't let go, it hurt too much.

***

HALIMAT

"I need to see a friend of mine who was admitted to the hospital. Please can you take me?" Halimat asked as she ate the last of her waffles. "You know my car is giving me issues. And you know you love my company."

He laughed. "Not a problem." He took a sip of his cold, bland coffee. "How's your dad? And how are things with your mum?"

She let out a deep sigh. "Dad is so much better now. My mum is another story. Ever since my dad and I last talked, I can't help but look at her with disdain. The whole thing still baffles me."

Femi had also found it shocking but then a lot of things were happening these days; men and women marrying animals amongst other strange things. Sin was definitely on the rise in this world.

"She's still your mother."

165

Halimat rolled her eyes. "Please save me the whole speech of how she's my Mum and I have to respect, honour, and love her. I don't need it."

His lips curled up in a smile as he teased, "You just saved me the need to give the speech since you gave it yourself."

She held up a hand to him. "Whatever. My point is why can't someone say she's a mother and shouldn't treat me that way? I have done nothing but love her all my life and she finds pleasure in ticking me off."

"Okay."

She narrowed her eyes. "Okay? Is that all you're going to say?"

"Is there something more you would like me to say?"

She shifted her eyes from him and gave a brief nod, causing him to chuckle. She could be so stubborn at times.

"She's your mother and shouldn't treat you that way, but sometimes we can't help how other people react or how they feel towards us. We try to give our best and even that isn't good enough. All you can do is accept them for who they are. Sometimes, we feel the other person needs to change, but if we look inwards as well, we see we also need a little of that change. When the love of Christ washes over us, we become more accommodating."

"You always give me the hard stuff." She pouted.

"Isn't that why you love my company?"

"Yeah, yeah," she said then suddenly grew sober. "I always used to wonder why she couldn't love me. If - maybe it was because I wasn't so smart then or I was the last born and they weren't expecting me. I don't know. I know you're going to say God hasn't forgotten me -"

"And He loves you Halimat. More than you know."

"You better be careful with the way you stare at me before I start crushing on you." She joked. He knew she said it to make the mood lighter. She tilted her head to the side. "Tell me again, why aren't you married?"

He threw his head back and laughed.

"Seriously Femi. Why haven't you married yet? Is it because of that girl? Leave that girl who broke your heart and look for someone better *abeg*. She's not worth your love."

Minutes later, she excused herself to answer her phone. "Oh, okay, she's home. Alright, I will head there now. It's not a problem. You're welcome." She ended the call. "We can leave now but we are going to her husband's house since she's been discharged from the hospital."

"So this friend of yours," he began as he drove out of the shop, "Why was she in the hospital?"

"She had a miscarriage, just weeks before her wedding in August. Imagine."

"I thought you said she was going to her husband's house?"

Halimat chuckled "Gosh, I've forgotten how much of a moralist you are. She got pregnant before the marriage." She sighed. "It's really sad though. I've known them for years and they love each other a lot. I can imagine how much pain she would be experiencing right now."

"Are you thinking of your past?"

"Kind of. Sometimes, I feel bad about the abortion. It's funny how people who don't want babies have them, but those who want them can't. God works in mysterious ways." She looked out the window and missed the smile on Femi's face at her latter statement. The house wasn't hard to find and he parked under a tree to shelter him from the sun. "I'll wait for you."

"How can you wait outside? Let's go in together. Besides, I'll need support. I hate all these condolence visits. I usually don't know what to say."

Femi groaned but all the same, he opened his door and stepped out much to her glee. The security guard let them in. His oga had called to inform him to open the gate for Halimat. The house was modern and fashionably decorated. Halimat went ahead of him and knocked on the door. He was still looking around when he heard her voice and felt like his heart was in his throat.

"Peju?"

She looked sad. Distressed. But the shock on her face mirrored his. *Was she the friend who had a miscarriage?*

"Femi, what are you doing here?"

"Halimat is a... friend."

Peju's brow drew together as she frowned. "Halimat?" She fixed her gaze on Halimat. "Antonia, how did you meet Femi?"

Antonia?

"Wow. You guys know each other? Femi is a good friend of mine." She spun around to face him. "And yes, my name is also Antonia. Antonia Halimat Ali." She returned her gaze to Peju. "Can we come in? I don't think you should be standing much after what happened."

Lord, no!

***

ABDUL

It was a quarter past four when he finally got home. It was the earliest he could leave the office though he had called in every two hours to check on Peju. When she didn't answer his last two calls, he assumed she was sleeping, following the doctor's orders. But when he got home to see her hurdled at the foot of their bed and crying he got angry with himself for not getting home sooner.

Abdul tossed aside his jacket and went on his knees beside her. He wrapped his arms around her as she sobbed, her tears wetting his shirt. "Babe, please stop crying. Please." He wiped the tears from her cheek, but it was futile as fresh ones flowed down again. "Peju, you are hurting yourself. You need to rest."

She cried harder, mumbling words like *Why would God take my child away from me? Is this my punishment? How could God be so cruel to me?* Some of what she said didn't make sense to him, but he held her all the same.

"Peju don't do this to yourself." He had shed his tears in the confines of his office. He also shared the news with his mother who had exclaimed at the loss of her first grandchild. She had comforted him, saying Allah knew best and he should be strong for Peju.

"Baby, don't cry. We would have more-"

Peju pushed him away and said, "Leave me alone." When he did not attempt to leave her side, she screamed, "Leave me alone! I want to be alone." She shoved his hand away as he tried to touch her. The hurt look on his face must have gotten to her because she covered her face with her hands and said she was sorry.

168

"You don't understand how I feel. No one understands."

"Yes, I might not understand fully how you feel but Peju, it was our baby. You're not alone in this and I'm also hurt. Please, don't shut me out." He pleaded. "Please."

Her lips quivered as she dropped her hands in defeat and welcomed his arms. He drew her close to him once more and cried while he held on, rocking back and forth. He did that till sleep found her and eased her pain even if but for a moment.

***

OBA

Oba walked into the main church office. It was simple with a Formica desk and a black leather seat behind where a man sat, and two extra seats for visitors. The man behind the desk rose and walked over to him with a smile on his face.

"Good afternoon, Oba. It's good to have you here." He extended his hand to Oba and he took it. He guessed the man was in his early thirties at most. Timilehin had explained how they paired new believers with older ones in the faith who could effectively disciple and encourage them as they grew in their relationship with Christ. Oba thought it was great he'd been linked up with someone close to his age that he could relate with. Despite that, his subtle fears of the session were on his mind. Timilehin had encouraged him to attend.

"Please have a seat. My name is John Ngwube. I'm an Associate Pastor here at His Glory Centre. I will be your discipler, if there's a word like that, but see me more as a brother. Feel free to call me John."

Oba nodded.

"You gave your life to Christ, how do you feel?"

How did he feel? The corners of Oba's lips curled up as he thought back to the moments when he decided to accept Jesus. He knew when he walked down the aisle to the pulpit, with each heavy step he took, that he was making the right decision. A part of him was screaming at him to go in the opposite direction, that God wouldn't accept him. Yet, there was another voice, softer and calmer than the other, encouraging him to keep going forward. There was a peace that washed all over him as he made the prayer to accept Jesus as his Lord and Saviour and an immense joy took over the sorrow of previous minutes.

"I feel good. Great, actually."

John smiled at him, apparently enjoying the baffled look that was probably on his face. "You sound surprised. Is this your first time? Coming to Christ?"

Oba nodded. "Yes." He had grown up in a Christian home. His mother had instilled as much as she could about God and all that, but Oba had no interest in it then. After what happened in university with his ex, he shoved it aside completely.

"Awesome. Next question, what does it mean to be born again to the best of your knowledge?"

Oba scratched the back of the head. "I guess it means living a new life."

John nodded. "Exactly. Don't be ashamed to make a wrong answer. I want you to be completely free. We learn every day. There was a man in the Bible - you have a Bible?" Oba nodded. Timilehin had gifted him with a new one. "Okay. A man named Nicodemus approached Jesus asking how a man could be born again. Was he going back to his mother's womb? How could a person be born a second time? Jesus said a person had to be born from water and the Spirit. Human life comes from human parents, but spiritual life comes from the Spirit. And it can only be so if you believe in Jesus as your Lord and Saviour, not just that he was a prophet but He is the Son of God as written in John 3:16. Understand?"

Oba nodded. "Yeah."

"You just gave your life to Christ and have officially become a member of God's family. Just like when a baby is born into the world, you don't expect the baby to instantly start walking. It takes time, nurturing, encouraging and that's why I'm here. To help, not to condemn or judge you."

Oba nodded once more, growing confident and comfortable. He was eager to learn as much as he could and get the most from the session.

"Cool. So before we continue, tell me about you. What do you do for a living?"

"I'm a manager of a bank." When John raised his brow, Oba laughed. People were always surprised when he told them that and he would explain he rose through the ranks quickly because of his skills and hard work. "I'm engaged to be married next month. That's pretty much it."

"Congratulations on the engagement, but you don't sound too excited. Why's that?"

Oba shrugged. He didn't want to talk about it. "I'm a guy. It's mostly women who are crazy about that stuff." The lie didn't come easy to him, he felt a prodding in him to open up, but he wasn't ready to.

"Seriously? I'm also getting married in June and I'm psyched about it. But-" he leaned forward, "Let's put that aside and get back to our conversation. We can get back to that later. Do you know why you needed to be born again? In other words, I'm asking why you decided to become a Christian."

"Well, I know I have probably done things God wouldn't approve of, but then these last couple of days, I've been battling with regrets of things I did in my past. I needed healing. I needed something to ease the pain, and I knew I couldn't do it on my own. I felt it in my heart that God was calling me to come." He laughed, feeling slightly silly at his last words. *How can I say God asked me to come?* He shook his head, not wanting to say more.

"And you feel silly at what you just said?"

Oba frowned, wondering how he guessed right.

"I understand. The Bible says I stand at the door and knock, if any man hears my voice, and opens the door, I will come in to him, and will sup with him, and he with me. Yes, Oba. God called you to Himself and Heaven rejoiced over you. There are a lot of people who reject the call for salvation. Some don't see the need for a Saviour since they believe they are already good. But the truth is when Adam and Eve fell - that is the first man and woman God created - we all lost fellowship with God. When we were born into this world, we were born into sin. We were alive physically but dead spiritually. We became slaves to the devil. We lost a lot of our birthright as God's children. And people don't know that.

"The god of this world has blinded their eyes. But then, there's hope. God calls us to Him, to bridge the gap, to draw us back to a relationship with Him because He loves us. He's done the same thing for you, Oba, and He wants us all as His children to live a new life with Him. That's why God sent His only Son to die for us."

They spoke for over an hour and in between, Oba had requested a pen and notepad to jot down a lot of scripture references he wanted to search out.

"Any questions for me?" John asked when they were done for the day.

"You mentioned something earlier on about the god of this world. Is that the devil?"

"Yes, Satan is temporarily the god of this world, but he can only do as much as God, our Heavenly Father, permits him. Satan blinds people's eyes and minds so they don't see the truth that is in Jesus. They don't believe they need a Saviour. You get?" When Oba affirmed he did he was asked if there were any other questions.

Oba had taken in a lot already. He wanted to think. "No, but I'm sure I would the next time we meet."

John beamed. "I look forward to it." They scheduled their meeting for the following Saturday and parted ways.

The drive home was fast. He was tired and hungry but amazingly refreshed. It felt like he had been filled up with something more, something different, but couldn't put his finger on it.

His tummy grumbled a complaint, and just as he was about to make something to eat, Nene called to tell him she was coming over and would buy food on her way. Part of him wanted to tell her he would see her another day but she sounded adamant to come.

"Hi, baby. How was your day?" she asked, hugging him and pressing her chest hard against him. Her vanilla and cinnamon scented perfume intoxicating.

His body was responding to her in one way and his mind another. He pulled away from her lest he got carried away. "My day was cool. Yours?" He made to take the nylon bags from her but she pushed his hands away. He raised his hands in surrender and let her have her way. These days she wanted to play the doting housewife and bring food for him whenever possible. Maybe she was afraid he would change his mind.

"My day was okay. Went to work. I feel I'm going to get a promotion any day now."

"Cool." The smell of *ofada* soup drifted to him and his stomach grumbled. "So what did you do today?"

"I went to church." He looked at her, and a surprised face stared back.

"What for? Didn't you go last week?" It had been a week since he gave his life to Christ and he was yet to tell Nene.

"Dish the food and sit down. Let's talk." He saw the fear and guarded look on her face. She nodded and served the food, placed it in front of him and sat down. She didn't serve herself.

"You aren't eating?" he asked as he dug in.

Nene shook her head. "Not hungry. What do you want to talk about?"

Oba chewed on the soft *ponmo* and swallowed before answering. "I gave my life to Christ last week."

"Okay, so?"

"It means I'm born again."

She shrugged. "That doesn't matter." She narrowed her gaze at him. "Is this supposed to be an issue?"

"I'm hoping it won't be."

"Wait, were you expecting I would scream at you and be vexed that you are born again?"

"I didn't know what to expect."

She sighed in relief. "It's totally fine. I thought it was something about the wedding you wanted to talk about." She rose to her feet and pulled her top down to cover her navel. "That's nice."

"Is that all you have to say?"

She looked confused. "Is there anything else I should say?"

He shook his head and kept eating. "No. It's fine." Back at church, when Eliana had seen him, she had been genuinely happy for him, but here Nene was acting like it was no big deal. And it hurt. He knew it was wrong to compare the two of them since they were so different from each other. But he wished he could see the same joy in her as he had seen in Eliana. He shelved his thoughts and kept eating. Nene cleared the plates when they were done. He was hoping she would leave so he could spend time poring over the Bible and looking at the references Pastor John had given him.

But Nene had other plans. She took her seat beside him and placed her hand on his thigh. "It's been a while we had sex, Oba. Aren't you attracted to me anymore?"

"I am, but I'm tired right now. I need to rest."

"That has been your excuse for the last couple of weeks. Are you still annoyed with me?"

Does everything have to be about you?

He yawned. "I also need to read my Bible a little before I nap."

The devil doesn't like that you are now a Christian. Temptations will come your way but you must hold fast. The grace of God is always available in times of need. Those were Pastor John's words to him when he talked about having premarital sex.

Oba got up and tried to cover the bulge in his pants. It was too late. Smiling Nene had already noticed it. "Nene, please you need to leave. I will call you later in the week so we can hang out."

She rose as well. "*Biko* Oba. What have I done wrong again? I'm trying my best to appease you but it feels like whatever I do isn't good enough."

"I told you I need time."

"Time? How much? Weeks? Months? We are getting married next month! There's no time. Please just let go of the past, Oba. Forgive me and let's start a new life together." She placed her hands on his shoulders, gently turning him around to face her. She looked into his eyes; her lips pressed against his softly as she kissed him. He was quickly losing the battle as he accepted her kisses. The moment got heated as he wrapped his arms around her waist and her body leaned into his as she deepened the kiss.

Don't!

The sharp whisper made him draw back suddenly, gasping for breath. He cleaned the sides of his mouth, contemplating how close he got to failing God.

"Nene," he rasped out and cleared his throat. "Please give me time."

Her eyes were a mix of desire and sadness. "Okay. I'll be waiting."

***

ELIANA

An excited Eliana admired her birthday dress in the mirror - a black, tulle knee-length skirt and a burgundy long-sleeved top. Her hair had grown considerably into a teeny afro, so she had it styled and applied some make-up.

The night before, Eliana finally opened up to her mum about Peju and the miscarriage, knowing her mother would hear of the news eventually. Her reaction was expected.

"What is happening in this world? Why on earth would she want to get married to -" Her mother's words trailed off. She shook her head. *"And she was pregnant for this man as well? Is that why she wanted to get married to him?"*

Eliana shook her head, having insinuated the very same thing. "No. She's in love with him."

Her mother hissed loudly. "What kind of stupid love is that? That's how young Christian ladies go astray. Unlike minds can never get along. They would eventually have problems. I want you to get married Eliana, but please don't follow in your friend's footsteps. Please. I'm not desperate for grandkids."

Eliana blinked the thoughts of the conversation away. She knew Peju was hurting deeply from the loss of her child, and all Eliana could offer was comfort and pray for her silently in her heart to come to her senses.

She sighed and continued the process of getting herself ready for her outing. Timilehin was taking her out for her birthday despite her protests not to. It wasn't a date. If anything they were becoming good friends than anything else. She had accepted that there was no attraction between them. At least not on her side, which begged the question if she had to be attracted to someone if they were to be married. She had been attracted to Kene and they had kissed from time to time. She held back from giving herself totally to him.

But for Timilehin, there was nothing. Nada. Zilch. Was that a problem?

"You're looking good." Her father observed when she went to the living room to wait for Timilehin.

Eliana smiled. "Thank you, Daddy."

"Twenty-five. I can still remember when we did your naming ceremony. You were so tiny and now look at you, as beautiful as your mother. The day you get married will be a great day."

"Yes o! My gele will be *skentele skontolo*." Her mother chipped in.

Eliana laughed.

"So where are you going to?"

"Timilehin is taking me to the cinema." She shrugged. "Nothing spectacular."

Her father nodded. "He's the one you went out with that last time, correct?"

Eliana nodded. A knock on the door interrupted their conversation and Dimeji sprinted to see who it was. She turned around to find Timilehin and Oba standing beside her brother. They both greeted her parents while Eliana tried to contain the butterflies in her tummy.

"Big Sis! They brought cake for you." Dimeji said just as she noticed the large white box Timilehin carried.

Her eyes widened. "Oh, wow. Thank you."

"Go and drop it on the dining table," her mother instructed him.

Oba walked up to her and the butterflies' wings flapped even faster. "Happy birthday," he said, giving her a side-hug. "How does it feel to be a year older?"

Eliana gave a nervous laugh. "Good, I guess."

"Are you set?" Timilehin asked quietly.

Eliana nodded and was about to leave with them when her father asked to speak with her. "I'm not comfortable with you going out with two men. I know Timilehin well, but not Oba."

"They are cousins, Daddy."

"It doesn't matter. Just be careful."

Eliana nodded. "Yes Sir." She blew her mother a kiss and hurried out the door. The guys were already seated in the car. Timilehin was in the driver's seat and Oba leaning against the car and looking down at his phone. *Isn't that Oba's car?* As she approached the car, Oba pulled the back door open for her.

She laughed. "Seriously?"

"Yeah, it's your birthday. Enjoy being treated like a queen."

She got into his car and watched as Oba went around and took his seat beside Timilehin in front.

"O- Oba is coming too?" she stuttered her question at Timilehin. Meanwhile, her eyes stared at Oba from the rear-view mirror.

"Yup! Unfortunately," Timilehin joked. "Don't worry, we will all have fun and enjoy the day. Just relax."

Eliana sat back and her eyes gazing outside the window as Oba's car rolled forward. How was she going to relax, especially with the startling truth that she was really attracted to his cousin?

Chapter 15

ELIANA

"Did you enjoy the movie?" Timilehin asked as they indulged in mouthwatering ice-cream scoops.

Eliana nodded. "Yes, Civil War was awesome. Can't wait for the next Marvel film. It's going to be amazing!"

Oba raised his brow in surprise. "You like Marvel films?"

"Yeah. Courtesy of the brother."

"So how many of the films have you watched?"

"Just a few."

"Like?" Oba prodded.

"Iron Man 1 and 2, Thor 1 and Captain America: The First Avenger."

"Hmm. I would never have taken you to be a superhero movie fan."

"Well, there's a lot you don't know about me."

He laughed. "True."

She turned to Timilehin to ask a question and noticed his eyes on her, with a puzzled look on his face. She licked her lips, in case there was ice cream on them. "Is something wrong?"

Timilehin shifted his eyes from them. Frankly, he was doing a really poor job of hiding his puzzlement. "No. There's nothing wrong. Just have a lot on my mind. Oba, how's it going with Pastor John?" He directed his question at his cousin. Eliana couldn't help the embarrassment that washed over her. *What's wrong with him?*

"He's really good. We were supposed to have our third session today but he cancelled because he had to attend to some family issues. His father is a senator right?"

Timilehin nodded. "Yeah, *dem* get plenty money but Pastor John *no dey* send *am. Na wetin* he talk one time like that. How many sessions do you have with him?"

"12. The guy is good at teaching."

Eliana bobbed her head. "That's Pastor John for you."

"I heard his cousin Daniel is also in the choir. He used to be the leader of the choir but things happened and he stepped down."

She didn't want to retell how the whole incident had exploded in his face and caused a scandal in the church.

"What happened to the Daniel guy?" Oba questioned.

Timilehin answered. "People make mistakes. He made one that opened his *nyash* to the whole church and he was disciplined for it."

Oba frowned at that. "Why should he be disciplined in front of the whole church? That's not nice."

"True, but that's tough love. There are many things at stake when a church worker does wrong." Timilehin explained. "We're ambassadors of Christ meant to represent Him and not make a mockery of the character of Christ. The discipline isn't to send you out of the church like you're a vagabond. It's to cause a change in the person for the better."

"Oh," Oba said.

"Wow." Eliana blinked, not having thought of it that way. "Timilehin, you're deep *o*."

"Is it true Pastor John's fiancée is a gold digger?" Oba asked. He explained how he overheard a group of women talking about it in their car at the parking lot.

Timilehin snorted. "*Na* bad *belle*. People can talk *sha*."

"That's gossip," she joined in. "I told you before that a lot of women are jealous of him getting married. They wished it was them. Don't pay close attention to it. And even if it's true, who are we to judge? It's between him and God." She looked at Timilehin and smiled, grateful he had taught her that lesson way back with Peju. Thoughts of her friend suddenly made her sad.

"Don't think about it," Timilehin said, his eyes on her. They were gentle and full of understanding. "At least, not for today."

She nodded. *He knows me well.* "Thanks."

Oba cleared his throat and excused himself to use the toilet.

"Eliana -" Timilehin began then shook his head. "Never mind."

"What did you want to say?"

"It's not important. I'll ask some other time."

She looked at him with concerned eyes. "Are you sure?"

"Yes, Ma."

"You have been acting weird since you picked me from my house. Is everything okay?"

He tossed his spoon in his empty cup and used a lemon serviette to clean his mouth. "There's nothing wrong. I told you I had a lot on my mind."

"And you don't want to share it with me?"

He smiled at her. "Not yet."

"Okay *o*. When you're ready, you know my number."

"Most definitely."

The day went smoothly. They had a delicious lunch of Fried rice and chicken. Timilehin made her tummy hurt from laughter, and Oba, her heart leap with his smile.

***

OBA

Oba noticed the petite woman Pastor John was talking to after the service. He didn't want to miss him, so he sat a few seats from them and raised his head from his phone when he heard the lady raise her voice. From the little he could gather, they were not in agreement on something and he heard Pastor John call her *Ade*. He saw Pastor John talking and strained his ears to listen in.

"Adesewa, he would come around soon. I'm sorry but you have no say in his life anymore. I care about you, don't waste your life plotting revenge over a man. It's not worth it."

Revenge over a man?

The woman grabbed her bag from the empty seat beside her and got up. She looked pointedly at Oba as though to chastise him for eavesdropping. Oba shifted his gaze away. But he listened on. "I'm sorry pastor but I didn't come here for counselling sessions. And speaking of marriage, I heard you're getting married to Funlola. Isn't she beyond your league? She isn't exactly wife material considering her promiscuous ways."

"Thank you for your concern." Pastor John said, unfazed.

"Likewise."

Oba turned to see her walk out of the church with dark shades on. *What was that all about?*

"Hey, Oba. Sorry to have kept you waiting. Let's go to my office. Were you able to get something to eat?"

"No. It was a long queue and everything was sold out when it almost got to my turn."

"Ouch. Not to worry I will send for food." He pulled out his phone and called someone to buy a couple of snacks and drinks for them. "Right! Let's get down to business." John took his seat. "What chapter are you reading now?"

"Chapter four. The story of the Samaritan woman who had five husbands. That's something else. Why would she jump from one man to another?"

"Perhaps she was looking for something none of them could provide. An emptiness that can't be filled by any man or woman." He paused, looking intently at Oba. "Tell me, how's preparation for your wedding going?"

Oba should have seen that question coming. The man just had a way of blending conversations with ease. He shrugged. "It's moving on well."

"11th of June right? That's less than a month away. Can I ask, why do you want to marry Nene?"

He didn't know anymore. "I thought I loved her. She's a nice person, at least when she wants to be. And I already made a vow to marry her."

"So you're getting married because you promised to? That's very honourable of you, but it sounds like you'd rather not marry her. Talk to me, Oba. What's wrong?"

Oba shifted his eyes from John's and stared at the white wall behind him. A picture frame hung a few inches above his head that said, *Christ, Is All You Need.*

"She had an abortion without telling me. And unfortunately, it's now put a bridge in our relationship that's hard to get past. I'm not saying I'm perfect because I have my baggage." He cleared his throat. "I also had an abortion with an ex when I was still in the university. While it was mutual, the pain of that hurt so much that I vowed never to let it happen again. Then Nene tells me she aborted my child. How am I supposed to feel? Am I supposed to tell her it's not a problem and we can continue as nothing happened?" He shook his head. "That's what she wants but I can't. I can't even forgive myself for agreeing to the abortion so many years ago."

John heaved a sigh. "I'm sorry that happened to you. But Oba, do you know God has forgiven you?"

Oba looked up at the ceiling and bit on his lip, his eyes getting teary.

John continued, "God forgave you immediately you confessed Christ as your Lord and Saviour. He isn't holding it against you, brother. You're holding it against yourself."

"I feel guilty. . ." Oba said, glancing at his hands. "Like there's blood on my hands." Tears trailed down his cheeks.

"Second Corinthians 5 verse 21 (KJV) says *for he hath made him to be sin for us, who knew no sin; that we might be made the righteousness of God in him.* Romans 8 verse 1, says *there's no more condemnation for them that are in Christ Jesus.* Read the New Century version as well. It says you are not judged guilty. Jesus didn't sin but He took our sins upon Himself so we could freely enter God's Presence. Jesus wiped off that blood on your hands and put it on Himself. He took our old selves with all our past mistakes, dead weight, flaws, and gave us new lives. We can never by our self make ourselves right with God. Oba, give the pains of your past to God. Let Him heal you and free you of the guilt."

Oba wiped the tears with the back of his hand as he reflected on the words shared for a few minutes. Pastor John's words felt like a warm blanket wrapped around him on a cold rainy day. Oba still had something else on his mind that required answers. "Can I ask a question?"

"Sure, go ahead."

"I kind of heard you're getting married soon and she's er— well people think she's wrong for you."

"I don't base my choices on what people say but what God says."

Oba was shocked. "And God says she's the woman for you?"

John smiled a little, leaned forward and clasped his hands in front of him. "I would have run the other way and completely avoided her if God didn't lead me to marry her. The kind of wife I had in mind was different but I trust God and believe He knows best. His plans for me are good all the time even when I can't see the big picture yet. I choose to believe that."

"How can God lead you to the person you should marry? God has other important things to concern Himself with."

"Proverbs 18 verse 22. *He who finds a wife finds a good thing and obtains favour from the Lord.* James 1 verse 17 says *every good and perfect gift comes from the Lord.* God is majestic, great. And even as great as He is, He's concerned about little things, even about what you wear to work or which route to take when driving. You enjoy all these benefits and more as you grow in your relationship with God. Marriage is really important.

"Hebrews 13 verse 4 talks about marriage being honoured by everyone. Some people do all sorts of things in their marriage and thereby bring dishonour and shame to what God created to be good and beautiful. I want you to read up the book of Ephesians 5 after you have read the next chapter of John, and when you come back we can talk more about it."

"Okay."

As Oba walked out of the church building, he left as a free man. The shackles of his past sins had been left behind; the knowledge of God's forgiveness, a gift he would cherish forever.

***

FEMI

Femi closed his eyes and took a deep breath. He was like that for a couple of minutes till he knew sleep wasn't coming his way any time soon, even though he willed it to. He opened his eyes and stared at the ceiling. The image and thoughts in his head wouldn't let him be. Peju looked broken and had the sad realization that she had been pregnant for her fiancé. He hadn't been wrong when he noted she had gained a little weight the last time they went out.

Was that why she was so self-conscious about the food and eating light?

He ran his hand over his face. "God, why? Why did you let this happen?"

The silence that followed frustrated him.

"God, why are You keeping quiet when I'm in desperate need of an answer?"

He expelled a breath.

Your thoughts are not My thoughts. Your ways, not My ways.

The scripture came to him swiftly. Femi understood what God was telling him. No matter how much God had done for calling us to Him, offering salvation and protecting His children from being snatched by the enemy, the choice was Man's to remain with Him or not. Peju had a choice. She was free to choose which way to go, and she chose the opposite direction of God.

She must love him then to have sex with him. He tried his best not to think of both of them together, making out and doing what only married people should do. Asides from that, he thought of how she may be feeling. He wondered if she cared how her relationship with God was like.

He propped his arm behind his head.

Then there was his friend, Antonia Halimat Ali. Who could have guessed she and Peju went to the same secondary school and had been friends once upon a time? When they left Peju the other day, he steered clear of any conversation that had to do with her. Halimat wanted to talk but respected his decision and plugged her ears as he drove back to the hospital. Understanding his need to be alone.

Why was it that each time he saw Peju, it always seemed like something bad had occurred? Like a dagger had pierced his heart.

Femi turned on his side and found the position more comfortable as he felt himself relax. He could damn it all and leave her to her life, but as much as he wanted to, it went against his nature. What he still felt for her. He had the urgent fervency to pray for her and he would. It was the least he could do.

***

PEJU

Peju turned on the gas cooker, heat seeping through the pot to the fish stew Abdul had prepared yesterday. She wasn't hungry but Abdul had insisted she eat something. He was keeping a close eye on her. He had even gone as far as to feed her the day before.

Things were a little strained between them, mostly because she had found comfort in solitude. Whenever Abdul tried to talk with her, she replied with mono-syllables and it frustrated him. He didn't know how to bridge the gap and she didn't know how to draw him close.

The smell of something burning wafted to her nose and she turned off the burner. She lifted the lid of the pot and peered into it. The stew was slightly burnt. Nothing disastrous. She closed the pot and rubbed the back of her neck. She couldn't believe Antonia and Femi were friends. Were they also romantically involved? The thought was ludicrous to her. Femi was too much of a Christian to be involved with her. He was too good for that.

And you aren't. You aren't good anymore, are you? You're being real to yourself. Real to your love for Abdul.

The words came heavily upon her along with a discomfort in her chest.

Femi offered words of consolation at her loss, after his shock wore off, and eventually kept to himself. Antonia did most of the talking, throwing questions Peju's way. She asked if she was okay and if there was anything she could help out with concerning the wedding. Maybe Femi wasn't interested in Antonia, but from the way they spoke, it seemed they were close.

Peju dished her food and sat at the lavish dining table. Her thoughts strolled back to Antonia and Femi. Even when they were leaving, he had looked at her with sadness and pain. She could still find tenderness in his eyes, what he had always had for her. Months later, she wondered, *What picture does he have of me now?*

Why do you care? It's none of his business. You aren't his wife or sister. The raspy whisper spoke across her heart.

But I'm his friend. I'm supposed to be his friend.

Don't kid yourself. You aren't his friend.

She shook her head. It was true. Why was she bothered about it? Whatever he thought of her was his business. *He can think whatever he wants.*

"Sweetheart?"

Peju looked up from her half-eaten plate of food; her appetite gone after the seventh spoon. Her stomach churned at the sight of his bare chest glistening with sweat. She figured he was done with his push-ups.

"Hi," she said in a whisper.

"Not hungry?"

"No."

He walked up close, pulled out a chair and sat down. On him was the familiar scent of his Cartier cologne that drove her crazy.

He took the spoon from her and tasted her food. "Did the stew burn?"

"Sorry about that. I was absent-minded."

"It's fine. I was just surprised. Anyway, how are you feeling?"

She leaned back on her chair. "I'm good." The bleeding had stopped and the pain had practically gone. Her lack of appetite had returned her flat tummy.

There was no trace of her previous pregnancy.

"Thank God." He leaned forward and kissed her lips. "You don't know how happy I am to hear that."

The emotional pain of the loss of her child was minimal. There was a thought brewing in her mind, but she wasn't going to bring it up just yet. She was waiting for the perfect time.

"Idris sends his love as do my family."

"Send my love back to them."

Abdul offered to clear the dishes and ordered her to go to bed and wait up. She obeyed. When he finally came into the dim-lit room his surprise and silent appreciation gladdened her and gave a boost to her confidence.

"I've missed you," she said in a shy voice. She was all dressed in the lingerie he once got her from Paris. "Let's make another baby."

Chapter 16

ABDUL

Abdul could barely contain his surprise. "What?"

"Let's have another baby," she repeated. "I know we can't replace the one we lost but we can try for another."

He searched her eyes. "Baby, you need to take it easy."

"Why? The doctor said we can try for another baby right away. Why do we have to wait?"

He removed her hand from his cheek and led her to the bed, sitting at the edge of it. "Peju -"

"Please, Abdul don't say no," she pleaded. "I want to have your children."

"And you will, love. Let's just do it right this time and focus on the wedding."

He felt her body tense immediately as she removed her hand from his. "What's that supposed to mean? What do you mean *let's do it right this time?*" She drew her robe close and covered herself, much to his regret. He had been looking forward to it but not for the reasons she wanted.

Abdul sighed inwardly. He didn't want them to argue. "I just think God didn't want us to have this child yet. That's all." He was hoping to cleanse himself during the Ramadan fast, to absolve himself of any sin he had committed. "I don't want you getting worked up with trying to get pregnant and juggling the stress of the wedding." Once again, he took her hand in his and when she tried drawing back, his grip was firm. He didn't want to give her the distance she desired. He was tired of the strain in their

188

relationship and wanted to get back what they had so badly.

"Habeebah, I love you. I love you so much I feel my heart will explode. I want the best for you. I promise you as soon as we say I do, I will carry you over my shoulder, rush you upstairs to our suite and make mad love to you. *Walahi*, you will get pregnant. With twins."

Peju laughed and looked away from him shyly.

His heart soared at the victory. Not one to waste a moment, he shifted close to her. He raised her chin so she could look him in his eyes. He loved the scent of coconut in her hair and ran his fingers down her thick, soft hair. "You mean a lot to me, Peju. I don't like to see you cry. I don't like it when you hurt. I want you to know I'm here for you every step of the way."

"I love you too, Abdul. You're right. I will wait till we get married."

He kissed her then. There was no love-making that night but they slept in each other's arms and that was good enough for him.

***

OBA

Oba had spent the last two weeks poring over the Bible, learning new things and having more questions. He was grateful Pastor John and Timilehin were available to answer them. During that time, he'd also had a lot to think about. A major breakthrough was letting go of his pain from the past, and finally forgiving himself. It had been an emotional experience for him but he felt at peace knowing God had truly forgiven him. This also gave Oba the push to forgive Nene. He decided to appease her with a dinner date.

He stared at her across the table as she swept her long brown hair to the side to look over the menu. She was gorgeous in her body-hugging red halter-neck dress and flawless makeup.

Things weren't the way they used to be, despite her trying her best. They hadn't been intimate with each other and she hadn't pressed him on it after the last time. When he called to invite her for dinner, she was elated and jumped at the idea immediately. He brought her back to the same restaurant as when she abruptly told him about the abortion.

She frowned and pursed her lips, then looked up at him. "I can't decide between the lamb and pork chops. Then I don't know if I want Fried rice or noodles. What are you ordering?

"Nene, I can't marry you." He blurted.

She jerked back like she had been slapped. A dazed look on her face. "What?"

He repeated what he said.

"W- why?" she managed to get out. "I thought you forgave me."

"I have forgiven you."

"Are you insane? Then why don't you want us to get married?"

He saw tears well up in her eyes and steeled himself for how emotional things were going to get.

God, please help me. "The truth is, I can't trust you Nene. And it's not just what you did. It also has to do with my past." He exhaled. "I didn't tell you this, but years ago, my ex and I agreed to an abortion. This was back in school. It hurt like crazy and I never wanted to go through that again. Yet, you went behind my back and had the abortion not thinking or knowing how much it would hurt me."

Her jaw went slack. "Oba, why didn't you tell me . . ."

"If I told you, would you have reconsidered having the abortion? Please, don't lie to me."

She made to nod, then shook her head, looking down at her hands. "No."

He sighed. "Nene, I truly forgive you but I don't love you anymore." There, he had finally said it. "I don't think I ever loved you the right way. The way God expects me to love you or rather, I can't love you the way He wants me to."

Her head snapped up. "God? God told you to break up with me?"

"I didn't say that."

Nene folded her arms across her chest giving him a glimpse of her cleavage. He shifted his eyes away. "So how are you expected to love me?" She asked in mockery.

The passage of Ephesians came to him then. "To love you unconditionally.

Can I love you the way Christ loves the church? Can I die for you?"

"Can you?" Her voice was barely a whisper.

Strength Lord. Give me strength. "No. I don't love you that deeply."

The torn look on her face pained him.

"I'm sorry, Nene."

"Is that the only reason you can't marry me? Love grows Oba. We can still love each other the way you said eventually."

"We don't share the same beliefs."

"Chill. Is it because I didn't follow you to church the other day that you're doing this? We both aren't frequent churchgoers. So what is the problem? Is it because you just grew an affinity for church that you want to use that as an excuse not to marry me? Our wedding is this Saturday for goodness sake!"

"I know," he said in a calm tone. "I will talk to your parents and mine will do the same." Oba had called his mother just that morning to break the news to her. She had shouted at him for wasting their time and money, but at the end of the day, with the help of his father, she was calmer now.

"I guess a broken engagement is better than a broken home. If you are sure this is what you want, then it's fine. Your father and I will try and make it to Lagos Monday morning and sort it out. I pray all goes well. But please - why this sudden change? Especially when it's two weeks to your wedding?"

"Let's just say God opened my eyes. She's not the woman for me."

He heard his mother gasp.

"I told you not to go for an Igbo girl. Have you told Nene yet?"

"I plan on doing that this evening."

"God be with you my son."

The slap on his cheek jolted him back to the present. He had expected it but would have expected not to be caught unaware.

"You are a terrible person, Oba Afolayan! How can you break up with me five days before our wedding?" Oba noticed a few heads turn to look at them. A particular woman gave Nene a piteous look before offering him one of disgust.

"Nene, I understand you are angry and hurt right now bu-"

"Is this revenge over the abortion?"

He shook his head. "No. I already said I forgive you."

She wiped the tears from her eyes with the back of her hand. "So you're really going to do this." She sniffed and said sadly, "We would have made a great power couple you know. Like Will and Jada Smith. And you're missing out on the best sex you can ever have in your life. You know that, right?"

He said nothing to that, not wanting to think in that direction. Of course, he was going to miss their crazy, passionate moments but that was all in his past. His silence angered her and she rose to her feet, tossing a glass of water in his face. "You're an ingrate! You will forever regret this, Oba. Go to hell with this place and it's bad *juju!*" With that, she stomped out.

Oba released a heavy sigh. That was phase one. Now, he had to think of how to break the news to her parents. That was if she didn't go home immediately and rant to her parents.

God, I need Your help.

He could imagine how pissed her father and mother would be. Right then, he remembered the scripture that spoke of God's grace being sufficient for him. *Sometimes when you need an answer from God, a scripture popping into your head at that time addressing your issue is answer enough,* Pastor John had said. Oba felt peace then, knowing God was fully behind him and would help him along the way as he faced what was in front of him.

***

ELIANA

It was the second week in June and Eliana had her work cut out for her. She was busy with Cr8tive Splash, and Bible study at church. Coupled with that, she also had to stand in for one of the teachers in the children's church who had recently given birth. Sundays were hectic for her. But there was joy in her heart as well, and she didn't know if she should feel the way she should.

There was a knock on the door and she glanced at her watch. Timilehin had mentioned stopping over from his cell meeting to talk. He was supposed to have arrived thirty minutes earlier. Timilehin wasn't one to be late but when he was, he always had a tangible reason.

"Hi," she greeted when she opened the door to find him at her doorstep.

"How far?"

"I *dey o*. How was the meeting?"

"It was good."

"What about your parents?"

"They went out. Dimeji's in his room."

Timilehin nodded. "Can we talk?"

She smiled and led him to the only three-seater sofa in their living room. "Sure. Would you like something to eat or drink first?"

"Water is fine."

She went to the kitchen, placed a glass and bottle of water on a tray and carried it to him. He had been distant over the last couple of weeks. They weren't gisting as much as they used to. She was surprised at how much she missed his company.

"Thank you."

"You're welcome."

There was an uncomfortable silence that followed and Eliana looked down at her chipped toenails. It had been a while she had a pedicure. *Need to fix that asap.*

"I want to ask you a question. It's been on my mind for a while now but I couldn't find a way to ask."

Her heart pounded. *I hope he's not going to ask me to marry him!* "Ask."

"Are you in love with my cousin?"

Her mouth fell open as she stared at him in shock. *Where did that come from?* She swallowed hard, her throat suddenly feeling very dry. "With Oba?"

Timilehin nodded.

She didn't see any teasing in his expression. She looked away from him. "Why would you think such a thing?"

He shrugged and clasped his hands. "Well, I have eyes and I see how you act when you're with him. I see the smile on your face and how you try to act calm and uninterested when his name comes up. And then my final proof was when I told you he wasn't getting married to Nene again. I knew then that you really liked him."

Eliana didn't know what to say. Could she confess her feelings? Could she say how much she hoped he would notice her? She knew he was still growing in his relationship with God and was keeping her hopes and thoughts between her and God. And her diary of course!

"Eliana?"

"What do you want me to say?"

He smiled and said softly, "The truth."

She nodded. "I like Oba. He's a nice person."

"Do you love him?" He prodded.

God, I don't want to hurt Timilehin.

The truth shall set you free.

She blinked as the words settled in her heart. She glanced up at Timilehin and said her words carefully, "I like him. I care about him." She pursed her lips, pausing briefly. "Yes, I love him. I know it sounds stupid since he doesn't see me that way. I mean we are all friends and he just broke up with his fiancée so it's wrong for me to even think such. But I know I care for him." Eliana's hand went to her mouth, realizing she had probably said too much.

Timilehin smiled. "Don't be ashamed of how you feel. It's safe to say we were both praying God's will concerning him and Nene would come to pass. That has happened."

"You aren't annoyed?"

"Annoyed *ke*? I mean, it pain me small but *wetin man wan do*?" Her sceptical look made him add, "I'm cool with it dear. Somehow somehow I knew you guys would end up together."

"Really?"

He nodded and poured himself some water. He took a sip before gulping it all down.

"How did you know?"

He shrugged. "I just knew. And don't worry he will eventually come around. He just needs to settle everything going on with him."

"How's he doing?"

"He's cool. Nene's dad smashed his jaw with a stick in front of his parents and called them all manner of names." Eliana gasped. "Things could have turned out worse but thank God for taking control." He nudged her arm lightly. "Don't be worried, he's fine. Take my word for it. He will be in church this Sunday."

Eliana nodded. She knew she would still worry but she was not going to let her desire to see him ruin her.

After Timilehin left, she went to the kitchen to start dinner, knowing her parents would be back any minute. She grabbed two small onions from the heap at the top of the fridge and brought out the chopping board and knife from the drawers. Smiling to herself, she replayed her conversation with Timilehin and hoped for the best.

***

ANTONIA

"So what would you like me to call you, Antonia or Halimat?"

"Antonia."

"Why the initial name change?"

"My mother named me Antonia. The name change was my way of rebelling out of the hatred I had for her. But I don't hate her anymore. I just feel intense pity."

"Hmm, that's kind of worse."

She shrugged. "Oh well. I guess with time I will snap out of that as well. But you, how are you feeling?"

He knew she was asking about Peju. "I'm fine as I can be."

"You really love Peju, don't you?" It was more of a statement than a question. He didn't see the need to say anything. "I was there when it all started. Their love blossomed right before our eyes. They have always been crazy for each other and no one could come between them."

Femi saw the look in her eyes and could see what she was hiding. "Did you have a crush on Abdul too?"

She nodded. "It's that obvious?"

"Not really. I just put two and two together."

She laughed nervously. "Peju always suspected but there was no proof. A crush isn't love. At least it's not like the love they share. I'm cool though. I have accepted their relationship and I think you should as well."

Before he could answer, Nurse Eniola knocked and walked in. She greeted Antonia, dropped the file in her hands after explaining what it was for and exited the office. Antonia pointed at the door.

"She seems to be a nice woman. Maybe you should consider taking her out."

"You're not serious."

"I am She's good looking and respectful."

"Hmm . . ." he said as though considering it, but he knew it was never going to happen. He didn't want to tell her he had considered it more than once in the last few weeks but had restrained himself from doing so. He didn't date his employees.

"Femi, on a serious note forget about Peju. Move on with your life. Please."

Femi nodded. "She's been forgotten."

"Are you sure?"

"Yes." The truth of his statement broke his heart but he knew it was for the best. He was finally moving on. The cloud had finally lifted.

Chapter 17

ELIANA

20ᵗʰ of August, 2016

A lot has happened. Not just with me but with my friends etc. Let me start before I explode and lose steam for writing. Where should I start? Okay, my business has been good. I partnered with a guy who takes pictures of my finished work whenever he's available. My clients love what I deliver and I'm getting more referrals which means more work.

On this note, I have to confess, I haven't had time for my Wednesday Bible studies and Sister Stella has called a few times to talk to me about it. She says the other sisters miss my presence. I miss them too. I really do but I'm having a hard time balancing it all with work and other things.

Also worth noting... Oba and I have started hanging out. We are friends o! But he has hinted that he likes me and we would both see where this new thing leads to. I like him a lot and my parents are cool with him. We don't want to rush anything because I know he just came out of a rough relationship with his ex-fiancée and I don't want to be his rebound girl and I told him this. He said that can never happen. I am trying to believe that. We attended pastor John's wedding and it was sooo beautiful! Pastor John was very romantic and looked so in love with sister Funlola. The love in his eyes as he watched her come down the aisle was priceless. I can't help if I'm a helpless romantic! To top it off, his vows were so heartfelt.

Sigh.

I heard the reception had equally been beautiful and he presented his wife with a car. Their wedding was in late June. But then on a sad note, it broke my heart to hear Sister Funlola left him six weeks after. I don't understand why but Pastor John looks so broken! I pray God helps them.

Anyways. . .

Oba and I don't want to rush anything because he's still growing in faith but his hunger for God is glaring! Sigh.

It's Peju's wedding today. Uncle Femi introduced me to an Eniola babe that is a nurse in his hospital. She seems nice. While I'm happy for him, I wish Peju realized her mistake sooner and went back to him.

***

PEJU

The months flew by in a frenzy with plans and preparations for the wedding. Abdul's family flew in and were taken care of for the big day. Abdul's sisters had been very helpful with handling other minor details and making sure the gifts for guests were taken care of. All they wanted was for her to relax till the big day came. The traditional wedding was slated for eleven in the morning, followed by the white wedding ceremony at three in the afternoon and the wedding party.

Peju took a deep breath as she held her bouquet of white roses. Her hands were shaky and her heart pounded as the photographer took a couple of photos. This was the moment she had long been waiting for. She was getting married to the man of her dreams. Her one time love. The only man she had ever lived for. This was what she wanted right? So why was she so nervous?

"You're nervous." Abdul's mother said, staring at her in the gold-encrusted mirror. She looked gorgeous in her gold lace and rose *gele*.

Peju nodded. "Yes, Ma."

Mrs Layeni smiled and walked into the room. "There's no need to be my dear. This is just another ceremony. The both of you are already married since you performed the traditional rites."

Peju nodded again, recalling the traditional wedding earlier in the day and how Abdul had carried her following the Yoruba tradition.

"You look beautiful. I'm thankful to have you as a daughter. My son loves you so much and I've never seen him so happy. When both of you were following each other up and down in secondary school, I didn't really think this day would come. But I have learnt years means nothing when love is involved. Allah has set this day for you. My son really loves you and I know you feel the same way. I wish you both happiness. May Allah keep your love between each other strong and bless your union."

"Amen."

Abdul's mother brought out a little box from her gold purse and handed it to Peju.

"For me?"

"Yes, dear. Open it."

Peju lifted the lid and gasped at the exquisite pearl earrings that matched the pearl head vine wrapped around her hair bun.

"It's beautiful." Peju gazed up at her. "Thank you, Ma." She rose and with tears in her eyes, hugged the older woman. Her mother-in-law. Her new mother.

"You're welcome, darling." They pulled back from each other and Abdul's mother smiled at her. "I bought it specially for you."

Peju took off her earrings and put on the new set. They looked perfect with her subtle, natural make-up. Her dress was handmade with pearls on the embroidery. It was an off-shoulder style, revealing a little of her back and very little cleavage.

Her mother walked in then. "*Oya*, they are ready for you." She opened her wrapper and spread her legs to re-tie her wrapper properly. She greeted Abdul's mother. "*Omo mi*, you're looking takeaway."

"Thank you, Mummy."

"I hope my son won't faint when he sees you."

The three of them laughed light-heartedly.

Antonia walked into the room. She looked gorgeous in her rose gown that flowed down to her ankles, her gold peep-toe heels shining through.

Peju was glad she chose Antonia as her maid-of-honour. Antonia had helped so much over the last few months, Peju felt indebted to her. It was nice to be with someone she knew didn't judge her. She also didn't feel threatened by Antonia's old feelings for Abdul, knowing his heart was sold out to her.

"Your groom a-" Her hand went to her mouth when Peju faced her. "Awww, you look great Peju. I'm so happy for you." They hugged quickly. "*Oya*, your groom awaits you." They hurried her down the elevator to the hall where everyone was seated and waiting for the bride.

The song *I Was Made To Love You* by Gerald Levert was playing in the background as her paternal uncle held her hand and they walked down the aisle.

She smiled at a few of the guests along the way. The wedding had been strictly by invitation as the couple wanted only three hundred guests. It had been a struggle to keep it at that. Peju's mother wanted to invite up to hundred guests alone, telling her it would be wrong not to invite her father's family, but Peju had pleaded with her to limit the number. She also threatened to have them embarrassed with bouncers at the entrance.

Peju's eyes caught on to Titi, her secondary school friend, who had flown in from Dubai for the wedding. In her words, it was a wedding she wouldn't miss for the world. Peju was glad to reunite with her after so many years had passed. She had changed from the mousy person she knew and had become loud and boisterous; giving her and Abdul one story after another of how her life had been over the years. Stories that kept them entertained and laughing.

She looked straight ahead and her heart skipped a beat when she saw Abdul standing at the beautifully decorated altar looking handsome in a blue suit with black lapels and a white rose pinned to his jacket. His eyes brimming with love for her.

She smiled at him. *I love this man.*

Her eyes shifted and she saw Femi and Eliana. He was staring at her, with half a smile and sad eyes. She looked away. She could have sworn he shook his head. Why would he shake his head? Was he also against her wedding?

He's just jealous.

She focused her gaze on Abdul alone, her groom who looked dashing at the end of the aisle. He reached out for her hand and kissed it.

"Let us proceed," the minister said. Her mother had brought him from her church to solemnise the marriage.

"We are gathered here to witness and celebrate the joining of Olupeju and Abdullah. Marriage is an honourable thing. A beautiful thing and all things beautiful were created by God. This union is beautiful to God." She felt a small prick in her heart as he said that. "Today, these two lovely people have decided to come together to become one, to procreate, to replenish the earth. God is smiling down at them from heaven."

A few people clapped and shouted hallelujah.

"Now, knowing the reason for marriage you two must know that whatever God has joined together let no man put asunder." The minister faced Abdul. "Abdul, do you take this woman to be your lawfully wedded wife? To have and to hold? To cherish? To love forevermore until death?"

Abdul gazed into her eyes. "I do."

The minister faced Peju. "Do you Peju take this man to be your husband? To have and to hold. To respect his authority in your life and honour him? To love forevermore until death."

Peju swallowed hard and shifted her eyes to look at the small crowd. Why she did so she didn't know. She glanced at Femi who fixed his gaze at her, and this time she knew, she wasn't imagining it as he shook his head subtly at her.

"Peju?" Abdul drew her attention back to him and he saw the confused look in his eyes.

Say yes. This is the man you have loved for years. This is the man who loves you. Say yes. Everyone is looking. It's too late to change your mind.

She swallowed hard and nodded. "I - I do."

"With the power vested in me, I pronounce you husband and wife. Kiss your bride!"

Peju closed her eyes briefly as Abdul's lips claimed hers.

***

PEJU

"I spoke to Pastor John about the wedding," Peju said as she and Eliana relaxed in a restaurant after a meal.

"What did he say?"

Peju explained everything that happened. "He said he didn't think Abdul could love me the way Christ would want." She looked at Eliana. "I didn't understand what he meant. In what way could Abdul love me more? He bought a brand-new car for me despite me telling him not to. The car I said was an official car, sorry. He takes care of me, he's there for me. In what other way could Christ want him to love me?"

"Do you really want me to answer that?"

Peju nodded despite being scared of the truth. "I want to know."

"Love isn't about material things or simply doing the right things and saying I love you. Paul explained in Ephesians how Christ so loved the church that he gave Himself. In the same way, a husband should love his wife so much that he should be willing to give himself up for her. Most importantly, he should love her so much to be ready to present her to Jesus Christ without spot or wrinkles because she has been washed by the Word. Abdul can't do that. He can't love you so much to watch over you and be concerned about your spiritual growth so you make heaven. He can't do that if he doesn't know Christ."

"He can. He can give his life to Christ and do everything God expects of him."

Eliana shook her head. "You can't predict the future. What if he never believes in Christ? What if he pushes you to become a Muslim?"

"I will take my chances."

Peju opened her eyes, her vision blurred from tears. It was too late to go back. Too late to say no. She was now Mrs Abdul Layeni.

"I love you, baby," Abdul whispered against her lips amidst the hoots and applause. "Thanks for saying I do."

***

FEMI

She's a married woman.

Femi watched as Abdul lifted her off her feet and carried her down the aisle with Peju laughing and screaming for him to put her down. He whispered in her ears and her eyes widened in shock as she begged him to put her down. He did, but not without kissing her while the crowd went wild.

"Awww, they are so in love!" He heard a lady behind him exclaim in excitement. Next thing, he heard her say, "Tolu, hope you're taking notes."

Femi looked away from the newlyweds. He wasn't lying when he told Antonia that he had moved on. He had mentally, but emotionally it was still hard to see her marry someone else.

"The wedding was really beautiful," Eniola said beside him. He had invited her to accompany him. In the last few months, he had gotten to know her and Antonia had been right in her judgement. She was kind-hearted, respectful and loved God immensely. She was a likeable person so it wasn't hard for him to be attracted to her personality.

"Yes, it was."

"But I don't think the pastor got it right."

Femi looked down at Eniola and saw the frown on her face. "What do you mean?" He noted Abdul and Peju were making their way out of the hall and a few ushers were guiding the crowd to make their way to the reception venue which was on the next floor.

"If a Christian is marrying an unbeliever, God may not smile at them, especially if it's against His will. I don't know why some pastors can't stand up to the truth and not sugarcoat things. Anyways, it's done. I wish them both a happy life."

Femi said nothing about her statement. There was really nothing to say. They were already married so whatever was said, to him, was crying over spilt milk. "Thanks for agreeing to come with me."

She smiled at him, the fury in her eyes easing up. "Thanks for asking."

As they made their way to the reception he couldn't help but think if perhaps Eniola was Peju's replacement. If God had brought the young woman his way for that sole purpose.

***

OBA

"Have I told you how beautiful you look today?"

Eliana placed a finger on her chin, having a thoughtful look. "Not since ten in the morning when you picked me up." She shook her head. "No."

"Then I must make amends immediately. You look stunning."

She shifted her eyes from his, and he loved how she got whenever he paid her compliments. "Thank you."

"You're very welcome."

She turned her gaze to the couple and the smile disappeared from her face.

"You aren't happy for them."

Eliana faced him once more. "I don't know. I love Peju as a sister and it breaks my heart that this happened, but it's done already. I can only pray she enjoys her married life."

He nodded and glanced at the couple as they left. For a moment he thought she would say no. He guessed Eliana might have been praying for that but when she said yes he had heard Eliana's deep sigh and how her shoulder sagged. Oba couldn't help but think about what life would have been if he had married Nene. He lifted his hand and traced the small scar on his jaw. The memory of going over to Nene's parents came to mind. It had been a terrible day.

"You come to my house and tell me your son cannot marry my daughter?" Mr Okafor stated, his nostrils flared up from anger with grey hairs standing in them. "I ask on what grounds and you can't provide a concrete answer except that it was your son's decision? That's outright nonsense!"

"Mr Okafor," Oba's father began, "We understand how devastating this news

can be to your family but the children have a final say on whether they want to get married or not."

Shaking like a leaf in the wind, Nene's father uttered some words in Igbo. Oba was able to pick out a few words - stupid, family and rubbish in particular. Gritting his teeth, he kept his anger in check. He couldn't retort because he was the one at fault. He was the reason why his parents were being insulted. He should have called off the wedding weeks ago.

"Your son should open his mouth and tell me why he has decided not to marry my daughter and used her like a piece of rag after forcing her to have an abortion."

What? Oba shifted his eyes to Nene who sat at a corner on a lone chair, avoiding his eyes.

"Ehn?" Oba's mother sat up. "Abortion ke? Your daughter had an abortion for my son?"

Mr Okafor pointed his walking stick at Oba. "Isn't he sitting beside you? Ask him yourself. He had been sleeping with my daughter. He rubbed her of her purity as a woman."

"It takes two people to have sex, Mr Okafor." Oba's mother said, irritated. "You make it sound like my son raped her."

Mr Okafor scoffed. "It may have been rape for all we know. Who knows what conspired between the both of them."

Like never before, Oba badly wanted to slap the cheeky grin off Nene's face as she finally looked at him and went back to her sunken snout when his mother looked at her. He wondered what lies she had told her parents. There was a hard tap on his thigh and he realised his mother had been talking to him.

"Answer me, Oba! Did you tell Nene to have an abortion?"

"No Ma."

"Will you shut up your mouth, you stupid boy!" Mr Okafor shouted. His wife, who was standing in a close range, told him to calm down.

"I did not tell her to get an abortion. I would never tell her to do that, but it seems she has conveniently forgotten the truth. I didn't find out about the abortion until about a few weeks ago but she had it done close to a year ago."

"Are you saying my daughter lied to us?" Mrs Okafor asked, rising to her feet and pointing at her daughter who now had tears running down her cheeks. She *deserved a big award for her acting skills. "See how she is crying her eyes out because you broke her heart by refusing to marry her. Now, you add salt on top of injury by saying she is lying. I cannot believe I wanted my precious daughter to get married to an irresponsible man like you."*

"One thing I know about Nene is she tells the truth," Oba said with his gaze fixed on her. "Lies are not her thing."

"Stop trying to cajole her to lie to cover your sins! You are a useless boy!"

"Hold it there Ma-" His mother started but Oba's father cut her short with a raise of his hand.

"We are very sorry for everything that happened. Yes, our son disappointed your daughter and you have every right to be angry. Forgive us. On the other hand, Nene saying she was forced to have an abortion is news to us." Mr Afolayan turned his gaze on Nene. "Nene, please talk to us. Were you pregnant for Oba?"

She nodded.

"Did you have an abortion?"

She looked Oba in the eye and nodded again. Nene's mother exclaimed something in Igbo but it didn't deter Oba's father from his questioning. Oba was amazed at how calm he was.

"Was it Oba that talked you into having the abortion?"

She looked at Oba one more time, sniffed and shook her head. "No, Sir."

"What?" Nene's father shouted, but Oba was staring at Nene and was too slow to see the man ram the head of his walking stick into his jaw. There were screams and shouts and Oba could feel a liquid flow down his jaw to his neck. The pain was excruciating.

"Mr Okafor, would you stop this immediately!" Oba's father roared and Oba looked up at him. He hadn't seen his father so upset in years. "We came to plead with you to let us reason out what happened with our children, but since you have decided to be uncivilised about it, we will take our leave!" He looked at Nene and said in a calmer tone. "I wish you all the best my dear. Please, forgive my son."

Oba stared at Eliana. He didn't want to rush into a relationship just yet. He was willing to take it slow and grow in his relationship with God. He wanted to learn how to be a better man, to be the man God expected of him. Oba also wanted to be the kind of husband worthy of a woman like Eliana.

He wasn't completely certain, but he knew God had good plans for him and he prayed it included her. His cousin had given him the go-ahead to date her if he wanted to.

"But don't hurt her, Oba. Don't even think of playing around in bed with her." Timilehin had warned him explicitly and Oba didn't mind.

"I won't."

***

PEJU

"Are you happy?" Abdul asked as they swayed to the song *Heaven Sent* by Keisha Cole. Peju had long since changed from her wedding gown to her second dress, a modest gold piece with a fish-tailed bottom.

"Mmm-hmm... very happy." Her head was against his chest. Her eyes closed. She was tired but ecstatic All her last-minute fears had long since dissipated. There was no going back now that she was married.

He laughed. "For a minute I thought you were going to say no."

She drew back to stare at him. "Why would you think I would say no?"

"Because you looked uncertain. I may have interpreted it the wrong way. Maybe you were just nervous."

"I was but I shook it off and said yes. I love you and I look forward to spending the next fifty years with you and our children."

Abdul smirked. "50 years yeah? Okay, *nau.*"

"I loved Antonia's speech."

"About how we were playing love in the classroom? I can't believe she remembered that time a teacher flogged us in front of the whole school when we were caught making out."

Peju laughed. "And that didn't stop you from sending me a cake the next day even if it wasn't my birthday. Gosh, you have always been romantic!"

"Yeah, baby. That's me, Mr Romantic."

"I also loved the best man's speech." Idris had talked about the way Abdul kept talking about a girl back in Nigeria that he was crazy about. A girl that would vex him but the following day, he would still go back for more of her love.

"I can't believe this happened." She held him tighter as they danced, enjoying the moment. "You don't know how many times I dreamed about it."

"Me too."

They danced some more till he had to attend to a few things.

"May I?"

She spun around and saw Femi looking dapper in a grey suit.

She nodded and he took her hand in his, putting a reasonable distance between the both of them. She bit her lip, hoping Abdul wouldn't read a wrong meaning to it.

"Congratulations once again."

"Thank you, Femi. Thanks for coming."

He hesitated a little then said, "It broke my heart, seeing you marry him, but I wouldn't have missed it for the world. I wish both of you a happy life. I have to leave now and head to the hospital."

She nodded. "Is that your girlfriend?" She hinted at the lady who sat next to Eliana. She was short, dark and on the plumpy side. She was also beautiful.

"Why are you asking?"

Peju blinked, taken aback by the question. "I'm just asking."

"Really?"

She nodded but knew it was a lie. She wanted to know if he had moved on with his life.

Why do you care? She queried herself.

"She's a friend, for now."

The music stopped then and the live band kicked off, disrupting the serenity the previous music had brought.

"I see. Good for you."

He smiled, leaned close and brushed his lips against her forehead and whispered, "Take care Peju." He turned his back on her and walked away. Peju suddenly had a sinking feeling in her stomach, feeling as though God

Himself had finally tossed her aside and walked out of her life.

***

ANTONIA

Antonia got home late at night. Her feet were killing her and she was exhausted. She just wanted to have a warm shower, lay on her bed and sleep off. Titi was also complaining of the same thing as she took off her shoes and sat on the only couch in her bedroom.

"That wedding was lit!"

"Yeah." Antonia moved her head from one side to the other to relieve the knots in her neck. She'd tried her best to hide her disappointment. She was also ashamed of how she felt. She was supposed to be happy for them. She *was* happy for them.

"Baby girl, it's you that's left. It's a shame the best man was married. You guys looked yummy together."

Antonia rolled her eyes as she took off her jewellery. "You this babe *sha.*"

"Seriously! If I was still single I would have snatched him up like this." Titi snapped her fingers.

"You need help."

"And you need a man," Titi countered. "I can't stop telling the story of how I met my husband. My boss asked me to deliver a package to a client's house. I go there, deliver the package. Mind you, this boy was fine!" Antonia rolled her eyes. "- and the dude was walking me out when next thing, he calls out Smallie. See me thinking it's one cute small puppy o. If you see the monstrosity of a thing that appeared out of nowhere. Big and black dog. I just fainted and when I woke up, I was lying on his couch and gazing into his eyes. I just knew he was the one for me."

Antonia hissed. "Your story sounds too polished."

"It's not. It's a one-in-a-million kind of meeting."

Shaking her head, Antonia brought out her phone and was surprised to see ten missed calls from her sisters. *That's strange.* She tapped on the call button and returned Esther's call. The wail on the other end of the phone when she picked brought a wave of fear over her.

"Esther, what's wrong?"

Her sister finally uttered a few words and Antonia let out a small scream as her phone fell from her hand to the floor. Titi rushed to her side.

"Toni, what's wrong?"

Antonia's lips moved but nothing came out. The only thing that came easily was the tears.

"Please talk to me! Who the hell called you?"

"M-my," she sniffed, "father is dead."

Chapter 18

ELIANA

"As an apricot tree stands out in the forest, my lover stands above the young men in town. All I want is to sit in his shade, to taste and savor his delicious love", Song of Solomon 2 verse 3 (MSG). Eliana recited the words in her head. There was no doubt about it. She was completely smitten by Oba, but she wasn't certain what he felt about her. Yes, she knew he cared about her and all that but was he interested in moving their relationship to the next level? Or were they going to remain friends? Recently, he had been acting strange, eager to leave whenever she approached him and Timilehin. Staring at her with certainty. They hadn't spoken about it yet but she had a feeling that was part of what they were going to talk about on their first date. He had finally asked her out a week ago when he called her after his baptismal class.

It was a beautiful day to be at Lekki Conservation Centre, a park in Lagos. They had toured the place and were resting their legs while seated on a bench. They talked and he shared his past with her. About the abortions and how the guilt hunted him for years till he finally let God in. He also gave her full details of his break-up with Nene.

"Are you over her?"

"Mentally and emotionally, yes. But a part of me remembers the intimacy we once shared. We had a very sexual relationship."

What does he mean by very sexual?

As though he read her thoughts he answered, "We had sex a lot. What I thought was love was lust."

Eliana licked her lips. "Okay, so you are still sexually attracted to her?"

Oba nodded. "Kind of. I miss what happened, not that I miss her. Do you understand?"

She nodded. She understood but fear gripped her heart as she remembered what Kene did to her. Was that why he was avoiding her? Was he back with Nene?

"Want to share what you're thinking?"

"I just remembered my ex. He got another girl pregnant while we were in a relationship."

"And you're afraid I would do the same to you?"

She stared down at her hands. "Yes."

"I know you've noticed how I've been dodging you and acting weird for a while now. I've been nursing the thought that I'm not good enough for you." Her brows went up. She never thought of that. "But I want to give you my word that I will try my best not to. I don't want to sin against God and I don't want to hurt you. God willing, I'm going to work hard at not falling into temptation."

She gazed into his eyes then and said softly, "It's only by God's grace. If you ever think you can do it on your own, you will fall the next minute."

"Yeah, true."

There was a comfortable silence between them.

"So what do you want from me?" Eliana asked after a few minutes.

"What do I want?" He released a breath. "I want you to be my girlfriend. I want to be in a relationship with you. I want to court you. I know I'm not exactly a strong Christian brother like the other guys in church, or like Timilehin, but I'm willing to learn. I want to be the man God wants me to be. Not just for Him but you as well."

Eliana felt like her heart was going to jump out of her chest and do somersaults. *God, is this what I've been waiting for all this while? Is this Your will or mine? I don't want it if it's mine. I want only Your will even if it hurts. Only Yours, Jesus . . .*

Be still and know I am God. I make all things beautiful in it's time.

She closed her eyes as the words came to her.

"Did I say something wrong?" he asked, breaking into her thoughts.

She opened her eyes and found his on hers, a frown on his face. She let out a little laugh. "No. You didn't. What you said was beautiful." *It took my breath away. . .*

"But?"

"No buts. Yes, I would love to go out with you, it's just that I have some personal rules."

"Rules?"

"Yes. I believe in a relationship with no kissing and no sex."

"No kissing?"

Eliana held her hands. *I'm sure he thinks I'm weird.* She released a breath. How was she going to explain? "I don't want to get involved in anything physical. I did that in my last relationship and I had to stop when I realized I couldn't handle it." *Now he's going to think I'm a small girl.* She groaned inwardly. "I want to abstain from anything sexual till marriage."

"Wow. That's a huge deal."

Her heart plummeted. Was he going to say he wasn't interested any longer? *If he does that's his business.*

"I have never been in a relationship where there was no lip-locking but -"

"But?" she repeated.

"As I said I'm willing to learn and God will help me. At least, I can hug you *ba?*"

She laughed, her heart soaring at his willingness to accept her for what she stood for. "Sure."

***

It's been a month since the wedding. As expected, the big social event was featured on *Bella Naija* with loads of comments on how beautiful Peju's dresses were, how handsome Abdul was and on the stunning décor. In grand style, Abdul had also whisked her away to Seychelles for their two weeks honeymoon before returning to work. They both decided it was best she partner with him in his business than be his personal assistant, but till they found a replacement, she was going to keep doing her work.

Usually, their days were routine. They would wake up at five in the morning, tease each other a little and make love, then rush to take turns showering all before heading out for work. Sometimes, they made each other breakfast and other times they went hungry till they had the time to get something later in the day. They got home at different times on rare occasions and enjoyed candle-lit dinner together. There were other occasions where Abdul came home really late and had dinner by himself. Sometimes, she would sit with him, other times, she was already asleep.

* * *

PEJU

Peju horned for a bus to get out of her way as the conductor hurried passengers to get in. Tired, she knew that day was going to end with one of those late nights.

So how did she view married life?

It was great. It was amazing being married to a man like Abdul. He was fun and they didn't get tired of seeing each other practically every hour of the day. It wasn't like she hadn't been living with him before, so there was no big deal about it. Her marriage was everything she thought it would be and more.

But there was an emptiness within her. It was a hollow feeling that wouldn't go away, despite how wonderful her marriage was or how doting her husband behaved. She couldn't shake the feeling that she had probably made a mistake.

A sigh escaped her lips. There were times she locked herself in the bathroom and cried as if the sadness and despair would disappear as the tears came down. She couldn't let Abdul see her. Or else how would she explain to him why she felt the way she did? He would think it was his fault.

She switched lanes and turned into the street of their house. All she could do was occupy herself with the next thing - try her best to get pregnant. A baby would fill up the deep abyss in her.

* * *

OBA

"What are you doing here?"

"Relax, I'm just here to talk." She leaned away from the wall. "Can I come in?"

Somewhere in his head, he knew it would be a bad idea to let her in but he still stepped aside and watched as she walked past him.

"So why are you here?"

"I wanted to see how you're doing. Is there any harm in that?"

"You could have called."

"I know but I thought it would be better to see you in person. Besides, you might not pick my calls."

Oba raised a brow. "At least try first."

She dropped her bag on the floor and ambled over to him. "How's your jaw?" She touched his chin and turned his head to look at it.

"Fine." He took her hand off his face. She was close enough for him to see her cleavage and he forced his eyes away from them and swallowed hard. All of a sudden the temperature of the room felt hot and he felt a trickle of sweat on his forehead. "Nene, you have seen how I am. You can go now."

"Oba, I've missed you."

"I haven't." He saw how his words hurt her.

"You know you really hurt me when you cancelled our wedding and I only

215

did what I did because I wanted to get back at you. I'm sorry."

"Me too." He backed away from her and sat on a couch, wanting to put as much distance between them as he could.

She strolled in his direction, and while he thought she would sit beside him, she chose his lap instead.

"Nene, what are you doing?"

"I want you, Oba. Even if it's just one last time. Let me show you how much you mean to me."

Flee!

He pulled her hands away from his neck. "No need." He shoved her aside and got up quickly. "I need you to leave."

She pouted. "Oba *nau*. This isn't fair." She got up and pulled off the cropped top she had on. He blinked rapidly at the sight of her flat tummy with the piercing on her belly button he used to love and the red underwear she had on that was barely covering her chest. "You know we had good times together. We would have crazy sex." Her hand went below his belt, and he closed his eyes and moaned a little. She brought her lips close to his.

A kiss won't hurt, would it? Just a little . . .

Don't give in son. For by means of a whorish woman a man is brought to a piece of bread: and the adulteress will hunt for the precious life.

The words were impressed upon his heart and he grabbed her hand tightly, causing her to scream from pain, and he pushed her aside.

She stood looking at him, mouth agape, with a hand on her wrist. "Are you insane?"

"I told you I'm not interested! Why is it so difficult for you to understand?"

"Is that why you want to manhandle me?" She picked her top from the floor where she flung it and put it on. "What's wrong with you? We never had this problem before. Even when we had our fights and broke up, it only took a few days of sex to put us back on track."

He ran a hand over his head. "This is different. We are *never* getting back together. Whatever we had is now in the past. Please, Nene, I didn't ask you to come."

She shrugged and shoved her hands in her back pocket. "I know. I- I thought we could talk and sort everything out."

He kept quiet. There was no need to repeat over and over again that there was nothing to sort out. Instead, he listened to what she had to say.

"I had to switch off my phone for a week, so people could stop calling to ask what happened or apologise about it and rain curses on your head." She laughed. "I kind of enjoyed them insulting you but later on, it irritated me and I had to tell them to get lost." Oba raised a brow at the expletive she added and she waved a hand in dismissal. "That's just to tell you how pissed I was."

"I'm truly sorry about everything."

She scoffed. "At least it wasn't at the altar you did it before they video it and share it on all social handles. That would have ruined my entire life."

"What about your parents?"

"They were going to say they found out you had HIV, so they called off the wedding but knew it would look bad on me as well."

"So what did they say?"

"That you had mental problems running in your family."

Oba covered his eyes and shook his head.

Nene picked her bag from the floor and got out a brush. "You deserve it."

He nodded. "I agree. It's all my fault."

She jerked back, surprised at his admittance. She held a thoughtful look as they both walked out the door and stood by her car. "I don't know what brought this sudden change in you. Maybe someone in your village has jazzed you."

He laughed. "Nope, it's only Jesus that jazzed me with His love."

There was Eliana as well. He had come close to doing the unthinkable and risking her trust in him. Risking their relationship. But he wasn't going to mention Eliana and get Nene riled up.

Nene didn't need to know. And quite frankly, it wasn't her business.

"You are serious about this Christian thing." Nene shook her head in wonder. "Are you now trying to say you're better than the rest of us that go to church because you are behaving all holier than thou?"

Oba remembered what Pastor John said about people not understanding his decision to leave a life free from sin and the ways of the world. He would be mocked and insulted because he was willing to take a stand but it was all a test of his faith; his belief in his relationship with God.

"No." He folded his arms across his chest. "I have my problems and struggles and they won't magically go away, but I'm willing to do things the right way. The way God expects of me. Being a Christian isn't just acknowledging there's a God or Jesus is His Son, but giving Him total control of your life and wanting to live life His way."

She looked away from his gaze and got into her car without a word.

Something came to heart and he spoke up, "My leaving you has nothing to do with you as a person. You're a wonderful woman. Beautiful. Intelligent. Loyal. And I know you will be a great wife to someone else."

"Are you *whining* me?"

"No. I'm being real."

Her lips curled up in a sad smile as her car engine came to life. "All the best, Oba. Enjoy your new life."

She drove off without waiting for a reply. As she left, there was a joy in him, as if God was smiling down at him. Oba knew then he had won the battle.

* * *

ANTONIA

God, why did you do this to me?

There was no answer, and deep down, Antonia expected none. The sound of footsteps against tiles caused her to raise her head from where she lay on the couch. Her heart dropped as she saw her mother making her way to her. She looked haggard and had rejected eating for the last few days when the sadness kicked in that she was never going to see her husband again.

Antonia wasn't in the mood for her rantings, so she rose to her feet. Esther and Miriam thought it best to sleep over from time to time since their mother didn't want to leave her house. Antonia had volunteered because she knew it was something her father would have wanted her to do.

But it didn't mean she was going to endure her insults.

"Where are you going to?" her mother asked.

Antonia gave her a wary look. "To my room."

"You don't have to go. I wouldn't disturb you." Her mother took her sit in daddy's favourite chair and did what she always did. Stare at his picture until the tears started coming down in heavy heaps till she was drained and slept off.

Antonia sat back down. She heard a sniff and knew it had begun.

"Tell me fun memories you had of Daddy."

The crying stopped and Mrs Ali turned to look at her in bewilderment. "What?"

Antonia repeated her question.

Mrs Ali didn't talk for a while, when she tried to tears came instead. Antonia waited. "Your father was a very generous man. He loved to make others happy when they were down. He was a true gentleman; standing up for me when his family fought against me going to church. There were times he showed me the true meaning of what it meant to love even with all of my ways. You know he gave his life to Christ on his death bed."

Antonia's head snapped up. *Her father gave his life to Christ? Did he become a Christian?* "H- How did it happen?"

Her mother gulped as another wave of tears consumed her. "He told me how he often thought of the after-life. Where he would go to. If heaven was where he would end up. He expressed his doubts. He had lived in the shadows of Christianity but never owned up to it." She paused as though the next words were hard to say. "H- he to- told me to pray for him."

Antonia laughed at her mother's brokenness and said, "I think he made a mistake."

"What's that supposed to mean?"

Figure it out yourself. "Forget it. It's best to remember the good things he did. The kind man he was and celebrate. I have cried. I have questioned God, but none of it brought Daddy back. You cannot keep starving yourself. You have to be strong for Esther and Miriam."

"Only Esther and Miriam?"

"They need you." Antonia was sure her mother got the hidden meaning behind her words.

"You don't need me because I was a bad mother."

"You were a terrible mother," Antonia whispered to herself.

"I loved you -"

"You hated me! You treated me like shit! Like I wasn't your daughter but a total stranger."

Her mother nodded. "Yes. Yes and I'm sorry. I did what I did because of my stupidity. I am a horrible mother. A horrible person. The last thing your father told me was to amend my ways. Bridge the gap between the both of us. Please forgive me, Antonia."

Antonia shook her head. "No. You just say three words and you expect it to wipe away all the years you mistreated me? That you forced me to eat cold food while my *sisters* ate better? What about the time you rubbed my lips against the floor for using your lip-gloss but Esther was free to do so."

"I'm so-"

Antonia covered her ears. "No! I don't want to hear it."

She walked out on her mother and slammed the door of her room, locking it. She wasn't going to forgive her mother.

Chapter 19

PEJU

It was Abdul's birthday and the couple decided to host a few friends for dinner. Friends were Eliana, Oba, Idris and his wife, Tahira. Antonia had called to cancel. Peju felt bad it was the day of her wedding her father had passed. When she and Abdul heard about it when they got back from their trip, he made sure they went straight to her house from the airport. Her friend had looked broken and dejected. She had a drained despondency about her. Peju took her in her arms and hugged her as she shed a few tears. She offered words of comfort to her, telling her it was all going to be okay. It would take some time, but the pain would eventually pass.

Peju wiped away beads of sweat from her brow and went back to turning the *Amala*. With each turn came more regret of not hiring a caterer. When she was certain it was cooked, she scooped about ten sizeable balls and wrapped each in white nylons. The soup was ready, along with the Fried rice and peppered turkey. The cake had been delivered earlier on in the morning.

She felt his arms go around her waist as he hugged her from behind and kissed the nape of her neck.

"Hmm, you smell of spices and all sorts of deliciousness. Well done love."

"Thank you, birthday boy." He took the spatula from her hands and turned her around to face him. Peju's insides made somersaults at the sight of him, clean-shaven and his hair wet from just having a shower. He leaned close and kissed her lips.

"I taste chicken."

"Is that all?" She cocked her head, grinning up at him.

He raised his brow at her invitation and kissed her again, licking his lips with a thoughtful look. "Salt?"

She laughed and jabbed in the arm. "That's too easy."

"At least I guessed right *nau*."

"Yeah, yeah." Turning her back to him, she resumed clearing the sink. "You would have said crayfish."

"*Haba*. Crayfish *loun loun*." He stole a piece of turkey from the heap, her shouts of protests following suit. Without hesitating, he reminded her he was the birthday boy. That the title came with privileges, after all. She rolled her eyes at him and shooed him out of the kitchen while she hurried with the rest of the meal.

The hours flew by quickly and their guests arrived. Everyone raved about the food and had Peju uttering a lot of thank-yous. The whole setting seemed strange and at the same time funny. Her friends and Abdul's friends. The only conversation they could have was about general life issues. There was an instance when Oba mentioned something relating to religion that had Idris in disagreement. Oba had apologised but the tension in the room hadn't dissipated as quickly as Peju would have liked.

* * *

PEJU

"I think that's all," Eliana said as she wiped her hands with a napkin.

Everyone had gone home except Eliana and Oba. Eliana had offered to help clear the table and put away the leftovers.

"Yeah, that's all."

Peju closed the lid of the storage bowl and put it away in the fridge. "Thanks so much for helping out. I'm so tired."

Eliana rubbed her back softly. "You're welcome."

"So *gist* me *nau*," Peju said, leaning against the kitchen counter. "How are things with you and Oba?" Though they hadn't spoken in a while, she was glad to see how happy her friend was. Glad with an inkling of envy. The peace on Eliana's face and inner confidence made her jealous.

"Really good." Eliana gave a lopsided grin. "He asked me to be his girlfriend."

Peju raised a brow at her. "And I'm sure you said yes."

"Duh!"

They shared a laugh.

"How are you and Abdul? Is it everything you dreamed it would be?"

"Yeah." Peju shrugged and leaned away from the counter. "We're good. Married life is pretty simple."

"So you're happy right?"

"Don't I sound happy?"

"Not exactly."

"Well, I a*m* happy. We're good."

Elaina nodded. "Cool."

"Let's get back to the boys and see what they're up to." Peju gestured for Eliana to lead the way while she followed. Abdul and Oba were seating in front of the TV discussing football. Technically, Abdul was doing most of the talking. Oba didn't look interested.

"Abdul, stop disturbing him with football *jor*. He's not into sport."

Abdul's jaw dropped and he turned sharply at Oba. "You don't like sports?"

Oba nodded apologetically.

"Why?" Abdul queried and Oba shrugged, explaining that he never quite took an interest in it. Dazed, Abdul turned back to the TV.

"It's getting late." Eliana picked her bag beside her boyfriend who stood.

"Yeah. I'll walk you guys out," Peju said while Abdul, briefly took his eyes off the TV, shook hands with Oba and went back to the football match.

"Can we talk a little?" Peju asked her as they made their way to the door. Oba ahead of them.

"Okay. Let's go outside to talk."

"What about Oba?"

Eliana winked at her. "He will wait for me in the car."

* * *

ELIANA

"Eliana!"

Eliana turned at the sound of her name to see Stella jogging down to her. She raised her hand above her eyes to block out the sun.

"Sorry," she began, catching her breath, "I saw you walk out of the children's church and dashed over. It seems you're in a hurry."

"Yes. I'm supposed to be home by 7 for family dinner."

"Oh. Okay, I would love for us to sit down and talk one of these days if that's okay with you?"

Hope all is well. Eliana nodded. "Of course it's fine I just have to figure out when that would be because of my schedule. When would you like to meet up?"

"Tomorrow afternoon after service?" Stella suggested, looking hopeful she would agree. Eliana knew it was mostly after service that she could spend time with Oba. "I'm not too sure."

Stella clasped her hands. "I promise I wouldn't take too much of your time. Like an hour."

Eliana raised a brow. "An hour?"

"Yes. It's not much, is it? We have a lot to talk about."

Eliana sighed in defeat. "Alright."

"Awesome! See you after service at 12."

As she took a bus home, she wondered what Stella wanted to talk to her about. Maybe she wanted to find out why she wasn't attending their women's Bible study anymore. *But I already explained it to her.* She shook her head, pushing it aside. She would hear what Stella had to say the next day, but what she hadn't counted on was what she had in mind to say to her.

* * *

ELIANA

"You want to know what my love for Jesus is like?" Eliana asked, perplexed.

Stella nodded. "Yes." She adjusted her skirt and splayed a scarf over her lap. "You can think about it before answering if you want to."

There was nothing to think about. "My love for Jesus is solid." Yes, she wasn't attending many Bible study sessions or reading her Bible that often. Sometimes, she was forced to choose between reading her Bible and spending time with Oba after he closed late from work. She had chosen the latter in some cases. Then, there were times she had a job to do that required her to work late into the night and Oba understood enough to let her do her thing.

But when it's time to spend time with Me you don't tell him?

Eliana felt the lump in her throat at the truth. She kept pushing aside her time for God with the excuse that He would understand.

And I just spoke with Peju the other day about going back to her First Love while she was drifting away from Him.

"Solid. That's good. I'm just concerned about you. I remember when you would be the first to volunteer for a program or be eager to go on evangelism and your passion for our Bible study. It seems like your fire for God is waning."

Eliana didn't like how the conversation was going. "Just because I don't come for Bible study?" she asked in defence.

"Not just that. I'm not saying this because I want to increase membership or anything. The Bible study group is growing. I want to see the vibrant Eliana I always admired and prayed to emulate."

Eliana's eyes widened. Did she want *to emulate me?*

Stella continued, "You see, when I started attending church, I was emotionally tired and spiritually empty. I felt like something was missing in my life. I knew I was a Christian but my relationship with God had dwindled. I just got married to Lawrence and I was so happy. Head over heels in love with this hunk of a man." Eliana smiled a little, totally understanding what she might have been feeling because of her feelings for Oba. "But I was so caught up with my role as a new wife and having a baby that there was no time to read my Bible or spend time with God. I was drawing upon the nutrients and resources of past times and wasn't taking in the new."

"I got depressed. One day, I snapped at Lawrence and instead of snapping back, he told me to talk to God about whatever I was facing. But I was angry at him. He was having his Bible study, he was cool with God and I wasn't. I couldn't even relate with my First Husband. . . God. So one day in church, when I couldn't take it any more, I wept and cried out for God to help me. And He did. He laid it upon my heart ways I could prioritise my time and have time for Him. At first, it was a struggle, but I gradually got the hang of it." Stella brought out two folded sheets of paper from her bag and handed one to Eliana.

"I printed this out from the internet. I don't know if it's a true story or not but it passed across a message to me and I would like us to read it together."

Eliana looked down at the paper and read,

A Call to Intimacy: Once Upon a Lover

They say looks are deceiving, so she must have deceived me numerous times with her seductiveness, her words of affirmation and deep concern. After all, that was what I wanted and she offered it to me on a platter of gold.

That was when my death had begun.

The title of the song, 'Killing me softly' became a reality to me. How could I have known she was a lady in the morning and an astute prostitute at night?

The words of Lady Wisdom had spoken to me over and over again. But what was wisdom in the presence of pleasure, no matter how short-lived? What was common sense in the place of a night of passion? What was sensible thinking in the place of uncontrollable urges?

It started with a thought and then the seed grew in my heart and my actions followed after. I was led astray - but at my own will. I knew right from wrong but still made the choice to follow. I thought I was in love. I thought she had everything I wanted but she could never satisfy my need as I realised probably, maybe, life was better off with my first love. . .

Now I have lost everything. My first love that I had abandoned to chase a life of passion and desires. How had it happened? I thought she was too boring. I was bored and tired of the same 'ole thing. But now I realize things were much better with her, her consistency in life was of comfort to me; her loyalty and faithful love far more than I could handle. So why had I strayed? Why was the story of the good times now known as 'once upon a time'? I needed to go back to her because she was truly the love of my life. And my only hope now is if she would have me back.

But then, I had also drifted from my true Lover; the Lover of my soul . . .The person who loves me for better was now a distant thought. How had I come to this place? I've had one too many with whom I devoted my attention and care but this one was special and different.

I had lost my devotion and dedication to God and chased after a goddess in a skirt; I lost all focus and drifted further away from Him. The only way back was to retrace my footsteps and go back. And so I did just that, I went back to Him and confessed my sins with a sorrowful heart and asked for His forgiveness. From

Him, I got the courage to approach my wife of ten years begging and pleading for her to take me back.

How often do we stray from God and place other things highly than Him? The gods of the Old Testament may not be the same ones as now; the money, spouse, fame, sin, our work for God; which could all very well be present-day gods. We remember how forgiving and kind He is but sometimes tend to forget we are to fear Him for He is the Consuming Fire. Gradually, our fear for God dissipates and we are left with nothing. We are left to do things our way, guided by ourselves.

Don't lose sight of your Lover. Don't let the story be once upon a time, rather, let it be a happily ever after.

And when he was in affliction, he besought the LORD his God, and humbled himself greatly before the God of his fathers,

And prayed unto him: and he was intreated of him, and heard his supplication, and brought him again to Jerusalem into his kingdom. Then Manasseh knew that the LORD he was God. 2 Chronicles 33 vs 12-13 KJV

"Wow," Eliana uttered and glanced up at Stella's smiling face. "This is beautiful." She especially loved the part of letting her story with God end with a happily ever after. It reminded her of what Jesus said in a few parables, *Well done good and faithful servant.*

"Yes. It's pretty direct. The author was saying as regards other life activities it's easy to shift our focus from God. It's easy for us to get carried away with life and the excitement of a relationship but we need to always place God first. Before we get married, He's first. When we get married, He's still first. He's our First Love and He should be given that respect. Do you understand?"

"Yeah, I do." It was like a wake-up call for her. God was trying to get her attention- to know how she was gradually drifting from Him.

Stella's smile deepened. "It's easy to drift from God. It's so subtle and at times unconscious, because one day we are skipping our devotion and the next day we are rushing off to work without praying. We sometimes hide it under the guise that God would understand. And yeah, He does understand. There are times when we are so weak and tired and He gives us room to rest in His Presence. He's a loving God and knows our frailties, but it doesn't excuse us from taking advantage of Him. It's a struggle at first, to get things right, but you have to be willing to make things work. Hebrews 2 verse 1 encourages us to hold on to what we've heard lest we drift past them."

Eliana felt the sting of tears in her eyes. "Thanks for sharing this with me. I really appreciate it."

"It's fine dear. Thank God for the grace to yield to Him. We are sisters in Christ and we need to be there for one another." She shrugged her slim shoulders. "Who knows if it's me that would need to hear this message the next time."

They both laughed.

As Stella made her way out of the church confines, offering to drop Eliana at a convenient place to get a ride home, Eliana was inwardly thanking God for pulling her back before she drifted too far. She only hoped Peju would find her way back as well.

* * *

OBA

"Did you tell Eliana?"

"No. How can I tell her Nene came over to my house to seduce me? After I gave her my word about being loyal to her."

Timilehin frowned in confusion. "Guy, *wetin* you *dey* talk? You didn't do anything with Nene."

"I wanted to. I was close to kissing her."

"But you didn't. That's a good thing. You were able to control yourself. Part of being in a relationship is being open with each other. Sharing your weaknesses and struggles."

Oba rolled his eyes. "You have started again."

"*Na you sabi.* Me I know what I'm saying."

"So what do you suggest?"

"Tell her. Explain what happened and she will understand and encourage you. What if Nene pulls another stunt and tells Eliana you guys had sex? That would make her lose trust in you."

Oba released a sigh. "Okay. I will tell her later today. She's at church, said she had a meeting with someone."

"Things are going okay between you guys? After you don *port* my babe." Oba glanced at Timilehin and didn't see any sign of anger or jealousy.

Oba smiled and answered, "Yup."

Oba had spoken to his mum some days back, finally breaking the news to her about Eliana. She had been somewhat sceptical, rebuking the spirit of Samson from him. He hadn't been offended until he asked Timilehin who Samson was and his cousin laughed to his contentment before telling him Samson was a guy in the Bible who loved women and told his parents to give him a certain woman as his wife or he would die. Oba realized his mother wasn't completely convinced after the lovely things he said about her.

"Just be careful with all these women you're carrying about. Shebi you said you're a Christian. Please, take things easy. There are a lot of things you need to dissociate yourself from."

"Yes, Ma," he had said, not wanting to get into an argument with her.

"Please Oba, I don't want to have to come to Lagos to help break another engagement and they do something worse to you."

"Yes, Ma."

* * *

FEMI

"You look terrible," Femi told Antonia a moment after she opened the door for him.

"Thank you." She turned around and made her way back to the living room where a half bowl of cookies and cream ice cream sat waiting for her, along with a nice action movie. Her spoon was in between her mouth and the bowl when she noticed Femi was taking in the mess. A far cry from the neat freak she was.

"Please sit down and stop analysing everything."

Femi apologised, sought out a sofa with a few clothes on it and dumped it on the floor based on her instructions. She spooned the ice - cream into her mouth and released a moan of pleasure.

"Please don't tell me you ate it to that."

Antonia grinned and stuck out her tongue.

Femi laughed. "Good to know you still have a sense of humour."

"Save the doctor-patient thing and be a friend. I'm not in the mood for lectures or what's good for me." She took another spoon full.

"How are you doing?"

"I've been better. My father is dead. My mother is pretending to be a saint. The man I always wanted is now married. My life is meaningless." She gave a mirthless laugh. "I know I said you should get over Peju but *abeg*, it's hard."

Why did it have to be on the same day Abdul got married that her father died? Why was it the one day she was too busy to check her phone that life happened? Antonia made a face and dropped her spoon in the bowl, pushing it aside. Looking at it made her feel sick.

"I feel bloated. Am I not supposed to feel super high right now?"

Femi laughed. "No. Taking ice cream won't make you feel high because of a sugar rush. Well, not immediately. The sugar in ice cream is mostly coated with fat and it will take a while before the energy kicks in."

Antonia hissed.

She got off the floor and went to sit next to him and placed her head on his broad shoulder. She saw him as a big brother. A confidant. Without preamble, she began, "She said he became a Christian on his death bed. That there would have been a few contentions from my father's side of the family because they wanted him buried the next day and she wasn't in the right frame of mind to fight them."

"This is your mother?"

She nodded. "She said he asked her to pray for him." She laughed. "Can you believe that?"

"You feel she had no right to lead him to Christ?"

"I feel she was living a life of pretence. She proclaimed to be one thing and yet acted another way."

"But your father knew that and accepted her that way."

Antonia rolled her eyes. "For reasons, I don't know. She wants me to forgive her. She doesn't deserve it."

"But your father did?"

Antonia lifted her head to look at him with angry, tear-filled eyes. "My father was a nice man!"

"Nice doesn't mean perfect. Nice doesn't mean right in God's eyes."

She scoffed. "So my mum is right in God's eyes even with all her flaws?"

Femi nodded.

"Then your God is weird."

"My God is love. He loves us despite the mistakes we make. He doesn't turn His back on us."

* * *

PEJU

"How was church?" Abdul asked her when she finally got home and collapsed on their bed. She took a bite of the red apple she grabbed from the kitchen on her way to the bedroom. She had sort of gotten used to Abdul's forced, healthy eating habit while she was pregnant.

Who knew? She could even be pregnant now.

"Fine. The Bible study was really good. Refreshing." She was glad she had attended. It was good to see a few sisters and listen to them dissect the Word of God, though Peju herself didn't contribute much to the study. She preferred to be more of an observer.

Maybe next week I would.

"So you're happy."

She laughed, dropping the apple on a white serviette beside her side of the bed. "Of course I'm happy. Why wouldn't I be?" She dropped her bag at the foot of the bed and began taking off her clothes. It had been a long day and she was tired. She just wanted to have a nice shower, eat and go to sleep. Strong hands came on her shoulder and she smiled as Abdul rubbed them tenderly. She closed her eyes and moaned. Lately, his massaging skills had gotten better. "That feels so good."

"You know I love you like crazy."

"Mmm-hmm."

"You know I would do anything to make you happy."

Where is he going with this? "Uh-huh."

"You know I have never loved any woman as much as I love you. You know my love for you is legit."

She blinked her eyes open and turned around. "What are you getting at?"

"I remember telling you we shouldn't keep secrets from each other. I told you we have to be open with one another."

Peju saw the tears in his eyes and worried lines came on her face. *What's wrong?*

"I know you wish you didn't marry me."

A pang of guilt gripped her heart but she shook her head. "No."

He sighed. "I overheard your conversation with Eliana. I wanted to know why you were taking so long . . ."

233

She felt her heart drop as soon as the words left his lips. Did he hear her? He heard all the things she said? "Abdul, what did you hear?"

"Everything." His balled fist went to his mouth and he closed his eyes. After a moment, he dropped his hand and when he looked at her, the raw pain in his eyes wrenched her heart. "Why didn't you tell me you didn't want to get married? Why all the lies? Why couldn't you be straight with me that you weren't -" He looked up, took a deep breath and continued, "- that you weren't at peace with our relationship? Why Peju?"

"B- because I love you."

"Bullshit!"

Her eyes widened.

"Love? You love me and yet, you were afraid of getting married to me because you feel your Jesus won't accept me."

"But I still married you!"

"Oh, so you did me a favour by marrying me?" He clapped his hands. "Thank you."

She wrapped her arms around herself. "That's not what I meant."

"Please, explain."

"I was just scared. I love you, Abdul. What I told Eliana about were my fears. Those fears are gone."

He scoffed and put some distance between them. "You told your friend you *regretted* marrying me. That your life feels like a deep abyss that you keep sinking in with no hope of ever returning." Peju shook her head as he repeated the exact words she had said to Eliana. "You said you were empty and wondered if there was more to life. You felt you had disappointed God. Do you know how it feels hearing you say those words?"

"Abdul, I'm sorry. I only said that because of how I felt at the time. I wasn't going to church. I wasn't -"

"And is that my fault?" he interjected. "Did I stop you from going to church? Did I force you to become a Muslim and follow me to the mosque?" He pointed at her. "That's on you, not me."

She nodded and moved close to him. "I know. It's my fault. Please, forgive me."

234

"I'm leaving."

"No," she croaked and shook her head. "No, Abdul. I love you. I love you very much. I didn't mean what I sa-"

"Shut up!"

She flinched. He had never raised his voice at her. He had never insulted her.

He raised his hand. "Please," He said in a calmer tone, "Just shut up." He turned his back on her and took determined steps to their wardrobe, bringing out a hand suitcase.

She hesitated, for fear he would snap at her again, but when he threw a few shirts in, she gave in. "What are you doing?"

"Leaving."

Peju rushed to his side and took out the clothes he had put in and threw them back on the bed, rumpling them in the process. "No. You aren't leaving. We are going to talk about this."

Abdul took the clothes she threw on the bed and tossed them back in his bag. When she was about to repeat the process, he spoke to her in a dangerously low tone, "Don't provoke me."

She halted, her hands mid-way to grabbing his shirt. Abdul had never hit her and she didn't want him to start now. She drew her hands close to her and watched silently as he added a few trousers and ties, along with a few toiletries.

"W- where are you going to?"

"Wherever."

He put on his shoes and grabbed his car keys from the dressing table. "Please, don't call me." He walked out the door and she jumped when he slammed it shut. Her vision got blurred with the rush of tears and she sunk her weight at the edge of the bed.

"God, why are you punishing me?"

She closed her eyes and remembered that very morning when he had made love to her and stared at her, compelling her to look at him while it went on. She took note of his watery eyes but assumed it was because of how good it was. How perfectly their bodies were in sync. It had been a crazy, beautiful morning for her, but Abdul…

Peju gasped and took deep breaths and as a heavy wave of sorrow washed over her. Why had she opened up to Eliana? Why had she taken Abdul's advice and invited her? Why hadn't she fought the need to let out her deepest fears that brought her to where she was now?

It all feels like a bad dream. . .

Dazed, Peju walked down the stairs to the living room, recollecting how he had proposed. Her knees sunk to the ground, she looked up at their wedding portrait. Staring at how happy they were. It was all her fault this had happened.

"You are already married to him. There's no way out."

"I'm not asking for a way out. I just need," Peju waved her hand over her heart, *"this emptiness I feel to go away."*

Eliana smiled. "Then you need to get back to your First Love. You need to get back to God. He alone can take that away, Peju. Why are you running away from Him?"

"I'm not running. I'm just afraid and ashamed to go to Him. My life feels like I'm in a deep abyss with no hope of ever returning. I feel I disappointed God. I feel He has departed from me or rejected me. It almost makes me regret getting married. I mean, I'm married." She spread her hands, "What next? Is there more to life than this?"

"Go back to God first Peju. He has all the answers."

A God that despises your love for Abdul. Why do you want to go back?

Peju nodded. It was all her fault. The reality of his words finally kicked in and her world blacked out.

Chapter 20

ABDUL

The sound of girlish laughter jarred him from sleep. He blinked his eyes open, taking in his surroundings. There was a faint amount of light reflecting from the lime coloured curtains. He swung his eyes to the wall clock. *Past ten?* Abdul made to get up and winced at the pain in his neck. He hadn't slept too good. Hadn't been able to sleep properly for the last few days. Couldn't concentrate on work. In short, he hadn't been able to do much of anything.

It wasn't only his neck that ached.

His heart did as well.

No matter how much he tried to quench the pain with a drink or two, he ended up with a bad headache and only temporary relief to his pain. Stifling a yawn, he got out of bed. He took a leak in the toilet and brushed his teeth. Threw on a t-shirt and a pair of shorts and headed down the stairs.

The smell of waffles and hot chocolate drifted to his nostrils and his tummy grumbled. That was another thing, he wasn't eating much as well. He heard voices coming from the kitchen and headed there.

"Uncle Abdul!" Idris' daughter screamed at the sight of him and jumped down her chair and ran to him, her arms spread wide.

Grinning, Abdul stooped down and welcomed her in his arms. He felt a sharp pain in his chest. *I would have almost been a father if Peju was still pregnant.* "Baby girl, how are you?"

She giggled. "My name is not Baby girl. It's Fah-tima."

He touched the tip of her nose with his. "I know. But you're my baby girl, right?"

She nodded excitedly. "Yes. My daddy says I'm his little princess."

"Fatima, leave Uncle alone and come and finish your breakfast," Tahira instructed. Abdul kissed her cheek, and the little girl returned it before hurrying back to her small size yellow chair and table.

"Good morning," Idris said as Abdul stood to his feet.

"Good morning. Good morning Tahira." Abdul took a seat on a high stool at the granite kitchen counter.

"Good morning," Tahira replied. "Shall I serve your breakfast? Fatima said she wanted waffles this morning." She said, giving her daughter a knowing look while the little girl smiled widely. "So that's what we're all having. If you would rather have something else, I-"

Abdul shook his head. "It's fine. waffles are fine by me. I would love to eat whatever my baby girl is eating. " He turned and winked at Fatima.

Tahira nodded.

"Can I get a cup of coffee as well?" Abdul asked.

"Make that two," Idris said and she dutifully went about it after asking if Abdul wanted milk and sugar in his. Abdul ate his food in silence while listening to the conversation going on with the family. Fatima asked if he would play with her later on and Abdul had agreed despite her parents' disapproval of her disturbing him. When he was done he took care of his dishes, despite Tahira's protests.

"It's the least I can do," Abdul said, wiping his hands clean with a napkin.

"It won't happen again." She said and walked out of the kitchen with Fatima in tow.

"Is she vexing?"

Idris snorted. "Don't mind her. She just likes her things washed until it's sparkling clean. When you leave the kitchen she would come back and wash it. Just leave her things for her."

Abdul wondered how things would have been in their first year of marriage, recalling back in school how Idris was the tidiest person amongst them. Tahira was just another level. He kept his thoughts on that to himself.

Peju wasn't so clean conscious. He closed his eyes. God, he missed her. He missed waking up next to her in the mornings over the weekend when they could lazy about in bed and watch a movie or two, both of them playing rock, paper and scissors to see who would make breakfast. It was all wonderful. Their life was perfect. But she was unhappy. Unhappy because she felt she had disappointed God and Abdul was the reason why her life appeared to be out of sorts.

Idris cleared his throat. "Are you ready to talk about what happened?"

Abdul took a sip of his black coffee. "It's nothing."

"Come on, Abdul. You come to my house at midnight with a piece of hand luggage, eyes bloodshot and looking beat up. Now, you tell me it's nothing? What of Peju? Where is she?"

The sound of the name that once made him giddy with excitement now brought a sharp pain to his chest. "Idris, please I don't want to talk about it. If it's a problem being in your house just let me know and I will leave."

Idris looked pained at that. "*Haba.* I'm just concerned. Even Tahira is worried about you." He placed a hand on Abdul's shoulder. "You know you can talk to me, bro."

Abdul nodded and took another sip. How could a man explain his wife of barely two months was regretting their marriage? Or the fact that he had spent years loving her, dreaming of the possibility of them being united once more and sought her out to resume their relationship? And all for what? To have her living in regrets? Abdul couldn't bear it, that he was to blame for putting high hopes in a woman he hadn't seen in years and proposing just four months after their 'magical' reunion. He couldn't let up that he had been a fool to believe in a love that had only been a façade to her. He wondered if she ever loved him.

"Ab-"

"I said I don't want to talk!" He snapped at his friend who raised his hands in defeat. "I'm sorry." Abdul dropped the mug and heaved a sigh. "I'm not in the right frame of mind to talk. I just need to think."

Idris gave him a weary look. "I don't want to imagine what could have happened to put you in this state."

Abdul gazed out the window at the gorgeous view of the garden with all sorts of flowers. The grass was neatly trimmed. A mini playground placed in the middle. It all looked perfect. No flaws. Unfortunately, that wasn't how life was.

That wasn't how *his* life was.

"I appreciate your concern, but I don't want to talk about it yet. As I said, if it's a bother staying over I would stay in a hotel." Idris was already shaking his head. "I don't want to be an inconvenience to you guys."

"Guy, it's not a problem. You can stay as long as you want to. You're my brother. I know how you helped me back in school when things were tough and I wouldn't turn my back on you now when you need my help." Idris patted his back. "I've got your back."

Abdul gave a single nod. "It won't be long. I just need to gather my thoughts and plan my next move." He downed the remaining coffee and dropped the mug in the sink. "I'm heading out. I need to visit one or two people."

"Okay, bro."

Abdul could feel his friend's eyes on him as he walked out of the kitchen. He went to his room and had a much-needed shower. He dressed up, realising he would need a fresh batch of clothes soon. Tahira had been kind enough to do his laundry with the washing machine, but he needed some more clothes for work. He had the option of buying some new clothes or going home to pick a few but he wasn't ready to face his wife.

Wife. He closed his eyes. Did she still deserve to be called his wife?

Right now he wasn't sure of anything.

***

PEJU

Peju woke up with a headache, feeling like her head had been used as a mortar by a novice. She pushed herself off the cold tiles and used the back of her hand to wipe off a small trail of saliva on her cheek. An effort to open her eyes a little wider failed. They were tired and swollen from constantly crying for the last few days. She didn't know which pain was worse; the feeling God wasn't with her or losing Abdul.

Her husband had been gone for three days now and she had no idea where he was. He didn't pick her calls, he never returned them. When she drove to his office the day after the incident the security men refused to grant her access into the building. No matter how much she shouted at them and promised to have them sacked, they hadn't relented.

"Madam na oga talk sey make we no gree for u." One of the three had uttered after she had threatened to call the police and have them all arrested for insubordination. They had looked at her with questioning eyes, their curiosity piqued as to why their boss wouldn't let his wife into the building.

Filled with embarrassment, Peju had gotten into her car and driven off in a haste, lucky not to have been involved in an accident with her blurred vision as she drove like a madwoman. What would the newspapers have said? Woman dies over emotional turmoil? Peju cringed. She had snapped back to her senses when a Federal Road Safety official had pulled her over, staring at her strangely, requesting for her car documents. One glance at the rearview mirror told Peju why.

Her mascara had run down her eyes, she had a smeared lipstick stain on the right side of her mouth from wiping at her tears - she looked like a masquerade! After concluding all her documents were intact, the officer had warned Peju to keep off the road till she had comported herself.

Peju heaved a tired sigh.

She had sent him tons of messages, yet to no avail. Her whole body was weak from lack of appetite. The only reason she had been able to sleep a little was from deep fatigue.

She drew her knees close to her chest and rested her arms on it, her palms covering her face. What was she going to do? What was going on in Abdul's mind? She bit her lip as fresh tears formed in her eyes. She could imagine the pain he felt, knowing for sure if she were in his shoes she would be distraught and livid.

It would be silly of her to call either one of their parents for she would be forced to tell them what happened. Peju couldn't imagine what his parents would say to her. Prayers were her only solution and she wasn't sure God was listening to her, talk more of answering her. She looked up at the ceiling.

God, please just let him come home. I promise I'll be more faithful.

The sound of a horn at the gate jolted her from her thoughts and she prayed it was Abdul. She hoped to God he was ready to talk. To listen to her and also forgive her of her wrongs. Standing to her feet, she took hurried steps to the door and not the least bothered of her looks, she pulled the door open and her heart plummeted.

"Idris," she said with disappointment. His eyes trailed down her body and he looked away. Aware of her dressing, she pulled the flaps of her housecoat together to hide her sports bra and matching pants.

"Peju, good day."

"Abdul isn't here," she said, not bothering to reply to his greeting. He wasn't Abdul and she was in no mood to play hostess and entertain him. Asides from that she wanted to be alone.

"I know. Can I come in?"

Peju almost said no, but then nodded and shifted aside to let him in. Her hand went to her dishevelled hair to tame the wild edges. If it were another day and time, she would have excused herself to dress up, but she was more interested in why he came. He knew Abdul wasn't in the house with her.

She gestured for him to sit down.

"How are you doing?" he asked, his face masked with concern.

She slightly shrugged her shoulders. "I'm okay."

"Why did Abdul leave the house? Did anything happen between you guys?"

"Sort of." She looked down at her feet, thinking of the best way to ask him to leave.

"Would you like to explain what happened between you guys?"

She shook her head. "No."

He sighed. "Your husband is at my place."

Her head snapped up, a mixture of gladness and anger accosting her all at once. *He lied to me!* She had called Idris to ask if he knew Abdul's whereabouts but he had declined. He must have noticed her accusatory look when he immediately apologized. "I lied to you because he didn't want me to divulge his whereabouts."

"He's my husband."

"And he's my friend. My loyalty is to him." Peju looked away from him at his jab. "I'm sorry to have to say that."

"It's fine," she replied quietly. *Perhaps he's told Idris what happened?* She thought, but his next question thwarted her line of reasoning.

"What's going on with you guys? What happened? Abdul has refused to talk."

"It's just a little misunderstanding."

Idris raised his perfectly trimmed, waxed eyebrows. Peju had always been amused at how perfectly groomed he was. "A little misunderstanding?" He repeated. "I call leaving the toilet seat open or the cap of the toothpaste undone or something stupid, a little misunderstanding... a squabble. But this seems more than that. You guys have only been married for what - six weeks? - and you are already having major issues."

Peju felt her insides burn with anger at his tone. What right did he have to talk to her in that manner? To judge her? With an edge in her voice, she asked, "Why are you here? To accuse and blame me or help? If it's the former, you can take your leave."

He sighed in resignation. "I'm sorry if I sound harsh. I'm just concerned about him. I have never seen him like this. He picks at his food. Always moody and keeps to himself except for when he's with Fatima. His two best friends are beer and coffee but not as a combination. I came here because I'm concerned about him."

Peju remembered the raw pain in his eyes as he related her conversation with Eliana. He hurt and she was to blame. "I have to see him."

Idris shook his head. "I don't think that's a good idea just yet. He seems pretty pissed off."

"I wasn't asking for your opinion."

He sighed again. "Okay. Do what you want. I would advise you tread carefully." He brought out his phone and typed out something. He informed her he had sent his address to her phone.

"Thank you," she said in a clipped tone. She rose from her chair, signalling it was time for him to leave.

"You know I'm not the bad guy here," he said before she closed the door.

She wasn't too sure about that, but she reminded herself he was a close friend of Abdul and was equally concerned about him. "I know, thanks for everything."

He opened his mouth, shut it back and turned away. Peju shut the door and leaned against it. Abdul was at his friend's house at Ikoyi. She could have her bath and drive over. Idris's warning clanged in her head but she shoved it aside. Despite his strong belief in her husband's behaviour, she *knew* Abdul. He didn't get angry at her for long. Even if it seemed this was the longest he had ever been angry at her, he still loved her.

Not waiting to analyse the feeling of doubt creeping up on her, Peju hurried off to do the needful.

***

ELIANA

8th of October, 2016

It's been a struggle getting my life back on track. After meeting with Stella, I searched inwardly and realised I haven't been honest with myself. I told myself it was perfectly okay to miss a devotion or two, choosing Oba over my time with God ...now I know better and it's because of that I had to explain it to my boyfriend (*scream* sounds good to say that), why I didn't want him calling me at certain times. I was praying he would understand my need to balance my time and put my day to day activities around God and not the other way around. And surprisingly, he did.

It's not like I don't have the urge to check my phone immediately after I get up in the morning to see his messages. On two occasions, I gave in to the temptation and felt bad. Guilty. But I'm working on it. So far so good I'm working with a new schedule. If I have a job I'm pressed to do, I make sure I push it aside. I spend at least forty minutes with God and go about my business. I've learnt a few things as well. Who says God isn't into interior décor? God pointed me to the Old Testament where He gave Moses specific details on how His Temple should be built among other things. In other words, if He can do that. . . He can do much more for me in Cr8tive Splash!

And the best part is I get more inspiration after I spend quality time with God. But even with that, I also don't want to make it the reason why I go to Him. That because I want Him to inspire me that's why I spend time with Him.

I try to clear my mind from all worries about an uncompleted job or feeling inadequate and incapable of doing something mind-blowing, or when my creative juices are drained, and just worship and love up on Him. Life has never been better. Bless God for Stella and her yielding heart.

There was a knock on the door and without her affirming entrance, Dimeji walked in, a strong scent of cologne and after-shave, accompanying him. "Sis, do you think I look good in this combo?"

"Did you hear me tell you to enter my room?"

He scrunched his face up. "No."

"Then why did you come in?"

"I knocked *na.*" He said, perplexed.

Eliana rolled her eyes and muttered locking her door next time. "What do you want?"

"Do you think this combo looks good?"

She gave him a once-over from his long-sleeved, buttoned-down, light-blue shirt with a round-neck shirt underneath to his stylish, faded jeans that were ripped at the knees and grey sneakers. He had a nice haircut. The wild facial hairs from days before had been shaven, giving him a clean look. Eliana was amazed at how much he had shot up in the last couple of months. He was well over her height now.

Her baby brother was growing up.

"So?" he asked impatiently.

She blinked, remembering his question. "Where are you going to?"

He groaned. "That's not the answer *nau.*"

"I have to ask *jor.* If you're going to a classy restaurant you can't go dressed like that."

He scoffed. "Who said so? If I'm a billionaire, no one can tell me how to dress. They should just *goan* hug an electricity pole."

She rolled her eyes. *He's growing but is still mentally a child.* "Na you sabi. Where are you going to?"

"Cinema."

Her eyes narrowed at him. "By yourself?"

Dimeji looked away from her then, suddenly finding the pimple on his left cheek interesting.

"Answer me."

"No."

Elaina raised a brow. *This is getting interesting.* She had a feeling her brother was taking a girl out. "With who?"

He muttered something she didn't quite catch. She asked him to repeat it.

"Toyosi," he said a little louder.

"Who's Toyosi?"

"You don't know her. She's a classmate."

Eliana nodded, enjoying how uncomfortable her brother was.

"So?" he asked again. "Is what I'm wearing okay?"

She nodded. "It's cool."

He clapped his hands. "*Ope o!* Thanks, Big Sis." He turned to leave but she stopped him.

"So you like this girl?" she queried, wanting more information from him on his apparent crush.

He placed a palm on his face and shook his head. "Yes," he answered, his voice muffled.

She couldn't help the grin on her face. She laughed as she climbed out of her bed and ambled over to her brother. "Dimeji likes a girl!"

"Big Sis *nau!*"

"Sorry. Have fun at the cinema. Not too much fun, but have fun."

Chuckling to herself once he was out of her room, she laid back on her bed and finished writing in her journal. She only had a few more pages left and made a mental note to go to a book store to get another. It might not be as beautiful as what Peju gave her but it would get the work done. She laid on her back and closed her eyes, allowing herself to daydream a little of her boyfriend.

My boyfriend. It felt good. It was even better that God approved of her relationship.

Oba was different from other guys she had dated in the past. He was considerate of her needs, caring and understanding. Not that Kene wasn't all this but Oba took it to another level. Another thing was she knew he was crazy about her and not shy to show it. Eliana was the shy one. She preferred to be affectionate in private. But then, she was willing to come out of her shell a step at a time, recalling when she allowed him to hold her by the shoulders as they strolled in the mall. And at that moment she had felt the urge to kiss him; ready to break her resolve. But she held back. The time wasn't right, and she loved how he respected her in their relationship. Respected her wishes to refrain from anything beyond hugging and holding hands.

She didn't know if it was possible to keep falling in love with him, but she was. A few passages from Song of Solomon crept into her heart and she sought out the scripture on her phone, reading with the Message Version of the Bible.

Oh! Give me something refreshing to eat—and quickly! Apricots, raisins—anything. I'm about to faint with love! His left hand cradles my head, and his right arm encircles my waist! My dear lover glows with health— red-blooded, radiant! He's one in a million. There's no one quite like him! My golden one, pure and untarnished, with raven black curls tumbling across his shoulders. His eyes are like doves, soft and bright, but deep-set, brimming with meaning, like wells of water. His face is rugged, his beard smells like sage, His voice, his words, warm and reassuring. Fine muscles ripple beneath his skin, quiet and beautiful. His torso is the work of a sculptor, hard and smooth as ivory. He stands tall, like a cedar, strong and deep-rooted, A rugged mountain of a man, aromatic with wood and stone. His words are kisses, his kisses words. Everything about him delights me, thrills me through and through! That's my lover, that's my man, dear Jerusalem sisters.

She sighed, dreamily.

A lot of people probably felt Song of Solomon was to mirror Christ with the church and wasn't a book for couples, but Eliana liked to see it as a mix of the two. God had inspired that book of the Bible for a reason. And like Stella used to say, reading the Bible never stopped at surface level. One always had to dig deeper, be open to a new revelation the Holy Spirit was always willing to share.

Her ringtone discarded her thoughts and she picked it off the bed. "Hey. . ." she said softly.

"Hi dear. How are you?" Oba asked.

"I'm good." She asked how the training was; he had to go for office training over the weekend. He told her the training was a little enlightening to him but he would have preferred being with her.

"Me too. So no more issues at work?" He had mentioned a few of his colleagues were acting cold towards him because of his strictness on late coming and on lying in the book records.

"It's cool *jere*. God is fighting for me." He yawned. "There's something I've been meaning to tell you *sef*. I thought we would be able to hang out this weekend but it won't be possible because of this training. Maybe when we see next week."

Eliana chewed on the inside of her cheek, not happy she couldn't see him even at Sunday service.

"You can just say it now."

"It's best we see."

She frowned. Curious at what he had to say. "I would prefer if you told me now."

His hesitation over the phone was glaring and she felt he would still object to telling her when he blurted, "Nene came over to my place to see me." Eliana felt her breath get knocked out of her at his words. "We almost kissed but nothing happened. I was able to see to that. She wanted to see if we could still get back together. If I still loved her but I made it clear I was no longer interested in the relationship."

She said nothing.

"Babe, are you there? I'm sorry I should have told you earlier on bu-"

Eliana didn't know what to say to that. Didn't know when she tapped the red button and ended the call. She tossed her phone aside. It rang once more and she cut it off, putting it on silent mode. She didn't want to talk.

***

ANTONIA

My God is love . . .

Antonia had spent all day in her pyjamas lounging on her bed. She snacked on junk food and kept replaying what Femi had said to her. Thinking of what he meant and how God could be so loving and yet be a Consuming Fire. How God would expect her to love her enemies no matter what they did instead of paying an eye for an eye. How Femi had explained God's desire to woo her and have an intimate relationship with her. The way he spoke made her have goose-bumps. He had made God out to be a lover than a Great and Mighty Being to be feared.

It was in that state Abdul had called her, asking to come over to hers.

She had hesitated briefly but given in. A part of her was glad for an opportunity to see him. Not too long after she ended the call with him, Femi also called to tell her he was stopping by. She made a sprint for the bathroom, showered, brushed her teeth and got on a pair of Jean trousers and tank top. Her living room was a mess with all sorts of biscuits and chocolate wrappers at different places. She would be lucky if no rats had accepted the free invitation she might have sent out.

Abdul was first to arrive.

"Hi," he said when she pulled open her door for him.

"Hey. Where's Peju?" She peeked behind him to see if his wife was in the car.

"I came alone."

Antonia blinked. "Oh. Er - come in." She moved aside for him. "How's everything?" she asked after offering him something to drink, to which he declined.

"Fine. How are you holding up?"

She licked her lips and pulled a strand of hair behind her hair. "I'm pretty good. Holding up nicely. Thanks for asking." She cocked her head to the side. "What about you? How's marriage with the love of your life?"

"Not as I expected," he said flatly. "I wanted to ask a question. Did Peju happen to look weird on the wedding day?"

Weird? She frowned. "No, I didn't make such observations. Yeah, she looked nervous but then that's how all brides are on their wedding day," she joked but Abdul didn't share her laughter. Not even a tiny smile.

What's wrong?

"Why are you asking?"

He rubbed his palms on his legs and forced a smile. "I'm just trying to put two and two together. That's all."

"Are you sure? You know you can talk to me."

Abdul nodded and took his gaze off her to the glass table at the centre of the room. He remained quiet and she left him to his musings till he spoke again. "I think she regrets she married me."

Antonia's mouth gaped open. "How's that possible?" she asked after recovering from her shock. "Peju loves you more than anything in this world."

"I used to think the same thing."

"So what happened?" Antonia raised her legs and tucked them under her bum, interested in the greatest love she had ever known.

"I thought she was happy," he began quietly. "She wishes she didn't marry me. That her life is not as it should be and it's because God doesn't approve of our marriage."

"That can't be true. Pe-"

"I overheard her talking to her friend," Abdul cut in.

The knock on her door broke their conversation and Abdul raised a brow at her and she gave him an apologetic look. "Sorry, I'm expecting a friend. I didn't know you would be coming alone." She got off the chair and hurried to open the door for Femi. He held up a pink box and grinned at her.

"I come bearing gifts."

She laughed and nudged her head for him to come in.

"I wanted to bring so-" He stopped once he saw Abdul in her living room. He turned briefly, throwing a questioning look her way before facing Abdul once more.

"Abdul, this is Femi. Femi, Peju's husband Abdul Layeni."

Femi nodded and the two shook hands.

"We met at the wedding," Abdul said.

She smacked her forehead lightly. "Oh right. Please have your seat." Antonia thought Abdul wouldn't talk more about what was happening but he shocked her by bringing it up with Femi.

"You're a Christian, right? What issue does your God have with a Christian marrying otherwise?"

Chapter 21

FEMI

Femi had wondered at the pressing need to stop by Antonia's house while driving out of the church premises. He had just finished a talk for the teenagers on the cons of premarital sex. He had fought the thought of heading to her place because he had a lot of things pending on his plate, a date with Osaz and his wife being one of them.

But then God had other plans for him.

He looked at Antonia who shrugged, her expression saying *I don't know what's going on*. A series of thoughts crossed his mind. Were things okay at home? Was Peju okay? Were they in the midst of an argument?

God, is this why you brought me here?

He cleared his throat. "Well, it says in the Bible that if a woman marries, she should marry another believer."

"But my religion has no discrimination for a man to marry a woman that isn't a Muslim," he countered.

Femi prayed for the Spirit to give him the right words to say. "Are your women also given this liberty?"

The look Abdul gave him then could have been enough to shut him up and dissuade him from talking further, but Femi was unperturbed. He asked Antonia for a glass of water and had drunk half a glass when Abdul spoke again.

"No, they aren't." He leaned forward, resting his arms on his knees. "But

252

why the discrimination? What's the need? We are all humans. We have the same blood. What's the point of rules and regulations? We love each other, shouldn't that be enough?"

"I didn't write the Bible. I didn't give the set of instructions. God did. He said in His Word that we aren't like others who do not believe and we shouldn't be joined to them. For what do we as believers have in common with an unbeliever?"

"And who's an unbeliever?"

"Those who don't believe in Jesus," Femi simply said.

"Jesus is a prophet and messenger from God. I believe he exists."

"Jesus is more than a prophet or messenger of God. He's the Son of God."

Abdul scoffed. "God has a son? Where do you people get your ideologies from?" He rested his back on the seat. "You claim a God that's so great can have a Son?"

Femi's curled up in a smile. "And what stops a great God who's sovereign, who created the heaven and earth, you and I, from having a Son?"

Abdul simply shook his head and didn't reply.

"I'm not here to argue with you or have a debate. You asked and I'm telling you what I believe in."

"And you believe Jesus as the Son of God?"

"Yes. That's what makes me a believer."

Abdul shook his head again.

"Who told you what you believe?" Antonia asked in a low tone, intrigued by their conversation. She licked her lips. "I mean, people say it all the time but how do we know God has a Son and it's not just a bunch of lies people are trying to tell us."

Femi was inwardly firing up prayers to God for wisdom to say the right words. Just one wrong word could send everything out the window. He got out his phone, tapped his code and opened the NCV Bible App. "Matthew 16 says 'Then Jesus asked them, "And who do you say I am?" Simon Peter answered, "You are the Christ, the Son of the living God." Jesus answered, "You are blessed, Simon son of Jonah, because no person taught you that. My Father in heaven showed you who I am."

He lowered his phone. "It's in the Bible and I believe it. It's not about people simply talking about it. Believing in Jesus as the Son of God comes from the heart. Only God can give you this truth. The Bible says so and that's empirical proof. It's all about faith. I didn't see Adam, who was the first man ever created, but I believe he existed. I also believe I can't save myself and I need God. No matter how good I perceive I am I can never be as good as God wants me to be. That's why God sent His Son, Jesus."

Abdul looked at him in disbelief. "Doesn't it seem crazy to you that God would put his son in a woman just so he could become a man? Why didn't God just let his son drop from heaven and come and dwell amongst us and we would tell for a truth that he's truly divine and the son of God?"

"God is bound by His Word. He is also a God of order. Man is a spirit who was put in a body. God followed that same principle. He needed to be in a physical body to live on earth. He sent His Son, Jesus, who came through Mary to operate on earth. Jesus came with a purpose, to save us from our sins and close the gap that separated us from having a relationship with God." Femi listed out a couple of scriptures and explained as much as the Spirit gave him the ability to.

"So you have a relationship with Jesus? With God?"

Femi nodded. "Yes, I do."

Abdul waved his hand and said he wasn't interested in that line of discussion anymore. Femi didn't object to it, but he knew a seed had been sown somewhere in his heart.

"Back to this marriage thing, why would God say it's wrong for two people He created to not be together?"

"A lot of reasons."

"Like?"

"One reason is different values. Another is how to treat your wife. As a husband and a believer, we are expected to love our wives as Christ loved the church. Treat her as we would our bodies. Love her not in a selfish way but sacrificially and unconditionally."

"Is his love different from ours as well?" Abdul's tone was laced with sarcasm.

"Yes, Christ died for His Church and gave Himself for her."

"Are you telling me I can't love without being a Christian?"

"Yes and 1st John 4 says if we know God, we can love, but I have to say that God giving us Jesus, opened the door for us to be able to love as He does. You can't love like Jesus or God in your strength. It's humanly impossible to do so. So whatever love we have at the moment is a tiny fraction of what God has for us. It's a tiny part of *how* God expects us to love."

Femi happened to have a Bible in his car and Antonia offered to get it and returned in less than five minutes. He leafed through the worn pages to 1 Corinthians 7 where it spoke about marriage. He read a bit out of it and explained certain things to him. Abdul asked for permission to read it as well. He handed the opened Bible over to Abdul who sat and read.

Abdul was like that for a few minutes, poring over the scriptures till he asked Femi about the part of husbands and wives. When he was done, he asked Femi a question he hadn't seen coming. A question he knew would change the course of Peju's life forever if it happened.

***

PEJU

Taking a deep breath, she approached the Azeez's residence and honked at the black gate held by high fences. A slim, tall man dressed in uniform peeped from his window at the security post and came out from a small, side gate. He walked towards her car and bent at her side.

She wound down her window.

"Good afternoon, Ma." He gave a curt nod. "Who are you looking for?"

Peju held her breath at the foul smell emitting from his mouth. "I'm here to see Tahira Azeez, the madam of the house."

He narrowed his eyes at her. "Is she expecting you?"

"No, you can tell her Mrs Layeni is here to see her."

The security guard rose to his full stature and went back into the house. From his post, she saw him pick a phone and utter some things, gesticulating with his thin, long arms. He nodded, looked back at Peju and nodded once more.

She silently prayed Tahira wouldn't turn her back. Even if Tahira did so, Peju had made up her mind to sit in her car and wait until she saw her husband. The guard dropped the phone and walked to the gate. He walked out and stood by her door once more.

"Madam said your husband isn't here at the moment but if you would like to come in, you are welcome."

Peju sighed in relief and nodded. "Yes. Yes, I would like to come in."

He nodded, went back in and opened the gate for her. She drove in, admiring the large driveway and plush garden at the side. The house was nicely-built and Peju assumed it to be a four-bedroom duplex. It was the typical modern rich family home. She was also sure it had a swimming pool at the back with a barbecue grill.

The front door opened and Tahira stepped out, looking cute in boyfriend jeans and a blouse with a pink scarf on her head.

"Hi Peju," she said when Peju had parked and was at the front door.

Peju gave a weary smile. "Tahira, good afternoon."

Tahira stepped aside a bit to let her in. Peju again marvelled at the interior décor. The room was an interesting mix of modern and boho chic. There was a large bookcase at the corner of the living room with neatly arranged books of different sizes, three black and white framed pictures of each member of the family on one wall painted white. The grey couch had a mix of colourful throw-pillows and a tall, blue vase beside it. There was also a weird painting of colours splashed together on a white canvas.

Maybe it's supposed to be symbolic, Peju thought. Asides from the painting, which she didn't quite understand, Peju loved the room. Thinking Eliana would like it as well. If the circumstances were different Peju would have loved a tour of the house but right now she couldn't be bothered.

From the corner of her eye, she saw Fatima dressed in a swimming suit, standing behind the only red sofa in the parlour.

"Fatima, come out and say hello to Aunty Peju," her mother instructed.

The little girl came forward shyly and curtseyed. "G'aftanoon Ma."

"Good afternoon dear. How are you?"

Fatima said a shy "I'm fine."

"Don't you remember Uncle Abdul's wife? You were at the wedding."

Fatima looked up at Peju once more and went to hide behind her mother.

Tahira rolled her eyes. "Don't mind her. She's a little shy with strangers but would eventually be herself. What do I offer you?" She led the way to their large kitchen and pulled open the fridge. "I have water, Zobo, juice, punch or, er - some alcohol." She looked back at her. "Which would you prefer? Or I can make you some tea?"

Peju said punch was fine.

"Great! I just made this an hour ago, so it's fresh and tasty. Fatima, wait for a little so we can all go outside to the swimming pool." She brought out a jug of which contained a blue liquid and Peju hoped she hadn't made a wrong decision, but one sip of the cold drink was a pleasant relief to the heat outside.

"This is good." She took another sip and placed the mason glass cup down on the counter.

"Thank you. So how are things with you?" She asked as she poured herself a glass and another in a small, pink cup.

"Fine."

Tahira nodded and gestured to a sliding door behind her. "Let's go outback. It's cooler there and we can talk."

I don't want to talk. I just want to see my husband. But Peju couldn't say that. Moreover, it sounded like there was no room for her to reject the offer. They all went out the door while Fatima screamed with excitement and ran to the small size inflatable, kiddies pool; her mother explicitly warning her to stay away from the main pool as they sat down on the wicker loungers.

Peju watched Fatima and felt a lump in her throat. Her chest ached thinking of what might have been if her child had survived. Maybe she wouldn't be in a bad place at the moment. Maybe she would have been satisfied with her life and not harboured crazy thoughts; blaming her lack of fulfilment in life on her marriage.

"I guess Idris told you your husband was here. I had to talk him into telling you." Tahira turned in her chair to grace her with a concerned look. "I'm sorry I'm going to be very nosy here, but what happened with you two? Did you guys argue?"

Peju took her gaze away from her and stared at the trail of ants going to and fro from a flower pot that held a single yellow flower. She wasn't interested in talking with anyone asides from Abdul but she also needed an ally in the matter. She didn't want to tell Eliana about it, angry at herself for talking to her about her problems in the first place.

"Peju."

"Mmm," Peju brought her eyes back on her and sighed silently. "Yeah, we argued. A bad one." She sniffled. "I don't even know how to explain it. One minute, things were so good between us, then the next minute, it all sort of fell apart. I wanted to explain but he wasn't willing to listen."

Tahira nodded in understanding. "Truth is, I've never seen Abdul so withdrawn, so hurt. And I'm not in a position to judge or point fingers." She glanced at her daughter who was playing at the shallow end of the pool and directed her gaze back to Peju. "Marriage is like that sometimes. We argue, fight, get angry but it shouldn't be so bad that things fall apart. I know you may not want to talk to me about what happened but I want you to know you can be free with me."

Peju nodded and thanked her but she still wasn't going to talk. Even if she tried to explain the whole situation, Tahira wouldn't understand and might do what she didn't want. Judge her. Peju already made a mistake in divulging her sacred thoughts to Eliana. It was the reason why she was in this mess in the first place.

Tahira went back to watching her daughter, occasionally tapping at her phone. Peju realised how little she knew about Tahira. She was beautiful, slim, confident and looked like she was fiercely independent. Peju could imagine them being close friends with time.

Just to keep her mind off her depressing matter, even if for a moment she asked how Tahira and Idris met. What was their love story? Tahira laughed lightly. "Our love story was chaotic!" She laughed again. "We met at the University of Toronto in Canada. I was a complete snob and didn't allow

Idris to go ahead with his plans of wooing me. I had a focus. Go to school, get a little work experience and head back home. That was my plan and no man was going to come in my way."

Peju shifted in her seat, the story holding her interest.

"I knew Abdul first and he tried talking me into going out with his friend but I stalled for three more months. Idris couldn't wait that long. He was in a relationship with a girl and I wasn't bothered when Abdul broke the news to me. Then one day, a mutual friend of ours was having a birthday party at some club, and I got there. Do you know what Idris did? He grabbed me from behind and shoved his tongue down my throat."

Peju's brow went up.

"Mummy, I want water," Fatima broke into the conversation. She looked bored.

Tahira offered an apologetic look and they all went into the house. Fatima had her glass of water after towelling her body.

"So," Tahira continued once they were seated in the living room. "I slapped him hard."

Peju eyebrows drew together in surprise and Tahira laughed.

"He told me he was expecting it. I was too embarrassed to speak. His so-called *girlfriend -*" she enunciated the word with her fingers, "- was his cousin. He wanted to make me jealous but since that didn't happen, he took another approach. Long story short, it took another two months before I finally agreed to date him."

"He was patient."

Tahira gave a wistful look. "He still is. He told me the best is always worth waiting for and I was it for him."

Peju also remembered Abdul seeking her out when he returned. He was a good man. Better than most and she couldn't dare imagine life without him. The last three days had been sheer torture. She wanted him back home. She wanted to put an end to their misunderstandings. She wanted to let him know how much she loved him, irrespective of her thought of disappointing God. She knew all she had to do was focus her devotion on God and be with her husband; accepting him for who he was. She was a fool to not have dealt with her fears. She was at fault and Abdul had nothing to do with it.

"I wouldn't say married life is all perfect. We have our fights now and then. I have a compulsive disorder for cleanliness. Idris is neat too, but no match for me. So you can imagine how we would have managed, our first year of marriage was enough for either one of us to give up. We wondered if we could cope with each other. But we remembered why we got married in the first place. We remembered our goals and visions as individuals and as a family. I have my career and I never let it get in the way of my family. I'm working not because of the money but because of the dreams I had way back as a child. If tomorrow, I have to step back to be a full-time mum, then I would take it. Life happens and it's in phases and every moment is to be enjoyed."

Peju blinked at the ocean of wisdom Tahira had said. Not knowing how much her words had helped her. She reclined to her thoughts and prayed for the best. She had a new perspective and hopefully, her husband would give her a listening ear.

***

OBA

It was eight in the evening when he got to Eliana's place, having to leave the training earlier than planned. He was worried and at the same time, pissed off at her attitude. He badly wanted to believe her phone battery had died or the network had disappeared and not that she ended his call. Oba also knew she would have been a little hurt at what happened, but it wasn't like he had sex with Nene or he gave in to the temptation to kiss her. So why was she being dramatic? He eased his car in front of the familiar brown gate and killed the engine.

He greeted her parents and took a seat while Dimeji went to call her. She blinked in surprise when she saw him at first, then frowned. The anger Oba felt a few minutes back waned just from seeing her. He got up and walked to her as she crossed her arms.

"Hey."

"Good evening," she replied.

"Can we please talk outside?"

She nodded and told her parents she was outside. Oba bid them good night before following her out the door. Their next-door neighbours were laughing loudly and screaming excitedly at something. Whatever it was, Oba wished he could have that same emotion with Eliana. He hated the dejected look on her face and hated that it was somehow his fault. They went out to his car and leaned against the boot.

"How was your day?" he asked, choosing his words carefully.

"Just there."

"Okay. Anything special happen?"

"No."

Oba sighed. "I don't know what happened when I called, but all of a sudden I couldn't hear you anymore. Did you cut the call on me?"

She stared down at her green coated toe-nails. He didn't like the colour on her, but now was not the time to give his opinion. He heard a muffled yes in reply to his question.

"Why?"

"Because I was angry and what you said was painful."

He expelled a breath and ran his fingers over his itchy scalp. He was in desperate need of a shower and haircut. "That was why I wanted to tell you in person but you women don't like waiting. You want to hear the *gist* immediately."

She threw an angry stare at him. "This isn't *gist*. *Gist* is when we are talking about something important that happened to you at work, or when you're telling me what a colleague did or something. *Gist* is not when you tell me you and your ex-girlfriend almost made out."

What's the difference between gist and gossip? He raised his hands. "Okay, I'm sorry."

"I hear you."

"Nothing happened between us. Babe, I'm committing my heart to you.

I'm not playing in this relationship."

"Right," she said, turning her gaze from his. "You said you almost kissed her."

He spread his arms wide. "I'm a man, Eliana, not a robot. I have feelings. This is a woman I went out with for over two years. We were intimately involved."

"Why are you rubbing it in my face?"

The pained look on her face tore at him. "I'm not, sweetie. I just need you to understand where I'm coming from. I wouldn't intentionally harm you, love."

"I don't think I can compete with *her*," she said, as though she hadn't listened to a word he had just said.

Oba knew who she was referring to. He sighed and took her in his arms. She stiffened at his touch but he didn't back away. He loved holding her close. Loved the strawberry and minty smell of her natural locks and how soft it was against his cheek. Particularly, he loved how right she felt in his arms. There were no stirrings to have sex with her but a calming attraction that only gave room at being satisfied with just staring into her eyes and inhaling the same breath as she.

There was no doubt about it. He was in love.

Pastor John had taught him how a woman's body was to be respected because it was God's temple. That love wasn't about going against the Word of God and engaging in premarital sex. Love was willing to wait till the time was right.

"I'm not asking you to compete with her or be her. I like you for you, Eliana. I should have told you earlier but I was scared of how you would react. I'm sorry about what happened." He pulled back enough to raise her chin so he could stare into her eyes that glistened with tears. "*Ma binu si mi jor*. Forgive me."

Eliana looked away from him and rubbed her arms as a cool breeze blew their way. "When you told me what happened I couldn't think clearly. Then all sorts of thoughts were running through my mind."

"Like?" He queried, brushing a tear off her cheek.

"Like you still love her and you can't get over your attraction for her. That maybe you made a mistake for wanting to be with me." She shook her head and looked him in the eye. "Look Oba, I'm not desperate. I'm not keen on entering a relationship with you because I'm 25 and single. I would rather be single than be with a guy who is confused about what he wants."

He opened his mouth to counter her but instead closed his mouth, shoved his hands in his pockets and listened on.

"I care about you a lot. I really do, but I'm scared. I've experienced heartbreak once and I don't want to go through it again."

"So what do you want?"

"I want you to be sure of what you want."

"What if I say it's you?"

Eliana shook her head. "You don't have to answer now. Take a few days to think about it."

At that Oba disagreed. "A few days without seeing you? Seriously? Eliana, God sees my heart. I don't love Nene. I love you. Whatever attraction I felt for her is gradually becoming non-existent! What do I have to do to make you understand?"

Love is patient. . .

The words imprinted on his heart. But he didn't want to be patient. He needed her to know she was the most important person to him asides from God. The words resonated again in his heart and he grudgingly adhered to it. He had read 1 Corinthians 13 last week based on Pastor John's instructions. Oba had brought up the topic of love and asked questions about how God expected him to love. What His definition of love was. He had been amazed at what God expected of not just him but all who called themselves His children. Loving His way was beyond any human capabilities, but Pastor John had explained it wasn't for Oba to love on his own, but give God the room to love through him.

Lord, give me grace.

Another passage registered in his heart, the part about God's grace is sufficient for him no matter his weaknesses or struggles. God was there to give him strength.

"How long are we talking about here?"

"Two weeks?"

Oba almost protested again but nodded. "Okay. I'll give you time to think. I don't need any time. I know what I want."

Her look said she didn't believe him but she remained silent. Not wanting to argue.

"I care about you, Eliana. I really do. It goes beyond physical attractions. I trust God brought us together for a reason. Don't fight it." He gave her one more hug, and this time she hugged back. He then got into his car and drove off. On the road, he took the time to pray that God would take control and have His way. As thunder crackled in the skies, he assumed it was raining somewhere in Lagos, hoping he would get home first if at all it rained at his part of town.

***

ABDUL

It was a little chilly, so he basked in the natural breeze rather than turn on the air-conditioner. Abdul saw the car in the driveway once the guard opened the gate. He badly wanted to reverse and go someplace else. He wasn't ready to face her, but also knew the time would eventually come for him to do so. And as much as he didn't want to admit it to himself, deep down, he had missed her.

Her smile. Her laughter. Her soft lips. The way she chastised him when he left the toilet seat up and threatened to move to another room and he teased that he would follow her to the ends of the world.

Discarding his thoughts, he sighed and locked his car with a click of a button. He took his time till he got to the front door and rang the bell. The sound of footsteps approaching the door caused him to release a breath as he steeled himself against what was going to happen next. As he had guessed, she opened the door and stepped out to stand before him. She then shut the door behind her, as though barricading the door. His first desire was to hold her in his arms but he stood still, as though his feet were cemented to the ground.

"Hey," Peju said quietly.

Seeing her brought fresh pain to his heart and the memories flooded his mind. He looked her over and realised how much weight she had lost. She looked miserable and it sort of gave him a good feeling to know she was suffering as much as he was. She clasped her hands nervously. A loud sound of thunder roared over them. As if that was the push she needed, she spoke, "I'm sorry for blocking you this way. I- I just didn't want you to go away. How are you?"

"Been better."

She nodded. "Can we talk?"

"I thought we were already doing that." He felt a drop of rain on his forehead and he looked up at the skies. The clouds were heavy.

She gave a small laugh. "Yeah. Abdul, I'm sorry about everything. What you heard -"

"Was the truth," he cut in.

"Please, let me talk."

"Fine." He led the way to his car and they leaned against the doors. She was close, the smell of her perfume doing all sorts of things within him and he held back the desire coursing through him. He waited for her to talk as he saw a mosquito land on his arm.

She took a deep breath. "I'm sorry you heard all I said. It wasn't my intention for you to hear it. Moreover, it was silly and stupid of me to have all those thoughts. I guess I was just afraid of my life seeming meaningless and empty. But that has nothing to do with you, Abdul. It has nothing to do with my love for you. I love you. I have loved you since I was fifteen."

"Maybe it was just puppy love. Not the kind of love that's enough to get married."

Peju shook her head. "No. Our love isn't like that."

He killed the mosquito on his arm and cleaned the blood off on his trousers.

He turned to face her. "So what's our love like? Because it seems our love isn't enough for you. Do you know what I realised today? That I'm not man enough to make you happy. And I don't mean that sexually, materially or otherwise. I mean I am just not enough and I don't think I can ever be enough for you. Do you know how that makes me feel?"

"I under-"

He shook his head. "Please don't say that. Don't say you understand when you don't know how it feels to have your heart ripped by the one you gave it to." He looked away from her. "Please, don't say you understand."

"Okay, you're right. I may not know how you feel, but it hurts that I put you in that position. I put you in a position not to trust me and doubt my love for you, but I mean it, Abdul. I love you with all my heart."

He closed his eyes. *Love the human way is fickle. A tiny fraction of how God expects us to love.*

"Are you happy?"

"With you I am."

"Do you still feel empty?"

"That had nothing to do with you."

It has everything to do with me. He had all afternoon to think it over and kept coming to the same conclusion.

"Didn't you know what the Bible said about marrying an unbeliever before you did?"

"I did but I went against it for you. Because I love you."

Abdul closed his eyes briefly then opened them. "This is hard for me to say . . ." He faced her and felt a pain in his heart as he said his next words. "I want a divorce."

He heard a sharp intake of breath just as the rain began pouring. They both stood there staring at each other. Peju, more out of shock. The rain got heavier and he got out his car keys to open it and quickly got into the car. Peju's face was already wet as with some parts of her clothes. She was wiping the water off her face and he offered his handkerchief to aid the process. When she didn't take it, he did it himself.

"Please, don't do this Abdul. I-" Her voice broke and she sobbed. It broke his heart. He let her cry a bit till she was finally able to speak. "Don't you love me?"

"Of course I do."

"Then why are you doing this?" she croaked.

"Because I want you to be happy."

"I'm happy with you."

He wished it were true.

"Can you convert to Islam for me? For our love?"

There was a sharp intake of breath. "I thought you said you wouldn't force me to."

"I'm not forcing you. I only want you to make a choice."

"Between Christianity and Islam?"

"No. Between me and your devotion to Christianity."

She took her eyes off him and gazed away at the house. He turned as well and saw the curtain drop. *Was that Tahira spying on them?*

"You are asking for a difficult thing, Abdul." He brought his eyes back to her.

"You still have to choose."

"I - I will." She closed her eyes as though in pain. "I will choose you." She opened her eyes. "I will not choose you, Abdul."

Her words confirmed his sorrow and his reason for wanting a divorce. As he studied her, he saw the same sorrow that had been there for the last couple of months. He remembered her hesitation on their wedding day. He knew she wasn't happy. He knew the truth.

He put her hands in his and rubbed the back of her palms. His next words were going to hurt her as much as they did him. "I love you crazily, Peju. With all my heart. But this can't go on."

Chapter 22

ELIANA

It was hard seeing him go and she almost called him back, to cancel her requests and hug him. Almost. He said he loved her. Eliana bit her bottom lip. Her eyes stung with tears. She would have tossed aside her need for time but she felt it was best for the both of them. For him to really think and pray. To know if he wanted her in his life or he wanted Nene.

It started drizzling so she hurried into the house. She stood by the door, replaying their conversation in her head along with his mannerisms. He looked sorry. But she also had to apologise for ending the call on him. No matter what he did, he didn't deserve that. It was rude.

"Is everything okay?" her mother asked and her father lowered his newspaper to catch a glimpse of her. Eliana didn't like the attention. If her mother looked at her closely, it would warrant more questions. She didn't want that.

She nodded and forced a smile. "Yes, Mum. I'm going to my room."

"Won't you eat your dinner?"

"I will but I just need to sort some things out first." She took quick steps to her room before her mother could say anything else.

Locking the door behind her, she collapsed on her bed and shut her eyes. The pouring of rain against her window filled up the silence and she prayed Oba got home safely. Though it wasn't a long drive from Iponri to Yaba.

She let out a sigh. There was no use for tears. It wasn't like she broke up with him even if it felt like it. She just felt they both needed time to affirm their feelings for each other. To be sure they were making the right decision.

"God, what if he still loves Nene?"

Peace, be still.

Eliana heard the knock at her door before she could process the meaning of the words. Her mother called out if everything was okay.

"Yes Mum!"

Her words didn't seem to be proof enough because she was asked to open the door. Eliana grudgingly got up and ambled over to it. Her mother gave her a questioning look.

"Are you sure you're fine? Did anything happen between you and Oba?"

Eliana shrugged. "We're okay." Early last year, just a few days after her birthday, Kene had confessed to sleeping with a female colleague. Very much heartbroken she had told her mother everything. But not this time with Oba. She didn't want to keep running to her mother to sort out her problems or when things got bad. And it wasn't like things were bad. They just took time apart. If at all they went their separate ways, then it was okay. It would hurt but it would all be fine.

"So, there's no problem between you two?"

Eliana nodded.

"That's good to know. Your father was worried about you as well. He's the one that asked me to check up on you. He really likes Oba for you."

A smile crossed Eliana's lips when she told her parents Oba hadn't gotten married and had given his life to Christ. Her father had said in passing that probably God had arrested his head and heart.

"I like him too. He looks responsible and I can see he cares for you. I pray it all works out according to God's will."

"Amen."

"Your food would be getting cold." Her mother stood from her bed.

"I don't think I'm going to eat. I would clear the kitchen and have it as lunch once I get back from church."

"Alright."

After her mum exited her room, Eliana took her phone next to her pillow where she had left it when Dimeji told her she had a visitor. She tapped the phone to life and saw she had a text message.

I'm home. Forgot to renew my data and network is messed up. It was great seeing you today. You were a sight for sore eyes. Once again I'm sorry about everything and I meant what I said. The three letter words you failed to catch. I love you. I know you said we should take time apart and if calling or sending messages is part of the deal then I would respect your wishes. 2 wks o! Nothing more but of course it can be less. Good night dear.

P.s Thinking of you.

Eliana smiled and read the message at least two more times. She typed out a message.

Good to know you got home safe. I'm also sorry for cutting the call on you. Really rude of me. It was nice seeing you too. I'll think about it. :)

P.s I love you too.

She fell back on her bed, clutching her phone against her chest while grinning ear to ear.

***

PEJU

The weather was wet and cold. Peju shivered even though she was under a thick duvet. Abdul had carried her up to his room and Tahira made a cup of vanilla tea that was left untouched on the table beside her.

"Please take a little of the tea."

She didn't have the appetite to eat or drink. Her heart was broken in a million pieces.

Abdul sat by her side and his warm hand on her head sent shivers down her spine. She closed her eyes and swallowed hard. Her throat felt dry and her head throbbed. She felt so tired and all she wanted to do was sleep.

"Peju, please," he begged.

She made to get up but her joints ached. Abdul helped her seat up and held the cup close to her mouth so she could take a sip. It was now warm.

"When was the last time you ate?"

"Yesterday morning," she admitted.

"What?" He moved the mug closer to her lips and she took another sip. She loved how concerned he was even after telling her he was no longer interested in their marriage. *He's so good to me. God please don't let him leave me. I can't do without him. I need him.*

Thou shalt have no other gods before me.

He's not a god. He's my husband.

"I would tell Tahira to help make something for you. What would you like?"

Peju pushed the cup away gently. "Nothing."

"No, Peju you have to eat. You look weak and it appears you have a fever." He placed the back of his hand on her head. "I will ask her to make pepper-soup for you if it's possible."

"I don't want."

But Abdul wasn't paying attention to her weak protests. He got off the bed and headed out the door. She casually took in her environment. As expected, the room was also tastefully furnished with cool caramel porcelain tiles and a purple curtain but she was too exhausted to take in much of the room with all its loveliness. With a huge effort, she went back to lying on her back and stared at the wall with blurry eyes as she painfully reminded herself of Abdul's words. Back to their conversation in the car while they waited out the heavy pours of rain.

"It's not that I don't love you Peju. It's because I love you that I'm letting you go."

"I don't need you to do that. It was my choice to marry you. I said crazy things. I'm sorry. It might be hard but please forget them," she said desperately, her teeth chattering.

"I have forgiven you, Habeebah," he said softly. "Really, I have. It tears me to think of my life without you."

"Then don't do this."

He shifted his eyes from hers and looked out the window. "It has stopped raining and you're cold. Let's take you inside."

If he left her, there was no point of living. She couldn't imagine him with another woman. She would rather die. Abdul returned in less than an hour with a steaming bowl of what smelt like chicken soup and French bread. *Trust Tahira to go the extra mile.*

He helped her up despite her complaints of body pains. "Sorry, there were no ingredients for pepper-soup but she whopped this up quickly. You need to eat. I will give you pain relievers and you will have a good night rest."

The soup was delicious and he made sure she ate most of it before resigning to her plea to stop. She took the pills and lay back down. Abdul was clearing the plates to leave and she stopped him.

"Can you please lie beside me?"

She saw his hesitation but was pleased immensely when he dropped the tray on a footstool and reclined beside her. She moved close. The faint scent of his cologne made a tingling sensation in her tummy.

Peju lifted her gaze to him and he caught on to her silent message. Their kiss was slow. They kissed like two people unsure, but it later grew urgent and sensual. He stopped before things went further.

"Peju, you need to rest."

She shook her head. "No, I only need you." She placed her head on his chest and enjoyed as his racing heart gradually returned to a normal pace. "Divorce isn't an option, Abdul."

"Rest. We would talk in the morning."

"Would you stay with me?"

"Yes, now go to sleep."

She felt his warm lips press against her forehead as she finally obeyed.

***

ANTONIA

Esther wore a tired look that Tuesday afternoon. Their mother wasn't feeling too good. Antonia knew no matter how annoying the woman was, she didn't want anything to happen to her.

"Where's Jasmine?"

"She's sleeping in the parlour. Esther stepped out to buy recharge card down the street."

"So how's she feeling?" Antonia asked, taking off her shoes and together they moved to the kitchen to talk. Esther had called her while at work to stop by. Antonia hadn't been there for weeks. Preferring to put some distance from her mother so she could think. A lot had been on her mind these days. Mostly what Femi and Abdul had discussed. It prompted a lot of questions from her. Femi had answered them all. But there was one, in particular, she needed her mother to answer.

"She's better now. Thank God. She's sleeping. The doctor said she should rest and eat. It's sorrow over losing Daddy that's weighing her down. She's also been asking after you . . .and in a good way."

Antonia's brows went up.

"In a good way? Like how?"

Esther grabbed a bottle of water from the fridge and poured herself a glass. "When she talks about you, she says *my* Antonia."

"Are you sure she's not losing it?"

Her elder sister frowned at what she said and Antonia apologised. She opened the pots on the stove and her tummy grumbled at the sight of yam porridge and fried turkey stew.

"I think she wants to apologise for all the years of neglect. As Miriam and I should. For years, we watched Mummy do all she did and we remained quiet. We didn't defend you. We just accepted it."

"Please don't cry," Antonia told Esther when she got all teary-eyed. "It's okay. I don't think either of you could stand Mummy's caustic tongue." That was the same excuse she had given for them over the years.

"No, it's not okay. We were your big sisters and we let you down. I'm sorry." Esther stepped forward and pulled her to a hug.

Antonia hugged her back. Miriam met them like that and joined in on the sisterly bond. No words were needed. They were sisters, blood... family. When the moment was over, Miriam announced that she was going to fry prawn crackers and the three of them laughed. Back in the day, the crackers were their go-to snacks. Their father made sure the house was always stocked with several packs.

"Hope it's not expired *sha,*" Miriam said when she brought one out of the cupboard.

"Me, I won't eat *o!*" Esther said. "I'm a breastfeeding mother, before I give my baby poison to suck."

The room was stuffy and smelt stale. Antonia opened the windows to let in fresh air.

"Antonia?"

"Yes, it's me, Mummy. I'm sorry I woke you up. Just wanted to see how you were." She went to sit by her mother on a chair next to her bed.

"Have you been here for long?"

"No. Thirty minutes."

The bed creaked as her mother pushed herself off and sat up. She asked Antonia random questions: how was she? How was work? Her friends? There was little for both of them to say since they barely had a relationship with each other.

"Why did you marry Daddy?"

Her mother stared at her in confusion. "What do you mean?"

"Like you and Daddy believe differently, but why did you marry him?"

Antonia's mother adjusted the faded, gold ring on her fourth finger. The white stone on it had long lost its glimmer. "Your father was the only serious man who wanted to marry me. The rest were more interested in having sex. One night stands." She sighed. "But your father was different and it amazed me that someone as good-looking as him wanted to be with me. He was fair and handsome. He wasn't as tall as I would have wanted but since height was the only hindrance, I considered it inconsequential."

"Even religion?"

"Oh, I wasn't a Christian when we married. I wasn't really devoted to God and I didn't mind that he was a Muslim. He had a good-paying job. He was responsible, humble and a gentleman. If he liked, he could have been an atheist. I wasn't bothered. Back then, all those seemed unimportant. All that mattered was we were in love."

Antonia took a cold prawn cracker and nibbled at it. "So you became a Christian during marriage? How did Dad feel?" Her father already told her his side of the story but she was eager to hear her mother's. To understand what had triggered her mother's hatred for her.

"He was okay with it as long as it didn't affect our relationship with one another. I never pressured him into changing his lifestyle. I was respectful of his beliefs as he was of mine. During Ramadan periods, I made his meals for him, both *Iftar* and *Suhoor*." She smiled. "Your father didn't really like the dates he was to break with, so I was the one that ate them."

Antonia thought back to when as a child she asked her mother for some dates and she had blatantly refused. One day, Antonia had been smacked for eating them even though it was her father who gave her. She blinked the thoughts away.

"We lived a comfortable and peaceful life."

Until I was born. Antonia thought.

As though her mother read her mind she said, "When you were born, I got jealous of his affection for you. You were his carbon-copy. You took his caramel skin, pink lips and pointed nose. I saw how he smiled at you with joy and I knew in my heart his love for me was divided. And that was when I started harbouring jealousy towards you, my daughter. I'm sorry my dear."

Antonia felt a tear drop on the back of her hand.

"Forgive me."

"Mummy, I've forgiven you," she whispered.

"As long as God gives me life, I want to amend my ways. I want to be a better mother to you. Will you give me the chance to?

Chapter 23

ELIANA

February 11, 2017

Oba's mother arrived in Lagos and I went to see her. And yes, things are much better between Oba and me. We talked things over and dealt with some of my insecurities with his past.

On meeting Mrs A... honestly, I was nervous to see her. More than nervous. I was petrified! I went to the toilet close to five times! Maybe it's also because I kept drinking water and somewhere in my brain, I didn't realise there would be repercussions for my actions. We spoke for about an hour. She asked me a couple of questions and seemed happy with my answers. When she was hungry, I offered to make something for her, knowing Oba is a complete novice in the kitchen department. Trust me, his cooking is H-O-R-R-I-B-L-E. The other day he made a concoction of rice and it ended up with too much salt and the rice was HARD. Hian! I won't complain when he asks me to drink garri with him.

Anyway, I made Jollof-rice for his mother and she loved it. Her words, 'My son will get fat o!' What can I say? My mama taught me well :)

I'm glad Mrs A approves of our relationship. She even told me to call her from time to time so we can get to know each other better. Oba told her we weren't married yet. His mother asked him what he was waiting for.

In other news, Pastor John's wife has returned! There was a lot of commotion in church. Both church members and outsiders listened to the heartfelt story she gave on her life and why she left her husband. Pastor John was sitting in front cheering her on. I want a love like that. A selfless love. A love that is unconditional and not based on situations or circumstances. I know that kind of love doesn't come naturally and it's only God that can do it. Their story was a true representation of how much God loves us. Just like the story of the ninety-nine sheep the shepherd would leave to chase after the one that was missing! The shepherd could have been comfortable with the fact that he had 99 and it was only 1 missing. Not at all! He went after that sheep. Even if it meant fighting off a few wolves or facing hardships. He went after that 1 sheep.

I was once that one sheep and God sought after me and brought me home to Him. Hallelujah!

Peju . . . I'm praying for my friend. She's going through a hard time and I pray God strengthens her.

***

PEJU

Home. They say home is where the heart is. But what was the point of a home when the one you loved wasn't there? It was no longer a home but an empty house. A building that echoed what would have been.

Peju stared at a picture she and Abdul took eleven years ago in their school uniforms. He had his lips pressed against her cheek while she closed her eyes in laughter. She blinked back the tears and kept the picture in the shoebox where the rest were.

She had loved Abdul with her entire being and their recent separation was a blow she was still finding hard to recover from. Her heart ached and she didn't know how to get past the pain.

No matter how much she tried to change his mind, Abdul was adamant about getting the divorce. And she gave it to him. No amount of pleadings from her and her mother could change his mind. Not even his parents could talk him out of it. When his parents had demanded to know what happened, he said he didn't love her anymore. His words hadn't hurt much because in his eyes she could see the truth. He was just saying that, taking the blame upon himself to divert the problems away from her.

Which was a reason for her to love him more.

Peju had sobbed pathetically at his kind gesture.

His love was on the right path. Why couldn't they just be together? Why was God doing this to them and causing so much heartache? She had yelled at Femi, after storming into his office where a patient was currently being attended to, for sticking his nose in her business. Even when he explained he never advised Abdul to go ahead and divorce her, she hadn't believed him.

"I may love you but I'm not desperate. I'm not the kind of person to break up a home," he told her after pulling her out of his office to an empty room.

"Antonia told me the two of you spoke. What did you talk about? What did you say that made him want to divorce me?"

"He asked if his leaving you would bring you back on the right track."

Peju pushed him. "And you said yes?"

"No! I said no. His leaving you is not a remedy for you to get back with God. That it's between you and God. You two are already married and there's no going back."

She looked at him surreptitiously. "So what did he say?"

"He said he was to blame for running ahead to get married. That the mistake was his."

Tears gathered at the corners of her eyes.

He stepped forward to hug her but she raised her hand at him. "Please, I don't need you comforting me. I'm sure you prayed for this to happen. You and Eliana. I'm sure you purposely wanted my marriage to fail so you could gloat and say you told me so."

He shook his head and said softly, "Not at all Peju. I wouldn't do that to you."

"Oh please! In your heart you were wishing I didn't marry him-"

"But I wouldn't wish for your marriage to end. I tried talking him out of leaving you but it seemed he had his mind made up."

Peju closed the box and placed it on the bed. There was still a lot of cleaning to be done to get her new apartment in shape. Eliana and Oba had offered to help next weekend. This Saturday, they were having a youth hang-out at the beach and Eliana had talked Peju into going. Peju would have turned it down but she knew mingling with other people may do her good. She had been in seclusion ever since the divorce, staying away from prying eyes.

Even from church. Especially from church.

She recalled what her mother had said about His Glory Centre, *"I heard your pastor's wife was carrying her body up and down as a sex slave. Are you sure that the church is not responsible for the break of your marriage? With all the bad spirit hovering over them. You better start coming to my church."*

Peju shook her head. "No, Mummy. I'm okay where I am."

"Ah! You don't want to marry? You don't want to return to your husband?"

Peju had smiled then.

"I have already returned." Her mother took on a surprised look and immediately *Peju explained what she meant. "I have returned to God, Mummy. God is my first husband."*

The smile disappeared from her face. Her mother flicked her hand to the back of her head and snapped her fingers loudly, saying God forbid in Yoruba. "You want to be a nun?"

"That's not what I mean." Peju was too tired to explain and knew her mother *would drag the issue. "Never mind, Mummy."*

Peju got dressed for the hang-out and took a bus there. Abdul had wanted her to keep the car but she had refused it. It was harder still returning his ring.

The wind was a cool breeze and she wrapped her arms around her. She watched as the wave settled briefly. Something was calming about watching the turbulence of the sea. When people heard about her life, they would think it was chaotic, but the exterior didn't mirror the peace and joy in her heart.

She had gotten it all twisted.

Her first love was not the one who loved her since secondary school but the One who had loved her even before she was born. The One who had seen her through the pain of the last month. The one who is Love Himself.

She couldn't believe she had given God up just because of her love for Abdul. That she would deny Jesus because of an old flame. It was almost like nailing Him to the cross all over again and joining the Jews in chanting for His death and crucifixion.

Yes, she had loved Abdul. But he wasn't her everything. He wasn't who she was going to give everything up for.

Peju heard Eliana scream at a distance and turned in her direction, her lips curling in a smile as she saw Oba go down on his knees and bring out a small box from his pocket.

In two days, it would be a year since Abdul proposed to her.

"Love is beautiful, isn't it?" Femi asked. She hadn't heard him walk up to her.

"Very." She took her eyes off the newly engaged couple that brought back painful memories and focused them on Femi, looking super casual in a Hawaii shirt and khaki shorts. "But it also depends on who you love first, otherwise it becomes an idol."

Just like her love for Abdul.

Femi said nothing to what she said. There was no need to. He understood perfectly.

"Where's Eniola?" She asked, breaking the silence.

"She's with Timilehin."

"Shouldn't you be keeping her company?"

He laughed. "It's not my job."

She craned her neck, scanning the beach until her eyes found Timilehin laughing at something Eniola had said.

Peju kept her shock to herself.

"I-"

"Wh-"

They both started to speak.

"You go first," Femi said.

"Why did you love me?" She saw his raised brow and added, "If you don't want to tell me, it's okay. But I would rather know."

"You mean why do I love you?"

Her sharp intake of breath made him smile. *He still loved her? Why?*

"My love for you isn't a feeling that I willed to come and go."

"Even though I was married to Abdul?"

He nodded. "When you got married, I told myself I couldn't love you the way I wanted or desired to. I had to love you as a friend and not someone I wanted to spend the rest of my life with."

She looked away from him, confused.

"I'm trying to say it was a choice to love you, Peju."

"And it was also a choice for you to stop as well?" He said yes. "But you didn't?"

"Yes and no."

She turned to face him and the love in his eyes shook her. A loud horn blasted the air and she jerked, looking away from him again. Breaking the moment.

The youth leader was telling them to gather so they could take a group picture. Elaina came by her side, and Peju hugged her and said congratulations. There was a lot of pandemonium just to get everyone in the picture. All 70 plus of them. The photographer finally achieved the hard feat and called out 'say cheese!'

"Cheese!" everyone yelled.

Come away with Me. . .

The words were whispered against her heart despite the noise, and she whispered back. "I'm here, Lord. I'm here and I'm not going anywhere else. Take me wherever and I will follow." She was beginning to understand that God was interested in every part of her life. God loved every bit of her and she had been too blind, too preoccupied to notice.

Her time at different Bible study sessions taught her a lot. Last year, they had looked at Song of Solomon and certain verses had gripped her heart. The part that spoke of the Shulamite woman searching for her love. Enduring sleepless nights. His absence was a pain in her heart.

Peju knew what that felt like. She could remember how empty she felt when she had strayed from God. The joy in her heart when she finally returned to Him, just like the prodigal son. She didn't deserve God's love but He loved her still.

Tears built up at the corner of her eyes. Peju felt a gentle nudge on her shoulder and she looked up at Femi standing next to her, smiling down at her.

She smiled back.

[Vividly she pictured it] The voice of my beloved [shepherd]! Behold, he comes, leaping upon the mountains, bounding over the hills. My beloved is like a gazelle or a young hart. Behold, he stands behind the wall of our house, he looks in through the windows, he glances through the lattice.
My beloved speaks and says to me, Rise up, my love, my fair one, and come away.
Song of Solomon 2 verse 8-10 AMP

Click here to read more about Pastor John and his scandalous wife in 'Always One More Time'.

Click here to read the next book in the First Love Series.

Author's Note

Hi dear readers... friends,

Writing *Once Upon a First Love* was an amazing experience for me. Interestingly, this wasn't the story I wanted to write originally. I was working on another novel idea I was excited about, then one day I couldn't go on because there was no inspiration. It just wasn't flowing. The words wouldn't just come and I was sort of frustrated. Call it writer's block or whatever. I felt something was wrong somewhere and I decided to pray about it. It was then God made me realise I was writing for myself. The words I had laboured on were pushed aside and He explained to me my desire for wanting to write wasn't out of a love for Him, but to please myself.

That broke me. It was true and it's something I had been trying to avoid in all my years of writing.

He made me realise the reason I sought Him was because I wanted to write. I wanted the attention and pat on the back that my writing was good. I wanted to help people with my writing, but to what extent? To the extent that my relationship with God was suffering.

I realised my writing wasn't because I wanted to know Him more. It wasn't because I yearned to have a relationship with Him.

And I think some of us get caught in this from time to time. Where we love the gift more than the giver. Where we get caught up in the busyness of life. We love the life God gave us and leave Him behind. We claim to be so busy with our responsibilities at home, work, and even church, that there's no time to fellowship with God; the owner of our lives.

And so this book was brought to my heart to pen down after I did a U-turn and made my way back to God. He gave me the ideas and how to go about it. Even the resources needed in printing this book . . . God laid it in the hearts of special people to sponsor it. How amazing is God? Just like He said in His Word, He is Faithful when he calls. He will do it.

Writing this book taught me different things. Like I was sharing with a sister just before the book was released, I came to see love in another light. I began to understand love, in God's way, in another dimension and thus far, it's been helping me with my relationship with others.

Having a relationship with Him is a choice we have to make. A choice between the love of the world and our love for Him. A choice to want Him more than we want anything - spouse, children, jobs etc. This is really hard because you see others have these things but you don't. He's saying 'Keep your eyes on Me, Seek Me first'.

Peju struggled with her love for Abdul and devotion to God. She was torn between following her heart's desires and commitment to God. She made Jesus her Saviour but not Lord over her life. She wanted both worlds but as the adage goes, you can't eat your cake and have it. God is a Jealous Lover and anything. . . anything we place above Him is an idol. Her separation from God brought about an indifference in her choices and an emptiness only God could fill up.

Once you have decided to renew your walk with God, it doesn't just get better immediately. There's a process, and yes, life will suddenly become so demanding that you almost feel like 'what's the point?' But don't give up. Keep pressing forward. Like Eliana got distracted but was kept on track by Stella, so also as Christians, we need each other as accountability partners in our Christian race. One beautiful thing about this race is we aren't competing with each other but rather cheering ourselves on to reach our mutual goal - God's Kingdom.

My walk with God is different now and it can only get better.

If you need to talk or ask questions, feel free to send an email to me. If you haven't given your life to Christ and you're ready to do so then say these words, Lord Jesus, I believe You are the Son of God and I accept You to be my Lord and Saviour. Come into my heart and make it Your home in Jesus name, Amen.

Yay! Welcome to the Kingdom of God.

So happy for you!
    If you would love to find out how Pastor John ended up getting married to a 'prostitute', then by all means get a copy of **Always One More Time** on Okadabooks. It's a book App.

I would love to hear from you. Let's connect.

God loves you... more than you can imagine.

Till next time,

Tope Omotosho.

Contact the Author:

Facebook: Tope Omotosho

Instagram: @topeomotoshowrites

Email: Topeomotoshowrites@gmail.com

Website: www.lifegodandlove.com

Glossary

Olorun maje - God forbid

I no fit kee myself on top their mata - I can't kill myself because of their issues

Abi na spirit you dey chase? - Is it a spirit you're pursuing?

Na true na - It's true

Pele - sorry

Wahala/gobe - trouble

All join - It's all the same

Bukka - roadside restaurant

Gisted - talked

As-salamu alaykum - Peace be unto you

Insh'Allah - If Allah wills it

Haba - come on

Hold body - Satisfy

Kin fara bale - I should calm down

Se o n gbo mi - Are you listening to me?

So wetin mumsi talk - So what did mummy say?

Abi - Is it so?

Nyash - Bum

Abeg - Please

Time don go - Time has gone/ It's getting late

Wharever - Whatever

Ehn-ehn - Oh really

Shebi - Right?

Buba and sokoto - Yoruba male traditional wear; shirt and trouser

Nkan te so ko da - What you said is not good

Iro and buba - Yoruba female traditional wear; wrapper and blouse

How far? - What's up?

You guys don settle the mata - Have you guys settled the matter?

No be sermon - This isn't a sermon

Na koko - It's the real deal

Na today you take know? - Is it today you are figuring that out?

Haba/Ahan - Come on

Na bad belle - Haters

Walahi - I swear

Wetin man wan do - What can man do

Gele - Headtie

Omo mi - My child

Oya - let's get it on

Whining - teasing

Wetin you dey talk - what are you talking about?

Na you sabi - That's your business

After you don port my babe - After you have taken my babe

Madam na oga talk sey make we no gree fo u - Madam, our boss said we shouldn't let you in.

Ope o - Thanks

Ma binu si mi jor - Don't be angry with me, please

Ehen - Yes

Juju - black magic

Aso-ebi - Uniform dress traditionally worn in Nigeria during festive periods

E ya - Awww

Alagas - Chair-person

Skentele Skontolo - Flamboyant

Biko - Please

Loun Loun - far, far

Goan - Go and
Dem - them

Other Titles by Author

With These Shoes Book 2: Now You Know Where It Pinches!

Crumbled

He Sees Me (non-fiction)

My Conversations with God

Dance with Me (Available in paperback and Amazon Kindle)

Separated

Ready To Say I Do (non-fiction)

I'll Keep Loving You

Once Upon a First Love

Always One More Time

With These Shoes . . . I Thee Wed (Book 1)

E-books Can be gotten on OKadabooks.com and Bambooks.io

Once Upon a First Love and I'll Keep Loving You are available on Amazon Kindle and paperback.

Also by Tope Omotosho

Book 2 of Once Upon a First Love

I'll Keep Loving You

Peju faces difficult times in the days following her misunderstandings with heartthrob, Abdul Layeni. Her spirit is broken, her will damaged, but her passion for God is what keeps her going.

Femi shows himself to be a true friend and extends a shoulder to cry on, but will this show of comfort and Peju's vulnerable stance lead to more? This is especially when long time secrets come to light and threaten to rock her world.

I'll keep loving you brings you to the doors of loving relationships with promises for something fresh, deeper and never ending.

Made in the USA
Middletown, DE
28 February 2022

61922102R00177